Praise for *I̶ ̶*

"This book is full of wond(
love Ireland, I love books, and 1
Literature, so I love the Brontë sisters too. I felt like this book was written just for me to enjoy. Michelle Daly has a lovely writing style, with echoes of the Bronte sisters, as well as of Maeve Binchy, one of my favorite living writers. I hope there will be a sequel. I want to know what happens next to Colette and her family and friends.

This is a lovely book! Pack a copy in your suitcase the next time you're headed off on vacation. On second thought, why wait? Read it now."   ~ Bobbi Sheahan, Texas, USA

"A journey through childhood to lifelong friendships and all amazingly real! A tale told with amazing true to life observation and wit. Couldn't put the book down and look forward to reading it again in the future maybe by a stream in Ireland!"

~ Sheila DiPiazza Birminghan UK

"I love Charlotte Brontë, too, and I love this book! It's a delightful story that will hook you on page one & keep you there until the end. What a wonderful ride. I wanted to go with them and enjoy Ireland myself. A definite keeper!"

~ Sharon Hyatt Shearouse Florida USA

'Sweet, lovely read! Don't we all wish we could just chuck our everyday lives and move to a cottage in a tiny village in Ireland where the locals would welcome us with open arms? Once you start, it's like eating chocolates. You won't be able to stop. Very much enjoyed it."

~ Debbie Krencicki Lincoln, CA USA

"It has such warmth and a lovely theme of friendship and family ties running through it. The description of rural Ireland is so detailed it is obvious that the author has lived the life. It made me want to up sticks and move to Ireland! Very much recommended. What a lovely present for someone with—or without—Irish roots."

~ Jan Cruise Liverpool UK

More Praise...

"Set in these two vastly different environments, the novel's story is centred around the importance of friendship and family. No matter where Colette goes, her generous heart is always a warm, welcoming haven that can be a model for all of us. After reading *I Love Charlotte Brontë*, I'm left with the feeling that England and Ireland would be great fun to visit, especially if I could have Daly's Colette Murphy beside me. Her infectious laughter and open hearted approach to living would make it a magical trip."

~ SS Bazzinet Albuquerque USA

"The story is warm, charming, humorous, dramatic, and adventurous. I think the book also shows the strength women can have that is sometimes overlooked. The book is entwined around another book from the Victorian era, *Jane Eyre* by Charlotte Brontë, once you read this book, well you just have to read *Jane Eyre* too, they are like chocolate and peanut butter and compliment each other well!"

~ Erin I Stewart Rhinelander, WI USA

I Love Charlotte Brontë

Michelle Daly

I Love Charlotte Brontë

Michelle Daly

Michelle Daly • Liverpool

Front Cover by graphiczxdesigns.zenfolio.com
Book design and layout by MaryChris Bradley of The Book Team

ISBN 978-0-9570487-1-3 (trade paperback)
ISBN: 978-0-9570-4870-6 (ebook)

PUBLISHER'S NOTE

Contact the Author:
Email: michelleannedaly@yahoo.co.uk
Twitter: @MichelleDalyLiv
Facebook: facebook.com/michelleannedaly
Blog: michelledaly.blogspot.com

For my sister, Cathy.

"If all the world hated you and believed you wicked, while your own conscience approved of you and absolved you from guilt, you would not be without friends."

~ Charlotte Brontë

Michelle x x

Part 1

Liverpool 1990

~ 1 ~

I FINISHED WORK early and hurried out into the cold blustery afternoon.

It had been one of those days and, to top it all, I'd just had a row with Agnes. Bloody Agnes! "Do this, Colette! Do that, Colette!"

I had been fighting back the tears all morning, but when I reached my car on that cold January afternoon, I just couldn't help myself, and they began rolling down my cheeks.

I hadn't cried like this in years. Not since I'd watched Jane Eyre's heart being broken at the altar on her wedding day.

I took a tissue from my bag and pressed it to my lips, trying to muffle the agonized cries that came spewing from my mouth. Frightened of being discovered in such a state, I started the car and drove towards the nursing home exit. I looked up and down the busy road, wondering where to go. I needed a few minutes to calm down and try to make some kind of decision, so I turned left and pulled up at the first empty space, not realising until I had stopped that I was parked across somebody's driveway.

This time yesterday I had been strolling through the busy city centre, going from one boutique to another, lingering in Dorothy Perkins, as I tried on three different outfits, much to the chagrin of the sales girl who'd kept glancing at her watch, doing the countdown to closing.

I had hidden my secret well. Not even Eddie had guessed when my breasts had swelled and I had put on a little weight, that I was carrying his baby.

Marion was the only one who knew.

I thought about Eddie. Last night we'd had hardly been able to keep our hands off each other. You know the way it is? After a few drinks, we had abandoned our plans for a romantic candlelit dinner and gone back to his place, almost falling over each other trying to get to the bedroom. I hadn't seen him for two weeks, so it was like the first time all over again.

IT MUST HAVE taken him five seconds to remove his clothes and another ten to remove mine. As we lay in each other's arms he kissed my eyelids then my mouth and neck and slowly kissed his way down my body…

And then he said, "I love you, Trudy." Honestly, he did.

Ouch! I thought. *Did he just stick a knife through my heart?* I moved the car a few streets away and parked outside the empty bingo hall. Nobody was likely to see me there.

Red eyes stared back at me through the windscreen mirror. I hated anybody to see me crying. Still, I thought, if someone comes and knocks on the window, I could always pretend I'd been to a funeral. I could say it was my gran's, or even my mother's. I was told it's acceptable to use dead people as a sickie from work.

I remember once a girl at school had re-appeared after a few days' absence and told our teacher her father had died. She gained so much sympathy and was even excused from doing homework, until the following week, when he really was knocked over by a bus and killed.

I applied some more eye-shadow and lippy. Then I placed a hand gently on my stomach and thought about my little baby. The tears began rolling down my face again. How had I ended up in such a mess? I usually looked down upon people like me; people with unplanned pregnancies. Now I had a taste of my own medicine. The expression until you've walked a mile in my shoes, blah, blah, blah, sprang to mind.

Ten minutes later, I pulled up outside Marion's.

My poor bones ached. I hadn't slept all night and just when I was drifting off to sleep, next door's dog woke me up. Now I wanted to go home and crawl into bed. However, I would have to get past my over-protective brothers first and that would be difficult.

As I crossed the gravel path, my eyes automatically turned skywards, to the second floor of the old Edwardian house, but there was no sign of my friend. Sometimes the sound of a car brought her to the window, but not today. The only sign of life was her big ginger cat, sitting on the ledge and even he looked like an ornament. I took a deep breath, walked up the steps to the front door and rang the bell.

I looked back over my shoulder to the car. Should I make a dive for it? I asked myself. Marion had recently lost her mother and I was no company for a woman in mourning.

In a way I dreaded telling her about Eddie. Not that she was judgemental, because she wasn't. But she took time and thought things through, whereas I acted on impulse. Just as I was turning to go, I could see the blurred shape through the stained-glass panel, coming down the stairs.

I leaned against the wall and waited.

"I NEVER LIKED him anyway," Marion blurted after the story unfolded.

I shot her a look and she shrugged her shoulders and shook her head defensively.

"I know what you're thinking, Col., why didn't I say, but he was your feller, not mine."

"But still…"

"Things could have been worse. I mean you could have married him."

Oh, God, here I go again, I thought, taking a tissue from up my sleeve and wiping my eyes.

"Oh, come on, Col," she coaxed. "Isn't it better to find out now rather than later? You can do much better than him!"

"I bet there was more than one," I whinged wondering how I could have been so stupid. "And you!" I accused.

She looked as if I'd just slapped her across the face.

"Oh, thanks very much. What did I do?"

"Well," I said glumly, searching for words to justify my meanness. "Well, I don't suppose you really did anything but…but why didn't you like him?"

"I can't put my finger on anything. There was just something about him and hey, what about that money you lent him for the car? I hope he's giving you that back."

"I'd forgotten all about the money. It's not that important now and I don't really expect it back. I mean, he told me it was to pay off the car, but now that I've found out he's a liar, I realise he could have used it to back a horse, or maybe pay back maintenance for another baby he has stashed away somewhere else. One thing's for sure, he won't be paying anything for this little baby. It'll want for nothing. It'll be the most loved baby in the world."

Marion's face softened. "You'll make a great mum."

She lifted the box of Milk Tray off the table.

"Here, have a nut whirl and forget all your troubles."

Oh, all right then, I thought sulkily. As I leaned across to help myself, I had the most awful pain. I folded my arms across my stomach like you do when you have them awful stomach cramps.

Marion moved over to the couch and put her arm around my shoulders.

"You've gone awful pale. What's up?"

"I'll be all right in a minute."

"No you won't."

"I will."

"Oh, Col, maybe I should ring for an ambulance, or do you want me to ring your dad?"

"Oh, God, no. You mustn't! It's just the shock of everything. I'll be fine in a minute, honest, I will." But I wondered if I'd ever be fine again.

For a moment we sat in silence and then the pain began to ease and I could feel the tension leaving my body. I leaned back and relaxed.

"See," I muttered, feeling like a great weight had been lifted off my shoulders.

I asked if I could stay the night and of course she agreed.

"Hey, I got that Julie Walters' video out, you know, *Educating Rita?* You can watch it with me tonight. At least we can have a good laugh."

I began to giggle.

"See, I knew that would put a smile on your face," she said. "You just sit there and relax while I put the kettle on and make us a nice cup of tea. We can have a slice of that lovely cream cake I bought from St. John's Market this morning."

Old habits die hard, I told myself. Marion sounded just like her mum.

"I treated myself as well," she called from the kitchen. "I'll show you what I bought in a minute."

I glanced around the immaculately tidy room and couldn't help admiring Marion's orderly life; the comfy sofas with big flowery cushions and carefully matching lamp-shades. Then there were huge aspidistras in their ceramic pots, standing in the shade to avoid the bright sunlight which flooded most of the room. I picked up a magazine from the table and flicked through the pages. "I'll bet it's another teapot."

"Oh, you! You've gone and spoilt the surprise now," Marion said loudly.

"Wow, sorry, Marion," I giggled. "I don't know what made me think of teapots. I just took a wild guess. You know, seeing that you have been collecting them since time began. That must be about 300 you've got now."

"Nearly as big as your shoe collection," she reminded me and that shut me up for a while.

She came into the room carrying a tray and placed it on the coffee table.

"It's gone dark awful quick, hasn't it?" she asked, switching on the table lamp and closing the curtains, making the room all snug and cosy. "I'll put the telly on for you if you like. I think Oprah's on."

"Oh, go on then. It might be good," I said, watching her flick through the channels. I loved all those American talk shows and Oprah was my favourite.

"How was work, anyway?" she asked.

My mood suddenly changed and I was down in the dumps again. "It wasn't too bad but I had a row with Agnes because I got Peter to do Audrey's hair and Agnes insists on the hairdresser doing it. After all she is her sister-in-law."

"What's happened to the hairdresser?" She asked. I watched her wipe the screen with a cloth and stand back to make sure it was dust free.

"Nothing's happened to her. But she's not like the old one, is she? You'd think this one was doing the residents' hair for free, arriving at ten past eight in the morning in the middle of winter, expecting them to be up and ready to have their head stuck under a tap. Poor Millie Johnson nearly had a heart attack the other day and she had to be put straight to bed afterwards. She came here for a rest and we should be making sure she gets one. They don't even have time to have their breakfast and she charges them for the privilege. Peter does it for nothing and if she doesn't want to lose her customers she'll have to buck her ideas up and revolve around them not the other way around."

Marion plonked herself on the end of the chair and grinned at me. "I suppose you told Agnes all of that?"

"Well," I hesitated for a moment, "as a matter of fact I did and anyway," I said, holding the receiver in my hand ready to ring my brothers to inform them I wouldn't be home. "They have little enough money of their own without lining her pockets. She starts at the crack of dawn and has everyone done in about half an hour. She must be laughing all the way to the bank. And why does she have to cut their hair so short and do the perm so tight they end up looking like poodles? She'd be certified if she went out looking like that. Never do unto others what you wouldn't like done to yourself."

Marion began to laugh. I think she was sorry she'd opened her mouth.

Speaking to my brother was like being in a court of law. "Where are you going? Who are you going with? Where will you be sleeping?"

No sooner had I put the phone down than I found myself sliding to the floor in pain again.

"Marion," I groaned.

She came in from the kitchen and, without saying a word, she turned into nurse mode and gently helped me over to the couch. The seconds passed—there was no ease to the pain. No matter which way I positioned myself I was in agony.

Marion snatched the cushions from the chair and placed them at the end of the couch so I could lie down.

"Don't panic," she advised with a voice full of anxiety. "It'll be all right."

I was in no mood to argue and clutched my stomach as she lifted my legs and inched them up onto the couch.

"That bloody waster!" she snapped. "Look what he's done to you. Wait till I get my hands on him."

Me first! I thought. *Me first!*

Suddenly I felt a hot gush between my legs. I was only ten weeks gone and realised I must be miscarrying. I moaned and groaned as I lowered my legs onto the floor and sat up.

"There's nothing for it, Col, you're gonna have to go to hospital," she said, reaching for the phone. I knew she was right. She insisted on ringing for an ambulance but I insisted that she didn't and in the end she agreed to take me in the car.

I came out of the bathroom suitably padded and followed Marion into her mother's bedroom.

"My mum's got loads of stuff in here," she said, grabbing one of the many nearly new nightdresses from the chest of drawers. Standing on her toes, she lifted the purple dressing gown from behind the door and put them both into a bag.

A minute later we left the flat. The pains were getting stronger and I leaned heavily on my friend for support. When the front door opened, the outside security light flooded the forecourt and we slowly made our way to the car.

"Just take your time. It won't be long now, Col."

Fifteen minutes later we arrived at the Casualty Department, where the staff whisked me into a side room and examined me straight away.

"IT WAS MY fault," I whispered to Marion the following morning as she drove me home. "Maybe if I hadn't had that drink on Sunday night–or maybe it was when I lifted Mrs Parker into the bath instead of..."

"Colette," she gently interrupted. "It was nobody's fault." She reached across and squeezed my hand. "It just happened, that's all."

I SPENT ALMOST a week in bed pretending I had tonsillitis. I felt so depressed I could barely lift my head off the pillow. In fact, it took me all my time to eat the soup and ice cream my brothers carried up in relays. When I wasn't staring at the pink wallpaper, I was watching old Hollywood movies. The pain had eased and the bleeding had almost stopped but the ache in my heart got worse. Of course I hadn't wanted to get pregnant and, in a way, I felt relieved, but I had still conceived a child that was no more and I was overwhelmed with sadness.

Every day Marion came in like Florence Nightingale, laden with flowers, holiday brochures and big plans of going on a long deserved break some time when I felt better.

We (Eddie and I) had planned to go to Spain later on in the year if we could afford it, but I now realised he would probably go with somebody else.

Poor Marion was finding my brothers' concern for me more and more difficult to handle.

"Why won't she take any calls from Eddie?" I heard Billy ask her when she was getting ready to leave one evening. "He's been ringing nearly every day and she doesn't want to know. What's going on?"

"Oh, I think maybe she just needs a break," she answered.

"He hasn't upset her has he? 'Cause if he has I'll give him a break. I'll break his sodding neck."

"Oh dear." I whispered. I took my copy of *Jane Eyre* from under my pillow and began to read aloud. I had always enjoyed this form of reading and it helped to drown their voices.

Anyway, the next day we both laughed and cried through *Educating Rita* but, when I slipped *Wuthering Heights* into the video machine, Marion took it out again.

"Colette!" she complained. "I'll be crying all day if I watch this." But I knew she was thinking of me.

After she left I looked out of my bedroom window. My eyes rested on next door's garden with all the empty toy boxes, the remnants of the holiday, waiting to be collected by the bin men. I usually loved Christmas even though it held lots of sad memories, but not this one.

And just to make me feel worse, last night Billy had shown me a photo of my ex-teacher, Sister Margaret, in the *Liverpool Echo*, smiling as she gave her retirement speech. A smile which probably warmed the hearts of many but left me and a lot of other ex-pupils chilled to the bone with the memories of that sadistic nun. She was a bully through and through. I don't know which school she retired from but it wasn't the one I had attended.

Most children hated science or maths or even English but I had hated religion; God, how I hated religion. We had The Catechism every morning and God help us if we didn't know the answer to those questions.

Thirty six in the class and this nun always targeted the same girl. Don't get me wrong, I've met some lovely nuns in my time but this one was something else.

I closed my eyes and pictured my friend, Muriel, that day in class.

"Who made you?" Sister Margaret quietly asked her as she strolled between the lines of desks and stood behind Muriel's chair.

"God made me," Muriel whispered.

"Why did God make you?" she asked menacingly.

"God made me to…to…" I could see Muriel's shoulders tense as she waited for the assault but the clever nun purposely stood behind her so she wouldn't know which side of her head the smack was going to land. Then she suddenly moved away. Sister Margaret liked to surprise us.

"I can't hear you. Speak up," she roared, returning to the front of the class, tapping the ruler menacingly to the beat of Muriel's frightened heart. Eyes flashing around the room as everyone sat there like mannequins, hardly daring to breathe. Everybody knew Muriel knew the answers but she was so paralysed with fear she was unable to speak. My mouth felt dry. My sweaty palms were entwined in my pleated skirt and I wanted to go to the toilet. I noticed Muriel's lips begin to tremble with fear so, when I saw Sister Margaret look out of the window, I whispered the answer to her. But all the time the sly nun had been watching our reflection in the glass and flew like a bat across the room. A bony hand with a gold wedding ring, a symbol of her marriage to God, reached out and grabbed me from behind my desk by my hair, smacking the back of my legs until they stung then, after shaking me like a rag doll, dropped me back into my seat.

I had hidden in the toilets all playtime and cried behind the locked door. When I arrived home that evening I was still in shock. My wet knickers were now dried and smelly. I stepped out of them, crumpled them into a ball, and hid them under the mattress.

After tea I had spread my homework across the table when our neighbour, Teresa Regan, came rushing in. She must have given my dad the eye because he followed her into the kitchen and closed the door behind them. When they emerged a few minutes later, my dad's face was ashen.

"Is it true what happened today, pet? Did Sister Margaret really hit you?"

Tears dropped from my eyes and landed on my homework. I began to sob.

Teresa stooped down near me. "Has she hurt you, Queen?" She gently lifted my leg, making me cry out when she touched the tender skin. I nodded.

"But she hurts Muriel Colby more. She picks on her all the time because she lives in a Home and she's got no-one to speak up for her."

If there was one thing my dad couldn't tolerate it was a bully.

"Is that so, lass?" he asked in an angry voice.

Teresa tutted and took a pack of cigarettes out of her large apron pocket, sat on the edge of the chair and lit one.

"Isn't she a vicious cow? She makes me ashamed of being a Catholic. Anyway, I've heard that one only belts the Irish kids 'cause she thinks they're letting the side down. You know with God being Irish and all that," she said rolling her eyes.

Billy lifted his face out of the comic and began to giggle. "She's not an Irish kid."

"Hold your tongue, son!" Dad cautioned. "Half the people in Liverpool came from Ireland, including your grandparents, so let's have a bit of respect, hey?"

Billy looked pained but then I saw Teresa give him a sly wink. "Sure, he didn't mean anything did you, lad?"

Billy looked at my dad sadly.

"I know that," my dad said and gave Billy's hair a playful rub. "I'm just upset, son."

"I've been up to her myself before now," Teresa said, flicking her ash onto the fire. My dad knelt down beside me. "I'll see to it that she doesn't pick on either of you anymore. D'you understand me, love?" I nodded.

AFTER TERESA LEFT he sent our Billy to get the priest. Father Thomas had been our parish priest for thirty years. He'd married my parents back in 1955, baptised us three children, given each of us a shilling when we made our Holy Communion, and officiated at my mother's funeral.

When my mother died, the house had been filled with a sadness I had never felt before or since. It was Christmas Eve, and she had died at one o'clock in the afternoon. After we had arrived home in a taxi, I had sat on my father's knee and cried until I had fallen asleep exhausted, and he had put me to bed. When I woke later on, I crept downstairs. My dad and the priest were talking quietly. I tip-toed across the carpet in my bare feet and crouched down behind the Christmas tree until the priest left for midnight Mass. I climbed onto my father's knee and fell asleep against his wet face.

AN HOUR LATER Father Thomas was trying to calm my dad. "Now, Jack," he was saying, "there's no point in you storming into the school in the morning. Just leave it to me and I will sort it." But my dad was hell-bent on confronting her.

Sister Margaret was conspicuous by her absence at school the next morning and even more conspicuous was that she never returned to the school.

"Been transferred," were Father Thomas' words when he called to see us that same night.

~ 3 ~

WHEN I FINALLY dragged myself back into the land of the living, my brothers couldn't do enough for me.

I sat across the table and watched Billy tuck into his egg and bacon. He loved his food and, luckily for me, he was a dab hand in the kitchen. I peeled back the yoghurt top and took a spoonful.

Billy eyed it disapprovingly because I wouldn't let him cook me a breakfast.

"It's nice to see you back on your feet instead of being stuck in that miserable room."

I rested my carton on the table. "You're not kidding. I could do with changing that wallpaper and God, the shame of it; I can't believe I still had Duran Duran on the wall."

"Ha-ha, I always knew they were rubbish." He folded a piece of toast in half and dipped it into his egg.

"Oh, and what about you and Debbie Harry?"

"Now, now, Col, I don't discuss my relationship with Debbie Harry, with anybody."

"Oops, I'm sorry. I didn't mean to pry."

"I'll let you off."

"Thanks, Billy."

"Is Marion coming around today?"

"No, she's working, but she's been awful good. She spent loads of money on me when I was sick. And the way she went down to Marks and Spencer's and bought me those lovely pyjamas."

"You've got a good mate there, Col. And she'd probably say the same about you. But you women are like that, aren't you? You know what I mean? Good to each other."

"I suppose we are. We can sit and talk about anything, but you men can't, can you? You could stand in a pub talking for hours and you'd still come away knowing nothing about each other."

"We just go home and cry into our pillows every night." He placed his knife and fork on the side of his plate and looked over at the clock.

"Are you late?" I asked, scraping the last bit of yoghurt and licking the spoon all over.

"No. In any case, I'll get a cab."

"I can give you a lift, if you like. It's no bother. I don't have that much to do today except iron my dress for work tomorrow."

"No, ta. You don't need to go to all that trouble. What's the point in getting stuck in that traffic? Anyway, I'll decorate it for you if you like."

"What?"

"Why, your room, of course. What did you think I meant?" he asked kissing me on the forehead. "Anything for a princess—you pick out the paint or paper and I'll even buy it for you."

"Thanks Billy." I stood up and pushed back my chair. "I'll just make another cuppa."

I stood staring out of the kitchen window while I waited for the kettle to boil. A princess, he'd called me. I choked back the tears and instinctively touched my stomach and then, remembering, slowly removed my hand and let it drop to my side. When I returned with the tea, I could feel Billy scrutinizing me. I had to be careful with my brother because he didn't miss much.

"You're looking a bit pasty," he said, slipping into his overcoat and checking his pockets.

"I always do when I wear black."

"But you're as white as a ghost. Are you sure you're all right?"

I avoided his eyes and waved my hand dismissively. "Well, wouldn't you if you'd been lying on your back in bed for a week? I'll be fine. Honest." I wrapped my arms around him and gave him a hug. "I just need a bit of fresh air in my lungs and then I'll be raring to go."

He held me at arm's length. "Are you sure that's all it is?"

I nodded.

"There's nothing troubling you? Nobody's upset you or anything?"

"Bill…"

"Say no more. I believe you." He opened his wallet and pulled out some money. "Here," he said placing the notes in the palm of my hand. "Go and buy yourself something nice." Closing my fingers on the money he kissed my cheek and left.

The first place I headed was the shoe shop. I never bought less than two pairs. Like a child's in a toy store, my eyes usually lit up as soon as they hit the racks along the wall, but not this time. It was only when a tear dropped onto the shoes I was holding that I put my hand to my cheek and realised I was crying. I looked around self-consciously, re-placed the shoes on the shelf and left. Once again I was out in the hustle and bustle of the city centre. With the January sales almost over, a kind of gloom hung over the city. I walked on aimlessly, unaware of the curious glances from passers-by. Someone touched my arm.

"Are you alright, love?"

She was talking so loudly I felt everyone was watching me so I quickly crossed the road. I walked on and on until I realised that I was walking in the opposite direction to the car. Crossing back to the other side of the road, I hurried through Clayton Square, scattering a group of pigeons who were enjoying a bag of cold chips. I cut through St John's Market, all the time keeping my head down, anxious to reach the car before I met anybody I knew.

When I put the key in the door I could hear the phone ringing. I picked it up and sighed when I heard his voice.

"No," I told him, "there is nothing to talk about. No. No," I said answering his questions. "And stop ringing me, Eddie. I've told you, it's over."

"Just give me another chance?" he whined.

"Sorry," I told him, "I don't give men second chances."

Isn't that just typical, I thought as I hung up. The times I used to sit in my room and wait for him to ring. How the sound of his voice had brought music to my ears and now he left me feeling cold.

I lay on my bed that evening looking up at the ceiling. Be strong, I kept telling myself. He's garbage. Just get over it.

My old brown sewing machine caught my eye and I groaned at the pile of clothes stacked beside it, waiting to be repaired. I dragged myself off the bed and inspected the growing bundle, picking out a pair of boys' school trousers. Poor Teresa must be waiting on these, I thought, as I straightened out the leg and inspected the hem, and she hasn't liked to ask me because she knew I wasn't well.

With Teresa's brood, there was always a dress to take in or let out and a hem to let down. I sat down at the machine, changed the spool to a light grey and began stitching the hem. When the garment was finished, I picked out another and before I knew it two hours had passed and all the sewing was finished. No sooner had I delivered these than they'd be handing me a whole pile of other stuff to do. I didn't mind really. If I did it one night a week, I didn't get behind. It was the big orders that took up my time like when I made the bridesmaids' dresses for Teresa's eldest daughter. "Never again," I'd moaned to my brothers. The house had seemed to be filled with lilac satin but, when I saw the three girls walking down the aisle, my heart had soared with pride.

Nowadays I only take in repairs to help out the neighbours. The only creative sewing I do is making curtains and cushion covers and odd bits and bobs for around the house.

I tossed and turned in bed that night. I dreamt I'd won the pools until Billy woke me up. I didn't know whether to laugh or cry. He stood there scratching his head in the Mickey Mouse boxers I'd bought him for Christmas.

"Sorry to wake you, Col, only you were making so much noise shouting and cheering I thought you might wake the street up. In any case," he added, "it's nearly time to get up for work."

I choked down my disappointment and turned to face the wall. "Oh, thanks, Billy," I said in such a sarcastic voice I felt guilty afterwards. "Sometimes you're just so thoughtful."

I MUST HAVE drifted back to sleep because ten minutes later the alarm went off and instead of throwing the clock at the wall like I wanted to, I pressed the snooze button. "Sod off!" I snapped and snuggled back down under the covers. When it rang again I knew I had no choice so I threw back the quilt and dragged myself out of bed. Anyway, I asked myself as I stood under the cool water in the shower, what does it matter if I can't buy my dad and Billy and Tony a new house? And my little Irish friend that flat in Sefton Park, and that sleek black number I saw in the shop window in town for 600 pounds and maybe a little cottage somewhere in the country. I will just have to remain a poor unattached twenty-eight-year-old female.

I put my blue dress on over my lace underwear, brushed my hair back into a pony-tail and clipped on my identity badge and fob watch ready for my day's slog as a care assistant. Downstairs I filled the kettle and made toast. I liked my breakfast and now that I was returning to work I needed all the energy I could muster.

My dad and Tony were working an early shift but I hoped Billy had managed to go back to sleep after the fright I'd given him. He'd be up soon anyway to see to his beloved pigeons. He'd laugh later on when

I told him about my dream. I could just imagine him saying, "And that's the closest you'll ever get to winning. I've told you, Col, you'd have more luck on the horses."

I closed the front door behind me and went out into the cobbled street, dashing through the rain to open the car door.

When I'd driven two miles down the road, I could see Marion in the distance. I put on the indicator and slowed down near the bus stop, moving the newspaper off the seat and throwing it in the back.

"Sorry, Col, I'm like a drowned rat," she said shaking her umbrella and lowering herself into the car. "I've only just come out, you know. I watched from the window until I saw you coming down the road and I'm still drenched."

I couldn't help laughing and leaned forward to turn up the heater. "You'll be warm in no time."

"Everyone will be made up to see you back at work, Col, but are you sure you're ready?"

Is anybody really prepared for anything? I asked myself as I drove along. You just have to take what's dealt out to you and keep your chin up. It could have been worse. Just imagine if it had been born dead like Teresa's little girl, then I'd really have something to cry about. And what about poor Charlotte Brontë? She died when she was pregnant.

"Oh look, the sun's coming out. It looks like it might be a nice day, after all."

"Well, that'll make a change," I remarked.

"I feel awful cold lately in these stupid blue dresses," Marion said, trying to pull the cotton material over her knees. "Wouldn't you think Mr Richards would let us wear trousers? Lots of other nursing homes wear tunics and trousers and they look much nicer."

"Yeah," I agreed. "It does look a bit antwacky, especially with the black tights."

"I reckon that new owner's a kinky sod. He'd have us all in stilettos if he could get away with it."

"And stockings. I mean, have you seen the way he looks at us?"

I hated working for other people and having to do things I didn't agree with. I hadn't always felt like this. Most of my colleagues had been kind decent people. This morning I was returning to work with our horrible, newish staff nurse whom I had nick-named Annie Wilkes, from 'Misery'. If I had really won all that money, I could open my own home and take all my lovely residents with me. Some of them could have a vegetable patch and we could have our very own hairdresser…

"Erm, Colette…Colette…"

I quickly turned to Marion. "Oh, sorry, what were you saying?"

"Where were you? I was talking away to you, telling you all about the great sex I had with that man I met at the take-away last night, and you didn't hear a thing I said, did you?"

She picked up the bag of sweets from the dashboard and peeped inside.

"Hmm, I knew it wouldn't be long before you found them," I chided.

"Well, you know me and my sweet tooth. Ooh, I just feel like one of these though. I keep promising to go on a diet but you know what a pig I am. Can I have one?"

"Of course you can."

She opened the packet and picked out a black jelly baby, bit off its head and rested the bag on her lap.

"I don't know why you worry about your weight. You're so small."

"Yeah, but I wish I was smaller" my friend said wistfully.

"I wish I had a face like Michelle Pfeiffer but what can you do?"

"Anyway," Marion said, munching away, "I don't need to ask who you bought these sweets for, do I?"

"Oh, it's only a few jelly babies and you know when she loses her appetite, which she often does, then it's them jelly babies that keep the blood pumping through her veins."

We approached Acorn House, drove through the gates and parked the car at the side of the building.

"Oh, I don't believe it," Marion groaned, "Have you seen Eddie over the road? I mean, what makes him think he has the right to follow you around wherever you go?"

I glanced over and sighed when I saw the silver Aston Martin parked near the building.

Marion said, "Do you want me to tell him to go and get lost?"

"Oh, just take no notice of him. He'll soon get the message."

"Will he? I wouldn't be too sure about that, Col."

"You worry too much."

"And what happens if you meet another feller? I mean, look at him," she ordered, struggling to turn around and face him. "He's stalking you. It should be against the law."

"After my experience with him, I'm hardly going to be rushing into the arms of another man, am I?" I said, dragging Marion into the building. "Besides," I added sheepishly, "don't tell anybody, will you?"

She stopped and looked at me. "Tell anybody what?"

"Well…" I mumbled.

"Come on, what?"

"Well," I said, "I only went out with him because his name was Edward."

"Edward?"

"Yeah, you know? Mr Rochester, the man who married Jane Eyre?"

Marion rolled her eyes. "What are you like?"

"Shallow," I replied.

With ten minutes to spare, we power-walked down to the staff-room and joined the others for a quick coffee and cigarette. The room smelt like an old bar as we puffed our breaks away.

First thing I always did was change into my soft white shoes and lock the rest of my belongings into my locker. Once I walked through those doors into work of a morning, comfort was my priority, especially as I was on my feet for most of the day. I wouldn't be seen dead outside work in flat white shoes but inside, who cared? They were like gloves on my feet.

"Look, nobody's bothered to water the plants," Marion moaned, filling a mug with cold water and pouring it on what was left of a Busy Lizzy sitting on the window ledge.

I needed a drink more than the plants so I filled the kettle. "I'm not surprised," I told her, "They'll have to give us a bigger room or we'll all be dead within a year. At least my fags are mild." I turned to see Peter standing in the doorway.

"Did I just hear you right? Your fags are mild? I don't smoke at all, so how do you think I feel?"

"Shut up and sit down or I'll poison your coffee," I told him, putting another mug on the tray.

"Tetchy this morning, aren't we?" he said, slipping out of his leather jacket and hanging it in the locker. "I was just going to welcome you back and tell you how pleased I am that you're better but now I'm not so sure."

When Peter had first begun working at Acorn House, he was

painfully shy. Jokes would fly across the staff-room like ping pong balls and of course, we gave as good as we got, but poor Peter would often go for a walk instead of joining us. We hadn't realised how in his face we were.

"Will you not come in and have a cup of tea with us, Peter?" Sandy Harrison asked him one day when we reached the staff-room. "Oh, come on," she coaxed in her Belfast accent. She turned to the rest of us. "We all promise to be good, don't we?"

"Of course," we chorused.

So we toned it down for a while and coaxed him back into the fold and slowly he had become as bad as us and just as capable of holding his own.

"How's your sister?" I asked stirring my coffee.

"Late. The baby was due yesterday," he replied whilst making room for me at the table. The very mention of the baby filled my eyes with tears and I pretended to yawn.

"At least she lives near the hospital," Sandy remarked, "so she won't have too far to go. If she has it while you're off, don't forget to ring in and let us know, will you?"

"I won't."

"I've just started the last bootee," Sandy announced, "but you know what, Peter, I'll be so glad when they're finished and I can give them to you. Some nights when I'm sat at home on the couch knitting, you should see my dad scrutinizing me when he doesn't know I'm looking. I'm sure he thinks I'm pregnant."

Peter gave her a hug.

"By the way, did you go to see that flat or did they cancel again at the last minute?" I asked.

He shuddered at the memory. "Don't mention it. I mean, it would have been perfect if you don't mind damp running down the walls and cockroaches under your feet and sharing the bathroom with ten thousand other people."

"Oh, never mind. Something is bound to turn up sooner or later."

At 8a.m. the day shift assembled in the office, where the night staff handed over their report. I smiled when I saw Julie Watson. She had been a staff nurse on the night shift for four years, and all the residents loved her. Some said she spoilt them all, but I knew she just enjoyed them. If anybody was off their food, she would spend hours during the night coaxing them with yoghurts and rice pudding, or anything else they fancied. Sometimes she brought in an egg custard or trifle for Mrs Wally, because she was taking such a long time to recover from a broken hip.

"Right then," Julie smiled. "We had a fairly quiet night, until we discovered Mrs Miller had been in the bedrooms on her floor," she said, raising her eyebrows to indicate upstairs, "and taken some of the false teeth out of the mugs and put them in her handbag."

Everybody began to giggle.

"One thing about this job, there's never a dull moment," Sandy said, exchanging smiles with everybody. "I'm afraid you're going to have fun and games today because as you can imagine, she's mixed them all up and we don't know whose is which."

Agnes sighed wearily. "I thought the teeth were supposed to go in the medicine cabinets?"

"Oh, they are, but that still doesn't put them out of anybody's reach."

"But at least they'd be out of sight," Agnes argued.

"Oh, dear," Julie said. "If you knew Mrs Miller like we do, you'd understand. She knows what she's looking for and she'll find it. She's always been the same."

"Aye, that's true," Marion agreed. "She'd have the wax out of your ear if you didn't watch her."

Marion's remarks broke the tension and Julie continued. "I'm a bit concerned about Hilda Fay. When I went into her room to check on her at two o'clock this morning, she was still wide awake. She asked me to turn her heating off so I suggested maybe I should just lower it a little because I didn't want her to catch a cold but she was adamant." Julie's eyes watered a little. "She said it was just in case she died in the night. She thought if the room was too hot, we wouldn't be able to tell how long she had been dead."

"That's the trouble when they come in here," Marion remarked, "Some of them could live for another ten years but they don't see it like that. They're just waiting to die. It sounds like she needs a bit of cheering up."

"Cheering up?" Agnes repeated looking over the top of her glasses.

"We can only do so much. I mean, there are twenty-five of them and it's not a hotel."

"I think they realise that. In fact, they must sometimes wonder if they're living in a prison," I said as the meeting came to an end.

"I don't like her," Katy muttered when we were out in the corridor. "She pinches all their sweets." "Don't get me started," I warned.

MY FIRST PORT of call was to Maisie, my Irish friend. I know we weren't supposed to have favourites, but she was such a love, I couldn't help myself. Walking along the tiled corridor, I passed the kitchen and sniffed that delicious smell of fried bacon, then went on past the lift and into the first bedroom. In the early days, when Maisie had been more able, I had often taken her home, but a few months ago she'd suffered a stroke and lost the use of her speech, leaving a weakness down the right side of her body. This made home visits far more difficult.

Fortunately, her eyesight had not been affected and she read constantly. One of her possessions was the oldest most battered copy of Jane Eyre that I had ever seen. She read it like some would read a bible and woe betide anybody who touched it.

"Morning, Maisie," I said peeping around the door. I jammed it open with the doorstop and smiled at the old woman in the bed.

"Mm, it smells nice in here. It must be those roses," I said pecking her on the cheek. "It's still raining off and on, but it looks like it's going to brighten up later on."

The old lady's room looked out onto the oak tree in the garden. These days she spent most of the time confined to her bed so I'd made an effort to make her environment as interesting as possible. A bag of nuts hung from the lower branch of the tree and the squirrels had great fun entertaining her. On her last birthday I had bought her a bird table and she had an abundance of feathery friends calling throughout the day. Returning to the head of the bed, I stroked the old lady's wispy hair and she gave me such a lovely smile.

"And how are you this morning?" I asked turning on the radio and propping her up onto her pillows so she could see out into the garden. "Our Billy was asking after you last night, and he said he would call in to see you this Sunday."

Maisie struggled to lift her arm and pointed to the vase of flowers on the dresser.

"I know. He never forgets, does he? And you know our Billy is so tight but every week when he gets paid he always gives me the money for fresh flowers for you." I took her glasses from the top of the dresser and put them on her. "You know you're the only woman in his life, don't you?" I teased, taking a packet of sweets from under the tissues in her locker and popping one into her mouth. "This'll keep you going till Rally comes round with your breakfast. By the way, Maisie," I whispered, "if Agnes comes in here pinching your sweets, you let me know, won't you? I'm sure you'll find a way. Oh, and you'll never guess what happened to me last night? I dreamt I won the football pools." I looked out through the window into the distance. "It was wonderful. Aw, you wouldn't believe the plans I was about to make. All the things I was going to do for everyone…and for myself," I grinned. "And I didn't forget you either. You were getting a lovely flat in Sefton Park with your own nurse. Just think, I could have visited you on my days off and taken you to the lake to see all those lovely ducks and swans… But never mind," I said, squeezing her hand, "maybe next week."

I put another sweet into her mouth, picked up the glass jug and took it down to the kitchen and returned a few minutes later with fresh water.

"You'll enjoy your dinner today. It's your favourite. Roast beef and Yorkshire pudding." I straightened her bed cover and made her as comfortable as possible. "Well, Maisie, I'd better go and get some work done or I'll be getting the sack. I'll see you later."

After breakfast, I pottered about in Hilda Fay's room, sorting through her clothes and opening her bedroom window to let in some fresh air. Some of the residents didn't like their belongings being touched and, for those who were able, we respected their privacy and left them to keep their own rooms in order but, for the likes of Hilda and Maisie, they needed constant support. I stopped what I was doing when I heard raised voices coming from the room opposite and stood behind the door to listen.

"You'll do as I say, Fred," Agnes was saying. "You're not allowed back into your room until this evening."

I sat down on the bed. This was another rule introduced when she arrived six months ago. Poor Fred. All he wanted was a bit of peace and quiet.

"But what difference does it make where I sit?" I heard him ask. "Am I a bother to anybody?"

"That's not the point. We all have to do things we don't want to do. You're a grown man, Fred, you should know that."

"Oh, I know th-th-that all right. Do you want me t-t-to tell y-you about the wars I fought in and how I d-d-did what I didn't w-want to do?" "Now, now Fred, none of the self-pity, please. You got medals, didn't you?"

"I did." Fred's voice faltered. "I got three of them."

"Well then, you had your reward."

I felt my heart sink to my feet and went to the staff-room for a much needed cigarette. When I returned five minutes later, Agnes had moved on to her next casualty and was in Hilda's room telling her she should go and sit in the day room. I went in to give her a clean flannel and towel, and my eyes rested on the box of Roses in Agnes' hand.

"Good morning, Hilda. Ooh, has someone sent you chocolates?" I asked, trying to defuse the situation.

"Humph!" she scowled, "Chance would be a fine thing but then it's just as well, isn't it, because they would only be taken off me and locked away."

"Who are they for then?" I asked Agnes as we left the room together.

"At this particular moment they're not for anybody. I caught Fred eating them and he's not supposed to. I've told him I'm going to lock them in the office."

I was incredulous. "But Agnes, Fred is a grown man, not a child. Surely he's allowed to have a chocolate when he wants one. There's no medical reason for him not to do so."

"Well, Colette, he threw such a tantrum and if he's going to act like a child, then I'll treat him like one"

Bloody witch, I thought as I watched her walk away. When will she ever learn?

I turned back to see Hilda trying to catch my attention and followed her into her room. She reached under her pillow and pulled out a magazine. "Look what I've got for you."

Seeing her standing there with her jumper on back to front and slippers on the wrong feet, I wanted to cry. She constantly changed her clothes and by the end of the day she'd usually worn everything in her wardrobe. "Hilda, you're so thoughtful. I'll read it in my break and give it back to you later."

Hilda shook her head. "You keep it," she whispered. "I saved it especially because I know you like to do those crossword things. Only if I didn't put it away for you, she would take it."

"Who would?" I gently probed.

"You know who," she said crossly. "She takes everything. Every time Fred's son brings him something, as soon as he leaves she whips it away and it's never to be seen again. She thinks I don't know but I do. I might be old and a bit forgetful but I'm not daft."

I put my arms around her shoulders. "Listen, why don't you come and find Peter with me and you can ask him if he will perm your hair?"

"Good idea," she said excitedly. "Do you know I haven't had my hair washed for six months? I keep asking the staff but they're always too busy doing this and too busy doing that."

"Hilda, you'll get us hung," I giggled as she put her arm through mine and we went off in search of Peter.

~ 4 ~

UP UNTIL RECENTLY I had enjoyed my work at Acorn House and, like most things in life I had discovered it quite by accident. Never having known my grandparents, the world of the elderly was alien to me. One day, a few months after leaving school, I was taking some books back to the library for our Tony. When I came out, I saw Marion crossing the road. I hadn't known her that well. She'd been a newcomer during our final school year and hadn't quite become part of the clique. Sometimes she would join some of the class when they walked home after school, but she would eventually trail off to catch the bus home. All the kids used to think she was rich because she travelled four miles to school and paid the fares herself, but the truth was the school had a good name. It wasn't until Marion's first day of term that the education department told her mother that she was outside the catchment area and not entitled to the bus pass they had expected.

"What are you doing around here?" I asked when I caught her up. "I haven't seen you for ages. How are you getting on?"

Marion smiled shyly. "I am going for the bus home. I've been working in Tesco's." She indicated over the road. "I'm a cashier."

"So what's it like?" I asked.

"It's so boring, except on Friday nights, when I get paid."

We sat on the nearby wall. I took a pack of cigarettes out of my pocket and offered her one. I didn't know anybody my age who didn't smoke.

"Snap!" We laughed, producing the same lighters and locking our arms together as we lit each other's cigarettes.

"I was going to work in that Tesco's but then I got a job in an office in Victoria Street, not far from the main post office," I said.

"Do you like working there?"

"It's all right for now, and we have a laugh," I told her.

"Have you got a feller?"

"Nah," I answered, feeling self-conscious. "Have you?"

"I did have, but he turned out to be a right randy bugger. Every time we went out on a date, he kept trying to put his hand inside my coat."

"Ha, ha, ha. You should have broken his arm," I told her. I'd met a few like him in my time too.

"I wish I had now, but I sent him packing anyway."

"And broke his heart instead?"

"I doubt it. I saw him a few days later with another girl on his arm. She looked like a right you-know-what."

"She probably was."

On and on we gabbed until Marion looked at her watch and slid off the wall.

"It's a pity you don't live around here," I said. "We could have met up and gone to the pictures sometime."

"Oh, I know." She brightened. "Are you doing anything this Sunday?"

"Nothing in particular," I answered maybe a little too quickly. "Why?"

"I was wondering if you would like to come and see my gran with me. She lives in an old people's home."

I tried to hide my disappointment and stumbled with my answer but I could tell by the sad expression that she knew what I was thinking.

"It doesn't matter," she said quietly. "I shouldn't have asked you." Turning to go, she said, "I'll be seeing you then, Colette."

I watched her walk away and then ran to catch her up. What's the worst that could happen? I asked myself.

"I'm sorry. I didn't mean to upset you. I didn't even know your gran was in a home," I shouted, trying to drown the sound of the passing bus. "It's just that I'd be a bit nervous."

"What of?" she asked as she counted her change for the bus.

"That's just it. I don't know."

"It's not that important. I understand. If …"

"I'll come," I burst out.

Marion smiled. "Are you sure?"

I nodded and agreed to meet her the following Sunday afternoon.

"My mum usually does the visiting but she's on her first holiday to France. I promised her I'd do the visiting and, to be honest, I hate going on my own."

WE MET AS planned and went across town on the bus.

"My gran's been in this place for years," Marion informed me, rolling the bus ticket nervously around her fingers. "We used to have a nice little house in Seaforth, but we sold it and bought a flat so we could be nearer and visit her more often. Besides, my mum wanted a fresh start because the house had too many sad memories. I wouldn't mind, she cried buckets when we left, but she's used to it now." The bus stopped outside. When we were about to go into the building, Marion said to me, "Sometimes when I'm going home, my gran starts to cry after me. We just have to ignore her and keep going towards the door, because if we go back, she'll think she's coming home with us."

"Right," I said, following her into the foyer.

Marion's gran was so pleased to see her that she cried like a baby. "I knew you would come for me, Mother, but why isn't Father with you? Is he still in Burma?"

"Alzheimer's," Marion whispered, before leaning over to give her gran a kiss. Then she took some packets of biscuits and marshmallows out of her bag and put them into the shopping trolley, which her gran apparently took everywhere with her.

I nodded as if I understood but I was clueless. However, after a while the old lady stopped crying and I began to relax. And then the poor woman looked startled and sat up straight, demanding in a high-pitched voice to know who we were, and where we were from.

Marion glanced at me with eyes full of tears. "She forgets," she said resignedly.

Matron came over and Marion introduced me.

"We're short staffed today," she said, looking around to make sure none of the visitors heard her. "Would you two young girls mind giving me a hand?"

"Erm, I'm not sure I can stay," I murmured but my voice was barely audible and I don't think anybody heard me. To Marion, it was obviously a regular occurrence. There she was, removing her coat and rolling up her sleeves as if she meant business.

"She's a friend of my mum's," she informed me, "and if she gets stuck, I sometimes stay and help her out. Last year, loads of the staff were sick with flu and I used to come here straight from school and then my mum would pick me up on her way home."

I wasn't impressed. Oh, if it wasn't for our Tony and his stupid library books.... Fixing my gaze on the wall print of a little girl with an Alsatian dog, I wondered how I could get out of it. I was just about to mention that I had to get home for Benediction when the clock on the wall told me it would be over in ten minutes.

Matron returned and handed us both a pink overall. She smiled at us gratefully and said, "If you just give us a hand with the feeds at tea time, it would be a tremendous help. I've had one of the staff ring in sick. Sunday of all days! Still, it can't be helped. Now," she continued whilst we slipped on our new uniforms and buttoned them up, "lunch is early on a Sunday. We like to get it out of the way so the ladies and gentlemen are free to sit with their visitors. However, because of early lunch we do find they're ready for their tea at about four o'clock, and then they have a little supper and a drink before they go to bed."

She smiled at me and fixed the collar of my overall. "I am sure you'll manage beautifully."

Before I could answer, Marion leaned forward and whispered, "Don't worry, I'll show you the ropes."

"Now," Matron continued, "Annie in room 10 is poorly. She's a very slow eater at the best of times, but you mustn't rush her because she'll sense your impatience and you'll put her right off. Give her as much time as she needs, but the main thing is to get her to finish her drink. It's very important that she has plenty of fluids – but first things first – before you do anything, you can go into the kitchen and grab yourselves a cup of tea and something to eat. The cook's gone home but there's some birthday cake left over from yesterday in the fridge or, if you like … oh, come on." She beckoned and we followed her out of the room. "I'll show you. And don't worry about your gran. I'll keep an eye on her for ten minutes. Maybe, when you come back, you could help in the dining room and – Colette, is it?" I nodded. "Perhaps you would like to work on the corridor. You could start with Annie if you like?"

I waited until we were alone again and then I hissed to Marion, "I can't feed Annie! I wouldn't know what to do. What if she chokes while I'm feeding her?"

"Get some cake out of the fridge," she instructed whilst she filled the tea-pot and got some cups and saucers from the cupboard. "And don't worry about Annie. She's a little love. She used to be a school secretary. You should have seen her when she was first admitted to Walton a few months ago. My mum was ward sister at the time and she said Annie was covered in bed sores and she had shingles."

"Shingles?" I asked as we sat down opposite each other.

She screwed up her face. "Yeah, horrible things. She says everyone thinks they're like chickenpox until they've had them themselves. Then you soon find out. Instead of the chickenpox itch, it's like a bee is stinging you. It's supposed to be agony."

"Ooh, painful." I grimaced. "I got stung once. I put my shoe on and had the most unmerciful pain. I thought I'd stood on a needle or something and, when I slipped my foot back out of the shoe, there was a dead wasp hanging off the end of my toe. My brother said it must have been asleep in there so now I always shake my shoes before I put them on."

"Yuk, I don't blame you."

I nibbled at my cake half-heartedly. "What about her family?"

"She's no family. She's a spinster. It was the vicar from the Church of England school where she worked who kicked up a fuss about the way she was being neglected and then my mother told him about this place so, when she was stronger, they brought her here. You see my mum tells me all about this medical stuff because she thinks I'm going to train to be a nurse, but I haven't had the heart yet to tell her I'm not. I can't stand the sight of blood. I don't mind places like this but not a hospital ward, oh no."

We finished our tea and cake and went into the dining room to find Matron. Most of the residents were sitting at the tables, and she was lining up the Zimmer frames along the window, careful not to knock the flowery pot plants over. The entrance of us two young girls caused quite a distraction, and we were bombarded with compliments and kind remarks from people whose youth had become a distant memory.

I followed Matron down to Annie's room where she gently tapped on the door before going in.

"This is Colette, Annie and she's come to give you your tea. Isn't she a pretty young thing? You pull that chair over from the corner whilst I go and get Annie's tea," she instructed pleasantly.

When she returned, she placed the tray on the bedside table.

"Sit down," she gently instructed as she propped Annie's pillows. "Never stand over anybody when you are feeding them–always let them have eye contact–it's very important. And don't look so worried."

She picked up the beaker with the lid and showed me what to do.

"You'll be fine," she whispered in my ear. Then I was left alone with Annie.

"Have you been crying?" Marion asked when I returned to the lounge with an empty beaker and half-eaten trifle.

I could feel the tears brimming in my eyes again. I shook my head and tried to gain my composure. "I'm fine."

"Do you want to go home?"

I shook my head. "Don't tell that woman," I whispered, looking anxiously around me.

"Who? Oh, you mean Matron? She's on her tea break but what's up?"

"It doesn't matter."

"Course it does. Tell me," she insisted.

"I was thinking how sad it must be for them when they leave home. I mean, how do they decide what to bring and what to leave when they are moving from a house to a little room? They're surrounded by their life's possessions and only able to fit a few bits into a suit-case. Oh, I'm sorry," I quickly added. "I didn't mean about your gran."

"It wasn't like that, so don't worry. My gran didn't even know her own name when she came in here, let alone where she was. It was me and my mum that were sad, not her. Anyway, come on. I said we'd wash the pots."

Next thing I knew, four hours had passed and we were almost finished giving out supper when Marion handed me my coat. "Come on, Colette, if we hurry we can get the half-seven bus."

"Can I just finish giving Meg this bit of supper?" I asked, placing a tiny piece of sandwich between the old lady's lips.

"Sorry, we won't have time. Let someone else do it."

"But …"

"Oh, go on then, but try and hurry up."

I gave the old lady a sip of cocoa and wiped the drips from her chin with a tissue.

We were soon stepping onto the bus with a box of Milk Tray each, compliments of Matron.

"When's your mum back?" I asked, sliding into the seat next to Marion.

"About two in the morning and then she has the coach ride from

London, so I'll just have to wait till I hear the key turn in the door."

"You can come to ours for a few hours if you like and I'll get my dad to run you home."

Marion smiled shyly. "Thanks! I'd like that."

From that night on we had been almost inseparable.

When I got up the next morning, I was longing to go back to the home but I had to go to my poxy office job instead. I lost count of the homes I rode past on the bus on my way to town – homes I had driven past for months and never noticed but suddenly they all seemed to be shouting at me. There was one in particular, on the corner of the main road about three miles from where I lived. It looked like a big hotel with a sign outside saying, "Tudor House."

As the weeks passed, I began to look out for this spot and would look across the forecourt into the dining room and see the same four elderly people sitting at the table eating their breakfast. One day I had a sudden urge to get off the bus and go in. And so I did.

"Ooh, look at the cut of this one!" my brothers teased the following week when I came downstairs in my new pink uniform. I was chuffed as hell and could only smile as I pinned my new identity badge onto my dress. Miss Colette Murphy.

"You're working in the poshest home in town," our Billy informed me and he was right. The fancy foyer, with its designer sofas and plush carpet and nearly as many exotic plants as Kew Gardens, was a great first impression. Oh, yes, to the visitor it was a palace, but after a few days I came to the conclusion that I wouldn't leave my dog in there.

Pulled out of bed and dressed by the night staff at five in the morning, most of the residents slept through their breakfast. At eleven, when I gave out the coffee, I was not allowed to give them a biscuit in case it spoilt their dinner. When I sat down to feed someone, my chair was taken away. I was told that the staff were not paid to sit down.

One night, when I was putting one of the residents to bed, I was unable to find a nightdress.

"Where can I get one from?" I went downstairs and asked the two lazy staff members who were sitting in the office, looking through a catalogue.

"If it's not in her room then it's not back from the laundry," I was told.

"Can I borrow one from another room?"

One of them shook her head. "We're not allowed."

"Shall I put some clothes back on her?"

She sighed. "Just cover her up. She'll be fine."

Sod your rules, I thought as I returned to the old lady's room, wondering what the poor old bugger was paying all that money for.

When I arrived home that night, I couldn't stop crying.

"It's too sad," I told my dad. "I can't go back." I couldn't get the vision of poor Kathleen out of my mind. I told him what had happened.

"So what did you do?"

"I made sure no-one else was looking and I pinched a nightie from someone else's drawer and put it on her."

My dad sat next to me on the couch and put his arm around me. "You know, girl, this is a hard world and maybe, well, maybe you're just not tough enough to do this kind of work."

"I am," I said defensively. "I really enjoyed helping out at Acorn House where Marion's gran used to live." She had since died from a stroke.

"Well then, why don't you give them a ring?"

I did and I'd been there ever since.

WITH FOUR RESIDENTS to bath and two hospital appointments, we were kept busy all morning. Lunch hour was a very welcome break. It was pay day and, as usual, there was a buzz in the staff-room. I opened the envelope and scanned my deductions. "I must be bloody mad to work here," I joked, "And it doesn't look like I'll be going to Barbados again this month, either."

Marion laughed. She strolled over to the tea trolley in the corner. "What do you want, Col, tea or coffee?"

I waved my pay slip indignantly in the air. "I'll have a coffee with a large brandy in it." I took a pack of cigs from my bag. "Anyway," I said, placing one between my lips, "looks like it'll just be another night out on the town."

Marion giggled and placed the two black mugs on the table before sitting down.

"No, seriously though," I said. "Why is the pay in these places so bad? The people we are taking care of fought through wars and saved our country, so why doesn't the government subsidise our wages and show their appreciation for the work that we do and the important people we're looking after?"

"But they don't class them as important, do they?" Peter commented. "In fact, they're not valued at all. That's why this job has no credibility. Once an old person enters a care-home, it's like they have been wiped off the face of the earth."

Sandy Harrison put on lipstick at the mirror. "Right, who's coming for a drink?"

"I'm buggered," I moaned. "Not today, thanks."

I tipped some lotion on to my finger tips and rubbed it into my face.

"That feels better," I said, screwing the top back on the bottle.

Sandy leaned across the table and picked up the bottle. She grimaced when she read the label. "Holy Water from Lourdes?"

"No, silly," I told her. "It's Anne French and they don't sell it in handbag size anymore so I have my own little bottle and just keep topping it up."

"Well, I think there's nothing like good old soap and water to replenish you."

"I agree," I told her, "but I'm allergic to soap and if I put any on my face, I would just break out in a rash."

"Never mind," Sandy said. "Anyway, I'm off. Are you coming, Marion?"

"Sorry, Sandy, I'm buggered too. I think I'll give it a miss if you don't mind. I just feel like a bit of peace for half an hour. My head's banging after trying to sort out all those sets of teeth."

Sandy hung her bag over her shoulder and opened the door.

"Hang on," Marion said, pushing back her chair. "I'll walk as far as the shop with you." She took her purse out of her locker and followed Sandy out into the corridor.

Peter put on his leather jacket and straightened the collar. "Oh, surprise, surprise," he said, looking out of the window. "I'll be back in a minute."

I didn't pay him too much attention. It was a relief to be alone. However my solitude was short-lived when he returned a minute later with a bunch of flowers in his hand.

"Didn't you see the InterFlora van pull up?" he asked, handing me the bouquet.

"I did not," I snapped, looking at the flowers like they were a piece of mouldy dog food. Being bothered by Eddie at work was the last thing I needed and I hoped the stupid flowers were a one-off. Leaning back on my chair, I stretched over near the window and dropped them in the bin. Peter was aghast. He only saw the good in people.

"Don't put them in there," he cried, rescuing them and putting them on top of the changing lockers out of the way. "Maybe you'll change your mind and take them home with you."

"And maybe you'll start your periods tomorrow," I said, stumping out my cigarette. I watched him sign the back of his pay cheque ready to lodge it in the bank. He was still laughing when he left.

I opened the card to see what Eddie had to say for himself.

I love you! I dropped it into the ash tray and burnt it.

Marion knocked on the staffroom window and passed in two bags of chips. "Here, put these out and I'll go down to the kitchen and pinch some bread and butter."

So much for our diet, I thought, spreading them out on two plates. When lunch was over, Sandy and I lifted Maisie into her chair and wheeled her down to the day room to watch TV.

"Don't worry, Maisie," I said looking at my watch. "I won't forget about you. When the film is over, I'll bring you straight back to your room."

"She wouldn't come out for us the other day, you know," Sandy was saying as she folded the blanket over Maisie's knee. "Oh, you should have seen her face when I wheeled in the chair. She was waving towards the door for us to go but Agnes insisted and made her stay up until it was time for bed. By the end of the night, she was so tired and fed up. You could tell all she wanted to do was go to bed."

"God, Agnes is such a cow," I whispered. "Why does she have to be so mean?"

Hilda Fay's face lit up when Maisie arrived. She immediately offered her the remote control, a sure sign that she was the honoured guest for the afternoon. Even the budgie began to chirp until I fetched a blanket and covered its cage.

When the chosen film, *The Quiet Man*, started, I sat behind Maisie and brushed her hair. Ever since she had first been admitted to Acorn House with a broken arm eight years ago, I had always done her hair. Then it had bits of red still running through it. Now it was pure white. After a while I coiled the long strands around my hand and, taking the ivory comb out of my pocket, secured it into the bun.

"Back in a mo," I said and went down to the office. I opened the cupboard and stepped onto a stool, reaching for the tin of Roses, sliding them towards me until they fell into my hands.

"IT'S LIKE CHRISTMAS!" Hilda Fay said, unwrapping a sweet. "Did you used to get these for Christmas, Maisie?" God love her, I thought, she's a head full of memories she can't share with anybody.

The other residents joined the party in dribs and drabs and then we started getting requests for glasses of sherry.

Why not? I thought, unlocking the bar.

When Hilda's smile disappeared, I followed her glance and saw Agnes standing in the doorway.

"My, isn't this cosy?" she remarked, her presence suddenly filling the room, looking at each of their faces like she was memorising items on a quiz show.

"Why don't you come and sit with us?" someone suggested, "and you can watch the end of the film?"

"Chance would be a fine thing. Some of us have important things to do. I start my week's holiday tomorrow so I want to tidy up the office a bit."

"Would you like a sweet?" Fred asked, limping over to the table and taking the tin to her.

She smiled that irritating mechanical smile. "No, thank you very much, Fred, and you shouldn't really be having any either, should you? But because it's my birthday, I'll let you all off."

"Happy birthday!" they all chorused.

"Thank you." She smiled again, walking into the middle of the room. "And I want you all to be good this afternoon. No moans and groans please because my dear husband is taking me out for a meal and I want to leave a bit early."

I watched her leave the room and then turned to Sandy.

"I've got to do a night shift with her a week on Tuesday and I'm not looking forward to it."

"I don't blame you."

Agnes seemed to have cast a spell around the place. Maisie wanted to go back to bed and Hilda and Fred were gathering their bits and bobs together, preparing to return to their rooms. Even if they didn't like Agnes, they would have liked to have clubbed together and bought her a present. I suppose it was called doing the decent thing. Then I remembered the flowers. I hurried to the staff room and snatched them from the top of the locker and hurried back to the others.

"Right, then," I said to the glum faces. "Who would like to go and get Agnes so we can give her our birthday present?" Would you believe the room lit up like a Christmas tree!

When I arrived home, I hung my coat in the hall, kicked off my shoes and ran upstairs to put the water heater on for a hot bath. Then I went downstairs to get something to eat. Thanks to Billy, the fridge was always well stocked so I lifted out the cooked chicken and cut a few slices and sat in front of the TV for a while with my sandwich.

I was watering the plants on the kitchen window ledge when I heard the key in the front door. The merry voices told me they had probably come from the pub. Christmas, birthdays, any excuse. I laughed, resting the jug on the drain board and going in to greet them. Billy stood in the doorway. "Love me tender, love me true … Ah, hiya, Col." He greeted me by blowing me a kiss. "Thanks for my birthday present. It was luverly. Just what I wanted."

I laughed and reached out to hug him. "Happy birthday, brother, and, well, it wasn't exactly what you wanted, was it? I got you your second choice, remember?" I teased. "I couldn't afford to buy you a face lift." I gave him a kiss on the cheek.

"Ah, will ye listen to the way she talks to me?" he said, swinging around to face Tony. "And where's our dad? Isn't he in yet?"

I glanced at my watch. "He'll be home in about half an hour."

Tony sat down and opened the newspaper. He didn't mind a pint or two but, unlike Billy, no matter what the occasion, he hardly ever got drunk.

"Are you coming down to Flanagan's later on, Col?"

I nodded. "Ooh, I'm looking forward to it as long as you're paying," I said, fluttering my eyelashes.

"Of course we're paying," Tony answered. "As long as you're drinking orange juice."

"Huh! Don't I always?"

It took longer than usual to get ready. I just couldn't decide what to wear. And then Billy started tapping on the door, saying I was hogging the bathroom.

"Erm, are you all right in there, Col, only if you don't get a move on, I'm gonna to be late for my own birthday bash," he was saying.

"I'll be out in a tick," I called, piling my hair loosely on top of my head and securing it with a comb.

"That's what you said fifteen minutes ago."

I put the final touches to my eye make-up and gave myself a generous spray of Enigma. Billy must have heard me unlock the bathroom door and ran up the stairs two at a time. When he reached the top he whistled.

"Wow!" he gushed, looking me up and down. "Who's the lucky feller?"

Slinking along to my bedroom in my figure-hugging dress, I looked back over my shoulder at him. "Billy," I purred resting one hand on my hip, "there's no feller that lucky."

WHEN THE CAB pulled up outside our favourite Oriental restaurant, I paid the driver and we went up the two flights of stairs.

"God, it's empty," Marion remarked, as the waiter showed us to a table.

The young Chinese man smiled and said in a gentle voice, "That is because we have reserved the building especially for you, madam." She tried to hide her blushes. "Oh, will you listen to him? Go on, you smoothie," she said tapping him on the hand. "You're just after a big tip, aren't you?"

I wondered if our Catholic upbringing was responsible for us throwing compliments right back from where they came? I scoured the menu, though I don't know why I bothered, because I always ordered the same thing.

"I wonder where the twins are?" I said to Marion.

Tye and his twin sister usually worked together and, when the restaurant wasn't too busy, they would pull up chairs and tell us all about their life in Japan. Both were students at Liverpool University: Sachi studying English literature and Tye studying science. They stayed with their uncle and worked in his restaurant in their spare time.

"He must have heard you," Marion said, nodding towards the door.

"Hello, Tye." Marion smiled. "We were just talking about you. Have you come to try and get us drunk again?"

We ordered a bottle of wine.

"Where's Sachi tonight?" I asked when he returned to our table.

Tye laughed. "You notice how peaceful it is without her?" He filled our glasses and placed the bottle in the centre of the table.

"Oh, no! You know I didn't mean that."

Tye laughed again and surrendered his hands.

"Yes, only joking. My mother and father are arriving from Japan tomorrow and she is fluttering around like a bird," he said, demonstrating with his hands. "She is too excited so my uncle has given her the night off. She is having bath and washing hair."

"Wow, your mum and dad, are coming over?" I marvelled. "Have they been to Liverpool before?"

Tye shook his head.

"They'll have a great time," Marion assured him.

"They want to go and see…" He clicked his fingers trying to think of the place. "The…where the Beatles played?"

"The Cavern."

"Yes, and the Albert Dock and also to London to see Buckingham Palace."

"That'll be nice," Marion remarked. "If Lizzie's at home, she might even ask you in for tea."

Tye laughed again.

"I don't think so. And they want to go to Haw … Haworth in Yorkshire?"

"Ah, where Charlotte Brontë lived?"

"That's it. My sister likes her books and also the other sister …?"

"Emily?"

"It's lovely there," I told him. "It's like stepping back in time. It's so quaint and romantic. We went with the school, didn't we, Marion?"

"Mmm."

"When I stood at that graveyard in front of their house, I expected the front door to open and all of them to come walking out. Honest, you'd think you were in another century. It was so real and so untouched … oh, but I don't want to spoil it for them. They mightn't see what I saw. I'm probably just an old romantic but don't tell anybody," I warned. *Couldn't let people know I had a heart now, could I?*

"Yeah. You probably are being a bit over the top, Col. I mean I liked it, but I wouldn't go back there."

"Oh, I would."

A bell tinkled, signalling to Tye that the meal was ready. He disappeared into the kitchen and came out a few seconds later with a tray of steaming hot food.

"Where are your mum and dad staying, Tye?" I asked as I unfolded my napkin.

"They stay in Adelphi."

"Very nice."

"You must meet them before they return to Japan."

"Oh, we'd love to, wouldn't we, Col?" Marion exclaimed. "I've never been in the Adelphi before so that'll be an experience in itself. I'll have to brush up on my table manners, you know, work your way from the outside in or is it the inside out?" she asked me.

"I'm not sure. Maybe we should just have a sandwich, Marion."

A party of four arrived and Tye excused himself. It seemed so long since I'd had a decent night out that I'd forgotten how to conduct myself and drank the wine like lemonade. I was feeling happier than I'd felt in ages and was determined to let my hair down and enjoy myself. After we had eaten our meal, we finished off the wine and ended up going around the corner to the Odeon to watch *Pretty Woman*.

Of course, neither of us could stand Julia Roberts. *Too tall...too thin...her hair's too thick...her legs are too long...* But Richard Gere ... well, he was something else...

Marion was all dreamy-eyed when we came back out onto the busy street.

"Did you see the way he was looking at her with those gorgeous brown eyes?"

I looked to the right and left as we crossed the road, and there was Eddie sitting in his car. I pretended not to notice. Why should he spoil Marion's night? We stepped over the railings at St Georges Hall and walked down towards the museum. I smiled at the NO ENTRY traffic sign.

"I hope I dream about Richard Gere tonight," she said, "Just imagine, Col, if you try hard enough, you can spend the night with anyone you want and be anywhere in the world, can't you? I mean, if you think about them for long enough?"

I burst out laughing and gave her a shove. Sometimes she came out with the strangest things.

"I suppose it's a possibility but Marion, if that was true we'd never get out of bed, would we? I could do with somebody to dream about at night now that I'm on my own. In fact, I might even start practising myself and maybe I can spend the night with, erm, let me see ..." I thought for a moment. "I know. Lawrence Olivier when he played Heathcliff in *Wuthering Heights*. Not the real Heathcliff in the novel. He was hard and bitter and cruel. The only decent thing about him was his passion for Cathy. Oh, but Lawrence Olivier... I could tip-toe hand in hand across the moors with him and pretend to be Cathy and then when he snatches me into his arms and puts his beautiful mouth on mine, I could say, 'Oh, Heathcliff,' and faint and he could ca..."

"Col-e-ette!" Marion nudged me. "Everyone's looking at you."

"Oops, sorry," I giggled, "I just got carried away."

Somebody touched Marion's shoulder. "Hello there, girl, how's your mam? I haven't seen her for ages, she not sick or anything, is she?" It was Dicky Owens from the butcher shop near Marion's.

You'd think he'd have known.

"She's dead, Mr Owens," Marion replied.

"I'm sorry, girl, I had no idea!" he said, hurrying off into the night.

Marion wiped her eyes with a tissue. "All I seem to be doing lately is apologising, but I am really sorry, Col, I didn't mean to spoil your night."

"You haven't spoilt my night," I assured her as we walked past St John's Market and down into Church Street. "In fact, it's the best night I've had out in ages but for God's sake, Marion, will you stop feeling guilty for missing your mother?"

"Yeah," she sniffed, "but your mum died so young. At least mine had sixty-five birthdays and Christmasses. Sometimes when I'm with you I feel so selfish."

"Well, don't. After all, I hardly knew my mother. All I do know about her is that she came from Bolton. My dad never talks about her, you see. Most of the time it's as though she never existed, except on her birthday when we put fresh flowers on her grave."

"He's probably frightened of upsetting you, Col."

"It doesn't matter anymore. Anyway, are we going to Flannigan's or not?"

The drinking session was in full swing by the time we reached the pub. The noise and the heat were overwhelming. We made our way over to Billy's table, where we were given a ceremonious welcome.

No sooner had we sat down than Tony returned from the bar with a tray of drinks. "Come on, girls, get these down you." He handed Marion a vodka and tonic and me a whisky and coke.

I began to relax and enjoy the fun. Having my brothers around meant that Eddie wouldn't dare come near. "Seen anyone you fancy?" Marion joked.

"I don't think I'm interested any more. I've had enough of being tied down. I'm going to start having a bit of fun."

I knew my voice lacked conviction. Marion smiled and said nothing more.

I groaned when the band starting to sing another song. "Come on," I said, dragging Marion's arm. "Let's go and see if they can play any decent music." We went over to the stage and, when the music stopped, we chatted with the band.

THE NEXT MORNING, I woke up where my brothers had left me: fully clothed on the settee. My head ached and, feeling like any sudden movement might make it fall off, I looked around the room. Two armchairs had been put together in the corner and something resembling the shape of a body was covered with a blanket. I staggered over and lifted the cover. It was Marion. Then, like a zombie, I went into the kitchen for the Paracetamol.

"Who's Heathcliff?" Billy wanted to know when he got up later that morning. Even in his drunken state, my calling out as I lay on the couch during the night had disturbed his sleep.

Marion and I began to laugh as we slowly began to remember last night's antics.

"Well, come on then, who is he?" he demanded.

"Ooh," I mouthed to Marion.

"Hey, hang on," he said, the penny dropping. "He's not that mad bugger off the telly who's running round the fields all night in the snow looking for that dead woman, is he?"

That was it! We both roared laughing and for a few minutes we laughed so hard we were unable to speak.

"My poor head," I groaned, tears trickling down my face. "My, my, Billy," I managed to utter, "you've got a lovely way with words."

Marion gave me a mischievous grin before adopting an expression of great concern. "Hey, Billy, why do you ask anyway? You didn't dream about him, did you?"

"No, I bloody didn't."

"Thank God for that. I thought you were gonna tell us you were batting for the other side there, Billy."

I fixed the cushions under my head to make myself more comfy. "Anyway, where've you been?" I asked in a little girly voice. I covered myself over with the blanket and straightened the creases. "We've been waiting hours here for you to get up and cook us our breakfast."

Without answering, he walked behind the settee and tipped it back until, kicking and screaming, I rolled onto the floor.

~ 6 ~

I HUNG UP my coat and put the miniature torch into my breast pocket. With the extra layer of clothes, I was well prepared for the night ahead. Our Billy had cooked me a lovely roast dinner and put ham butties in my bag for my breaks.

Most of the residents were in bed, and only a handful had supper drinks. I hadn't seen Agnes since the handover and presumed she was in the office, sorting out the medication. I went around the building, checking that all the doors and windows were locked, and then put on a pan of milk for the Horlicks.

I groaned when I saw the pile of dirty washing in the laundry. I'd forgotten that all the beds are changed on a Tuesday. No wonder they couldn't get cover for the night; it was the busiest one of the week. I sorted through the heap and stuffed a load of duvet covers into the machine, put in the powder and switched it on and then I emptied the dish washer.

The light flashed on the kitchen wall so I went along the downstairs corridor to answer the bell. Agnes was already there when I arrived. It was the room next door to her office.

"Where's the fire?" I heard her ask as she stood there, blocking Maggie Simpson's doorway.

The sarcastic sod, I thought, returning to the kitchen to make the drinks. Poor Maggie won't be ringing again tonight. Where's the fire, indeed.

I did an extra room check that night and saw the relief on some of the faces when I popped my head around the door. I knew nobody would ring the bell whilst Agnes was on duty. Six of them wanted a drink and three hot water bottles needed filling.

I was busy in the kitchen when Agnes sauntered in to put her chicken curry takeaway on a plate. She looked at the tray of assorted drinks I was about to deliver.

"Who are they for?" she asked. As if she cared! I watched her spread the curry evenly across her plate and then lick her fingers.

"It's for those who are too nervous to ring the bell because you're on duty," I told her.

When I crept into Maisie's room, she was fast asleep so I removed her glasses, put the old notebook she had been reading onto her locker and covered her shoulders. She opened her sleepy eyes and smiled at me.

"Sorry if I woke you," I whispered.

She shook her head and beckoned me to lean closer. She pointed to the book and back to me.

"Oh, I didn't read it, Maisie."

She shook her head and repeated the actions.

"Do you want me to take it and read it?"

She smiled and rested her head back on the pillow.

It was 2 a.m. by the time I had finished my jobs. I could hear Agnes snoring when I passed the office to get a blanket. I hadn't seen her for hours.

I was tired and looked forward to this break. I plonked my bag on the floor in the lounge, pulled the cleanest armchair close to the gas fire, covered myself up with the blanket, took a bite of my butties and opened Maisie's red book.

Ireland 1930

IT WAS THE height of summer and nature was in full bloom. The flooded dirt track, now dried in the June heat, crunched underfoot as the men made their way home from the fields where they had been since the break of dawn. The sun beat down on their tired weather-worn faces, their hot sweaty bodies welcoming the soft breeze as they headed towards Tansey's, where they knew Paddy would have a warm welcome and a cool pint. A crowd was expected home from Liverpool and the men were looking forward to some good craic.

In the cottage on the hill, the sun shone through the tiny squared windows, spreading across the floor like a patchwork quilt. It had been a busy day and in between the baking and seeing to the animals, Josie had spent what little spare time she had getting ready for the barn dance.

An hour earlier Gertie had broken away from the rest of the cattle and trampled through the fence, onto Hanley's land. By the time the fugitive was discovered, the damage had been done, and after apologising profusely to her sour neighbour, Josie and I lead the calf home.

I straightened out the folds in my friend's blue satin dress, which had been so lovingly put together by her mother. She stepped into her new sandals and gave a twirl, laughing like a child when she spun around. Her long fair hair cascaded over her shoulders in soft springy waves, and her deep blue eyes glinted with excitement. Mrs O'Brien looked at her daughter with such pride. It was times like this I missed my mother, but I was lucky in some ways, because my best friend, Josie, was more like a sister.

"Oh, lass, you're a beauty. Jesus, Mary and Joseph, just look at you." Her rough hand stroked her daughter's soft, gentle skin. "Fit to dance in marble halls."

Josie looked at her mother sadly. How often she must have heard her sing that song. It was as if a black cloud descended on her and the dance was now a million miles away.

"Aw, mammy, why did you have to marry him; you should have married a prince instead of that..."

Mrs O'Brien turned away so we wouldn't see the pain in her eyes as her mind probably drifted back into the past – a past she preferred to forget.

My da told me that from the age of five she had walked with a limp, after her right leg had been badly mangled. He said she was still haunted by the memory of that awful day when she'd toppled off the horse and cart and by her mother's screams as she'd carried her into the doctor's. Within seconds of the cloth being placed over her nose, she had slowly drifted away from the nightmare and the pain. She'd spent months in a Dublin hospital, finally emerging with a permanent leg brace. Over the years she was constantly reminded of how lucky she was to be alive and how she had nearly bled to death on the doctor's table.

She had watched her friends marry one by one, something she had given up on. That is, until her father made Pat O'Brien an offer one night at his brother's wedding reception. Complaining of the disadvantages of being the second son with nothing to inherit but a ticket to England and, despite being five years younger than her, he took her father up on his offer. Everybody thought he was a good catch but Josie's mother felt humiliated. Marrying a man five years her junior caused her to shed many a tear before the wedding. But the decision had been made. There was no going back.

And so the marriage went ahead but Mrs O'Brien wasn't to know the years of heartache to come as one baby after another died in infancy. Josie was the fifth and last child who came into the world kicking and screaming. Even the midwife Kitty Saunders, declared that this one was here to stay.

Mrs O'Brien turned back to her daughter and forced a smile. "I could have gone to America and stayed with my cousin Margaret. I was just turned eighteen at the time and itching to get out into the world."

"Then why didn't you?" Josie pleaded, obviously desperate to understand.

Her mother's face melted into a smile. "Ah, musha, if I'd gone to America, I wouldn't have had you, would I? And God knows where I'd have ended up. Not everyone made their fortune in America. Oh no, there were hard times there too. And not everybody made it to America either. Didn't Pat O'Riley fall overboard during the crossing? So maybe it was for the best."

"But you wouldn't have married him."

"I know that. But good or bad, and God knows he has his faults, he is your father."

Josie looked down at the stone floor and I could see she was trying not to cry. "You don't need to remind me. Hasn't he told me almost every day of my life? Every time I step out of line he reminds me how this place, your place, not his place, will be left to the church, instead of me. And when he's not mouthing it, he's saying it through those wicked eyes. I hate him!"

Mrs O'Brien touched Josie's chin with her fingers and tilted her head to meet her eyes.

"Don't be cross," she whispered. "Hate makes people ugly. Eats away at their hearts like acid and makes them bitter and twisted. Come on now, just for me."

We went out into the sunshine and followed the kittens into the shed.

"Now, a ghrá, don't you come back here tonight, because you know he'll only start on you," her mother warned when we returned with a pan full of potatoes. Josie placed them in the sink to be scrubbed and went to see to the fire. "Stay at Maisie's. He'll be sober in the morning and won't give it another thought. After tonight, the place will be wedged with them all home from England, and there'll not be sight nor sound of him for days."

Josie nodded. "When will there ever be any peace in this house?" she whispered. "Why can't he just die? He's in the fields from morning till night. He has the strength of an ox."

Poor Josie! I think she feared he was going to live forever.

"An' if you must be chatting with Johnny, be discreet. You know what your father says."

"But, mammy, it isn't fair. The arguments are between him and Johnny's father, not us two, and all over a stupid animal that was probably cooked up for somebody's dinner long ago. What has it all to do with me and Johnny?"

Mrs O'Brien nodded. "I know, child, but you know the hate that's between those two men, and he'll not have his name mentioned in this house. That's the way it's always been and that's the way it always will be."

"I thought God lived up in heaven not here in this house," Josie responded, taking more sods out of the bucket and placing them on the back of the fire. "I will be careful, but only for your sake. One day I shall leave here and then I'll be free of him. I'll speak to whomever I want and choose my own friends and he'll know nothing about my life."

When she turned back to her mother and saw the pools in her eyes, she stopped dead in her tracks. "Oh, mammy," she whispered, throwing herself at her mother's feet and burying her head in her lap. "I'm sorry. I didn't mean to make you cry. I didn't mean what I said. I'll never go off and leave you. I promise."

"I know you won't, a ghrá. You're upset and don't mean half of what you're saying. Haven't I always told you you're the best daughter any mother could have? Haven't I?"

Josie nodded sheepishly.

"Come on now," her mother coaxed. "Swill your face and we'll have no more talk of it." She lifted the teapot from the centre of the table and poured herself another cup. "No doubt you and Maisie will be up half the night talking," she said, stirring in a spoonful of sugar, "so I don't expect you'll be fit to do any chores with me in the morning. We'll just see to the animals and leave the washing until the day after."

LATER ON THAT same day, I lay sprawled face down in the grass, deeply absorbed in my book. Every so often my black mongrel, Pilot, scrambled to her feet and wobbled off to the lake, eagerly lapping up the cool spring water. She was old and tired and needed to be in the shade on such a hot day. My da said we should put her out of her misery but I wouldn't let him.

"Go on home, girl," I told her. "Go on." I watched her trundle off before continuing to read.

The box of books had arrived from America a month ago and I had snatched every opportunity to escape to the peace and quiet at the back of the old cow-shed, devouring each story from cover to cover. Every book I finished was always better than the one before. But this last one really was the best and, for some reason, I had received two copies of the same book. I took a deep breath when I turned the page. "That's right, Jane," I whispered, as a tear dropped from the end of my nose and landed on the black ink. "Go back and find him. Go on, follow your heart."

On and on I read, losing all sense of time, transported into another world of long ago: a world of hardship, tragedy, determination and love.

Something tickled the back of my leg. Unable to turn myself away from the page, I scratched it idly and continued reading until a hand whipped the book from under my nose. I leapt to my feet with fright and glared at Arnie Tosh.

Ever since he'd arrived home from England two months ago, he'd strutted around like a peacock, believing he was a great catch but I had my own plans. I wasn't going to marry some old penniless farmer with a stone hut or become a nun and spend the rest of my days scrubbing wooden floors, indeed I wasn't.

I was going to marry a man just like Mr Rochester.

"Arnie Tosh, you big stupid eejit! Did you leave your brains back in England?"

I watched in horror as he threw my book high in the air. When I leapt up to grab the descending missile, his long arm reached out, and it fell easily into his hand. He tossed the book into the air again and this time I flew at him and belted him across the face nearly knocking his thick-rimmed glasses from his nose.

"Give me back my book!"

"Bejesus," he grinned, his eyes roaming up and down my body, "I didn't know you had such a temper on you."

"Well, you do now. Give me back my book," I hissed.

He continued to stand there smirking, one side of his face beginning to redden from the slap I'd just given him. Then, up he tossed it into the air and down it came. Up and down. Up and down.

I lifted my leg and kicked him as hard as I could, making him stagger back with a groan. An angry shove while he was still off balance sent him sprawling backwards into the grass.

"There! That'll teach you."

I had barely caught my breath when he was back on his feet, shaking the earth from his clothes, glancing around slyly to make sure nobody had witnessed the scene.

"Ah, Maisie," he laughed, showing his cigarette-stained teeth, "don't…"

"Never you mind, 'Ah, Maisie'. Those cows in that field behind you have more sense than you. You might think you're clever, but I know you're not, you – you ignorant Jeramous."

I wrung my hands and fought back the tears as he continued with his silly antics. "Give me back my Jane Eyre!" I yelled, lifting a broken stake from the ground, "or I'll crack your skull."

He stepped back and hid the book behind him. "Only if you'll have a dance with me tonight?"

"I mean it." I warned him but he continued laughing and then began to throw my book up in the air again. I looked at him in disgust. His pock-marked face was as hard and lumpy as a bog on a hot summer's day. The thoughts of his filthy hands soiling the best book I had ever read fuelled my anger and, before I realised what I was doing, I brought the wood down on his head.

CRACK!

He groaned and fell to the ground…

I JUMPED WITH fright as the piercing sound assaulted my ears, closed the book and dropped it into my bag. I was so disorientated, I just stood in the middle of the floor, and then I realised the burglar alarm was ringing.

The strong winds often triggered the system. I just needed to shut that awful din off fast. I could see the bells lighting up on the wall and my heart sank as I realised that was the end of my break. *Oh my God, I* thought, my head still in Ireland, *what a time to leave the story.*

I rushed down the corridor to the control panel.

"It's only me," Agnes said as I neared the front door. "I had to go out to the car and I forgot to turn off the alarm."

The kitchen was freezing when I went to fill the kettle. I knew there'd be a few needing a hot drink after being woken by that racket. I couldn't get Maisie off my mind; killing someone over a book. Sometimes I felt like killing people when they didn't return books I'd lent them. 'It's only a paper-back,' they'd moan, but it's far more than that to me. Maybe it's a book I'd like to read again sometime, and it's no longer available to buy in the shops, or maybe it's a story I absolutely adored and had wanted to share, expecting the borrower to do the decent thing and return it to me. That's why I no longer lent them out.

WHEN THE DAY shift came in, I was busy helping Fred to shave. I used to hate this task and it took months of practice before I stopped nicking someone's skin with the razor. At one time there could be three or four men walking around with bits of cotton wool mixed with blood stuck all over their neck and chins and I'd hear the staff laughingly ask if I had shaved them. Now I was a dab hand at it, even if I said so myself.

Agnes was handing over the night's report and it was time to go home, but I wasn't going anywhere. Not until I found out what happened to that annoying bugger who pinched Maisie's *Jane Eyre*.

When I left Fred's room, I bumped into Julie on the corridor.

"Morning, Colette. Did you have a good night?"

"It was okay, Julie, but I've got a bit of a headache and I was wondering if I could have a lie down in the respite room before I go home?"

"Certainly. The bed's empty until tomorrow. Would you like me to bring you a cup of tea and a couple of Paracetamol?"

"No, thanks. I'll be fine if I rest for half an hour."

I collected my things from the sitting room and I was soon opening the red book where I had left off...

~ ~ ~

I STOOD THERE, looking down at his body, and began shaking like a leaf. I hadn't meant to hurt him. It was only meant to be a threat. Oh, me and my temper!

I ran through the grass and hid behind a tree, almost breathless with fright. I stood there for ages with my back against the wood, too scared to face what I had done, then, I peeped around the side of the trunk and put my hand to my mouth in shock. He lay there stone dead, the blood trickling down his face.

My stomach heaved and I began to vomit violently. I'd never meant to kill him. And what was my da going to say when he found out I was a murderer?

Maybe they would hang me or send me to prison in Dublin for the rest of my life. I waited for a few minutes trying to pluck up some courage.

Somehow I had to get my book.

I took a deep breath and slowly put one foot in front of the other, all the while watching the dead man lying in the grass. When I reached the body, I very slowly stooped to retrieve the novel from the crook of his arm. Then I saw his chest rise and fall.

I never thought the sight of Arnie Tosh, *breathing* would put a smile on my face, but it did. I laughed aloud and turned to run home through the fields.

My father was hammering in the fence post when he caught sight of me running down the lane towards him.

"What's happened, lass?"

"Oh, Da, I was so busy reading my book, I forgot all about the dance and now I'll never be ready in time." I could hardly tell him what I had just done.

My da smiled with relief.

It was early evening when I climbed over the stone wall near Josie's. It hadn't taken me long to get ready and, with an hour to kill, I had escaped to my bedroom and finished reading my book. I hadn't cried so much in a long time; hadn't realized about love either. I thought people just married for convenience, and then had one child after another until they couldn't have any more, but not according to Charlotte Brontë. How did she think up such a story?

My eyes felt puffy despite bathing them in cold water.

They mustn't know I've been crying.

I strolled through the sheep-filled meadow and glanced up at the cottage. I was trying to concentrate on the night ahead but the sad image of Jane Eyre kept creeping into my mind.

"Ah, speak of the Devil," Mrs O'Brien greeted me when I popped my head around the door. "Come on, lass. Don't be shy. Come and let's have a look at you."

I stepped into the room and stood self-consciously, with my hands by my sides, waiting for the inspection.

Mrs O'Brien looked at me affectionately. I'd tied my frizzy red hair at the nape of my neck with a black velvet ribbon. My green dress, with the sash around the waist to match my hair ribbon, hung perfectly on my tall, slim body.

"If your mammy was alive she'd be so proud of you, a ghrá, Eighteen years of age," she muttered. "Where did the years go? Ara, they'll be fighting' over you both tonight. There'll be many hearts broken before you take your pick."

Josie sprang to her feet. "Oh, no, mammy, I know who I want. I've known for a long time and he's coming back from Liverpool tonight. He said so in his letter and he's not broken a promise to me yet. Not even—"

"Ah, musha, don't be building up your hopes," her mother interrupted. "You know sometimes when they cross the flash, they forget to return. I've seen too many broken hearts and—"

"Not my Johnny," she blurted, her face melting into an enormous smile. "And if the boat is late and he can't get back from England, he'll get word to me. I know he will." She sat down and pulled out a chair for me to sit beside her.

"I finished that book me uncle sent me, Mrs O'Brien, and it was wonderful," I whispered, opening the clasp on my bag and taking out the novel.

"Another one?" She cocked her head slightly so she could read the title. "Sure, you'll be as blind as a bat by the time you're twenty."

"Oh but this one was the best." I displayed the object with such pride one would have thought I'd written it myself. I could feel my eyes watering and my bottom lip began to tremble and then a great big tear rolled down my face and landed on the table with a little splash.

She reached out and squeezed my hand. She hated to see anybody cry. "Ah, musha, don't take on so, 'twas only a story after all. What was it that's upset you so? Did they all die in the end?" I had no chance to reply because she turned to Josie again. "Isn't there enough tragedy in the world without having to make it up?"

I shook my head. "Oh, no, Mrs O'Brien," I said, jumping to the author's defence. "It had a happy ending ... well, sort of," I decided, running my fingers along the name on the spine. "You see, they're both in love and it's other people and circumstances that drive them apart. They're both loyal and strong and honourable. Well," I said, as an afterthought, "she is more than him because he has a wife hidden away in the attic and it's a big secret and he doesn't tell anybody and she only finds out in the church on her wedding day when his real wife's brother's solicitor turns up from Jamaica and stops the ceremony right there and then."

Josie's mother opened her mouth to speak and then closed it again.

"Aw, but it's not as bad as it sounds, Mrs O'Brien."

"Good God in heaven," she finally muttered. "You better hadn't let Father Mullen see you reading books like that. He'll be shouting at you from the pulpit and bringing shame onto your family."

For a moment I wanted to laugh but quickly checked myself so as not to cause offense. I knew if Father Mullen looked at me sideways he'd live to regret it. Ever since he'd clouted my brother Jamie around the head in the presbytery and accidentally knocked him to the floor where he'd hit his head on the corner of the grate, requiring ten stitches, Father Mullen wouldn't dare come near us.

I tried to sound light-hearted when I said, "Father Mullen won't know and besides, me da is master in our house, not the priest, so just as long as I don't read them in church, he's nothing to worry about."

Mrs O'Brien folded her arms across her chest and grinned at me playfully. "It's your mother I'm looking at and listening to sitting right here in front of me. She had the face of an angel, too, and no more than yourself was a woman of few words but if she had a point to make she'd have argued with Our Lord."

I began to laugh softly and the others soon joined in. I turned my attention back to the book cover.

"I wish I could write like that, don't you, Josie?" I asked, nudging my friend. "I suppose you can only write about things you know and what do I know about love?"

Josie grinned. I knew she could count the books she'd read on one hand – she didn't share my passion for reading. "Maisie, have I not told you before?" she said, stirring the tea and placing a cup in front of me. "You read the books and then tell me the stories."

We laughed again and spent the next half hour chatting and catching up on all the local gossip.

"Oh, I nearly forgot," Mrs O'Brien said, shoving her chair back and limping over to the press in the corner. "Now I've got a little something for both of you and it's about time I gave them to you instead of leaving them here gathering dust. After all, when would I ever get the chance to wear them again and they'd look better on you two than me."

Josie and I exchanged glances before following her mother with our eyes. After rummaging through some old cloths, she closed the drawer and limped back over to us.

"Close your eyes," she said in her sing-song voice. We immediately obeyed and squeezed them tightly shut but I peeked and saw her taking hold of Josie's hand and placing something in her palm. Then she did the same to me. "You can open them now," she whispered.

Josie's harp brooch had two blue stones encrusted on the left-hand side, and the violin brooch I had been given had a ruby encrusted on the bow.

My friend's eyes filled with tears. "But, mammy, they're your pride and joy." Her voice was barely audible as she inspected the piece of jewellery, turning it one way and then the other.

"And so are you two and that's why I'm giving them to you. Now come on," she ordered, taking Josie's brooch and opening the clasp. "Let me pin them on you." She stood back to admire her daughter before moving on to me.

I wiped my eyes with the back of my hand and stood very still whilst the brooch was pinned to my dress. "It's beautiful, Mrs O'Brien," I whispered. "I shall never part with it."

The sound of the horse and cart made us all jump.

"Now go on with you quickly," she urged, clearing the cups and teapot off the table. "The less he knows the better."

I grabbed my bag from the table and slid the book inside. Then, like a pair of children, we held hands as we ran down the field, laughing hysterically when we reached the gate and ran into the lane, stopping only for a moment to make sure our brooches were fastened tightly.

THE FOLLOWING MORNING I dragged my tired legs up to Josie's. I could hear her mother playing the piano; that meant *he* was out. I smiled, replaying last night's events in my mind. I spent half the night dancing with an America who was leaving for Chicago in two days time.

"What's your name?" he'd asked me when we sat near the door for some fresh air. I smiled up into his handsome face.

"Jane." The name fell from my lips without any thought. "Jane

Eyre." I waited for him to laugh and tell me to be serious, but he didn't.

"May I write to you, Jane?"

My heart soared. He'd called me Jane!

"Of course you may, but if you send your letter c/o the post office, then it'll be sure to get to me."

He left soon after, travelling to Westport, to spend the last couple of days with an uncle and I wasn't sure if I would hear from him again. Handsome or not, I wasn't that interested in him, but the letter....

I would have to ask Lilly Hanley, just to be on the safe side. If she promised to keep any post for Jane Eyre a secret, I could offer to clean her shop every week, or serve behind the counter for an afternoon. Oh, I would do anything for her!

And then towards the end of the evening, who came through the door, but that Arnie Tosh. There he stood in his crumpled black suit, looking like he'd slept in it for a week; his dirty unshaven face a match with his bruised head. I thought I might have knocked some sense into him but I hadn't, because he still wouldn't leave me alone and kept leering over me with his drunken breath, until my brother spotted him and threatened to throw him in a cell overnight if he didn't leave me alone.

Josie caught sight of me and my dog through the window and came out clutching the egg basket. Off we went, arm in arm, to the chicken coop at the back of the cottage.

"What happened to you this morning?" I asked as I pinned my bushy hair behind my ears. "You must have risen with the sun. I woke up and you were gone. I thought you were in the kitchen and I was lying there like Lady Muck, expecting you to walk in with a mug of tea and a piece of bread, for my breakfast."

"Sorry, Maisie. I wanted to get home to see how mammy was and you looked so peaceful, I didn't want to disturb you." She opened the wire mesh door and we went inside and closed it after us.

"Stay there, girl," I instructed the panting dog, and she immediately flopped onto the ground. I turned back to Josie. "Well?" I asked shyly. "Are you going to tell me or not?"

Josie's eyes twinkled and she covered her blushing face with her hands, showing her nails almost bitten to the quick.

"Oh, Josie O'Brien, I do believe you're in love. Just look at you with them stars in your eyes! You can die of happiness, you know?"

We stooped down and placed the eggs in the basket.

"Oh, Maisie, is it that obvious?" she asked, avoiding my eyes.

"It is." I chuckled. "And last night you were dancing like you were the only two in the world. Someday I'm going get myself a feller but not from around here," I told her as I thought about Arnie Tosh.

Josie rested on her haunches. "I love him so much I'd give him my heart's blood, and if I tell you this you mustn't tell a soul."

"I promise." And just to prove it I made the sign of the cross and waited expectantly for Josie to reveal the big secret.

"He wants to marry me."

I stopped smiling. "But—but—what about your da? He won't be too pleased about that, will he? Isn't Johnny's name still a dirty word in your house?"

"With my da, everybody's name is a dirty word and, with a bit of luck, by the time I'm twenty-one he won't be around anyway."

"Oh, Josie, you've been wishing he was dead since you could talk. I'd say the old tyrant has plenty of years in him yet."

"Well, I can hope and pray and, when the time comes, he'll not stop me." And then her face softened. "Never mind about me. What about you? You spent a long time dancing with that swanky Yankee. I saw the way he was looking at you."

I gasped. Now it was my turn to be embarrassed. "Oh, Josie, now it's you that has to keep a secret. He says he's going to write to me but he doesn't know me real name." Josie looked confused. "What d'you mean, he doesn't know your real name. Who does he think you are?"

I couldn't speak for laughing and then I whispered, "Jane Eyre."

"Jane Eyre?" she roared. "Maisie O'Donnel, have you lost your mind? If your Jamie finds out, there'll be hell to play. You know how protective he is."

"Well, he won't ever find out," I whispered. "Unless you tell him, and I know you'll never do that, will you Josie?"

"Ara, no, of course not, but wouldn't it be grand if you married a Yank? Just think of all the holidays you'd have across the ocean, and all the goodies you could bring back for us."

I sighed. "I hardly know the man and you already have me married off. Besides, I'll not be marrying any Yank. I'm going to marry a gentleman like Mr Rochester, in the book."

"Maisie O'Donnel, you're such a dreamer."

"And why shouldn't I dream? Don't you know dreams can come true?"

EVERYBODY TOOK ADVANTAGE of the dry weather and worked from morning until night. The long grass had been cut and bailed and stacked in the hay shed along with the turf. I had been up since the crack of dawn, boiling water to fill the wash tub. My father had been on the back field all morning, knocking in new fence stakes and checking the barbed wire. Jamie was down at the Garda station. Their overalls had been soaking for days. I dipped them into fresh, hot, soapy water and began to scrub them clean. I had just finished squeezing them through the mangle and began to peg them on the line when I heard someone giggling and half turned to see one of the schoolchildren come running into the yard with two cats trailing her feet.

"Hello, Sara," I called through the wind to the chubby little girl. "I'll be with you in a tick."

"Morning, Maisie," the child greeted as she stood waiting by the back door. "Miss Hines wants to know would you ever take class today?"

"Indeed I would." I said, approaching the cottage. "With this lovely sunny day the good Lord has blessed us with we could have a picnic on the field and make daisy chains and do all the things we're not supposed to." She giggled when I rubbed her jet black curls and shuffled her into the kitchen. "Did your mammy make that pretty dress?" I asked, standing back to admire her.

"She did so! Don't you know my mammy makes all of my clothes? She even makes my daddy's shirts and trousers. My mammy can do anything. Honest to God, Maisie, she can." She watched me lift the lid off the cake tin and offer her a piece of chocolate sponge. She took a bite and licked her lips before she spoke. "She made it for Easter, but she said I am growing so fast that I can wear it all the time and don't have to save it for Sundays anymore." Her little hand absent-mindedly brushed the crumbs off her dress onto the floor as the two watchful cats ran in from the step and devoured them.

"That's the beauty of being the eldest of five girls and not the youngest," I told her.

"Oh, and I have to tell you, Mrs O'Leary couldn't come in because her Rosie had a baby girl at three o'clock this morning, and she was too tired to come in to class."

I rolled my eyes. "Another girl; sure, the poor woman will be running out of names, but I expect she'll keep on going until she gets her little boy."

"Keep on going where, Maisie?"

"Never you mind," I said offering another cake.

"Why haven't you got a feller, Maisie?" she asked, swinging her plump legs.

"I beg your pardon?"

"Well, my mammy says," she managed to say in between mouthfuls of cake, "it's because you have your head stuck in them books all the time but my daddy says there's time enough yet."

"Oh, is that so?" I placed a glass of milk in front of her. "Drink your milk and be off with you."

"Oh, can I not wait for you, Maisie?"

"Ara, no. You run on ahead and tell Miss Hines I'll be there in ten minutes."

After she'd left, I stepped into my lilac dress and fastened the buttons from the waist up, straightened my collar and put a clean handkerchief from the drawer into my pocket. I brushed my long hair over my shoulder and tied a ribbon around the end. A few minutes later, I left the house and wandered out through the village to the little school.

Miss Hines was the pulse of the village; a small, thin, formidable woman whose bark was worse than her bite. Rumour had it that she used to be a missionary nun and, after surviving a long illness in Africa, had left the order. Her cousin, Father Grady, in dire need of a teacher in the next village at the time, had gladly given her the little house, which had been left to the church and she, in turn, had accepted a nominal teaching fee along with the accommodation. Years of travelling on the far side of the world had made her skin rough and weather-worn. Her long grey hair, which some said reached the floor when it was loose, was tied into a bun at the nape of her neck. No matter how bad the weather, she cycled the five miles to school every day with her dog running alongside her. The creature would then wait patiently outside the building until it was time to return home.

I smiled when I thought about the old priest.

Miss Hines thought children should be seen and heard, and encouraged open debates on some very controversial subjects. When the priest heard she'd been discussing women's rights and telling them the story of the Suffragettes, fighting for women's right to vote, it was the last straw.

"That woman will have to go," I overheard Father Mullen telling Father Grady, but the truth was, apart from the part-time help, she was all they had. If they sacked Miss Hines, the school would have to close.

"Will you at least stop putting fancy ideas into their heads?" the stout little priest had asked her one day when I was helping out. I knew he couldn't care less if the school closed down. Father Mullen would have been quite happy for the children to stay at home and get their education from the pulpit at daily Mass.

A few weeks later, I was sitting in the corner of the classroom with the group of oldest children. Not a sound could be heard apart from my voice as I read loudly, glancing around occasionally when I turned the page to see so many pairs of eyes on me.

Miss Hines was sitting at her desk setting the weekend's homework when Father Mullen quietly entered the room. His sneaky eyes took in the scene and, after greeting Miss Hines, he strolled over to the group in the corner and, standing before me without either acknowledging me or the children, he stretched out his palm. With a nervous glance at Miss Hines as she approached us, I turned to the priest and placed the book in his hand.

Miss Hines ignored his bad manners and addressed the children.

"Say good afternoon to Father Mullen."

The children obeyed and received a muffled reply from the preoccupied priest as he stood before them, flicking angrily through the pages of the novel.

"What is this?" he hissed.

A stern look from Miss Hines stifled the children's giggles and she quickly suggested we go outside and play in the sunshine. When the last of the children had shuffled out, I quietly closed the door after us.

I could hear the priest through the open window. "Miss Hines, I asked you what this is?"

"Well, Father, unless I am sadly mistaken, it looks like a book to me."

I stood on tiptoe and watched the priest push the book in front of the teacher's face. Miss Hines glanced at the cover and smiled. "Ah, that's Jane Eyre. Why, have you not read it, Father?" She slowly moved around the room, placing a set of questions on each desk.

"Have I read Jane Eyre?" He sounded incredulous.

"Oh do forgive me, Father. It's just that when I think of such a brilliant young woman being half Irish, the Lord have mercy on her, but then you would already know that."

"Know what?"

"Why, that her Father, Patrick Brontë, came from Ireland, of course." She returned to her desk in front of the classroom and put the rest of the papers into the drawer.

"Yes, yes indeed," he lied.

I giggled when he sat down at one of the desks and took a handkerchief from his pocket to wipe his sweaty brow. Miss Hines sat down opposite him.

"He was born on St Patrick's Day, the oldest of ten children." The priest nodded. "My," she went on, "it's easy to see where Charlotte Brontë got her talent from. Her father was a graduate of Cambridge University. He did us very proud, didn't he, Father?"

"He did. God bless him."

Five minutes later, I watched the priest put up his hand and wave as he left the school yard. She does it every time, I marvelled: he comes in like a lion and goes out like a lamb.

"Is it true what you told Father Mullen?" I asked Miss Hines when we returned to the classroom. "I mean about Charlotte Brontë? Is she really half Irish?"

"She is indeed, child. Where on earth do you think she got her talent?"

On my way home that day, Lilly Hanley banged on the shop window and I hurried inside.

"I've got something for you," she said "and if your father finds out I'm encouraging you with these shenanigans, there'll be hell to play!"

She took a letter from her skirt pocket and handed it to me. "Here,

Jane bloody Eyre! I think this is for you."

~~~

SOMEONE TAPPED ON the door and stuck their head in. "Colette, Marion's on the phone." I leapt off the bed. I'd forgotten she was expecting me to call in on the way home.

"Oh, thanks, Julie. I should have rung her to say I'd be a bit late."

~ 8 ~

IT WAS SUNDAY and, despite the heavy snowfall, Tony and I picked Maisie up to bring her home for the day. When we arrived at the local church, the Mass was finishing but that didn't matter to Maisie. She had always enjoyed the privacy of an empty church where she lit her candles and said her prayers. It didn't matter to me either; I loved an empty church. Father Thomas had long since retired and, to me, nobody could ever replace him.

It was open house that day. My dad always made sure there was an extra 'drop' in for anyone who cared to call. News of Maisie's visit spread and many of my friends and neighbours dropped by to see her. With the long winters and her failing health, Maisie's visits were indeed a rare event and we went out of our way to make her day special and fussed around her like she was made of glass.

"Oh, look at the glow on her cheeks," Tony said, taking the empty glass from her. "No-one makes a hot toddy like my dad, do they Maisie?"

Just at that moment Joan from next door, still boasting her lovely tan from her holiday in Malta, popped her head around the door. She began to cry when saw the wedding ring Maisie had proudly displayed on her finger all her life now hung around her neck on a gold chain. Next was Teresa, on her way home from eleven o'clock Mass. She liked the odd tipple and enjoyed spending an hour or so with us before she went home to give her brood their Sunday lunch. Then Bridget Fahy, God love her, who sat and talked incessantly and prevented anybody else from getting a word in edgeways. Sometimes, if Father Lynch had time, he would pop in before Benediction.

After everyone had gone, Maisie sat at the table and watched Tony playing a game of solitaire whilst my dad and I put out the dinner.

I was such a slob in the kitchen. That's why everybody else usually insisted on doing the cooking. I didn't believe in clearing up as I went along. When I had finished one chore, I just left my mess behind and moved on to the next clear space. Potato peels, empty veg tins, an old used-up Bisto carton, an empty wine bottle were all cluttered along the worktop, making it difficult for my dad to find a place to carve the meat. I sang along to the radio and opened the vent in the window to let out the steam. After fanning myself for a few seconds, I sliced a bit off the butter and, with a drop of milk, I began to mash the potatoes. When they were ready, I scooped them into a dish and placed them in the oven underneath the roast potatoes.

"She's looking awful frail," my dad whispered gravely when he'd finished carving the meat. Laying the knife down, he wiped his hands on a piece of kitchen roll, and strolling over to the fridge, took out a can of lager. "You wouldn't notice it the same, love, because you see her every day at work." He clicked open the can and took a swig. "But, by Christ, she's gone down a lot."

I stopped what I was doing and watched him take down some more clean glasses from the cupboard and, after picking up the bottle from the table, pour Maisie some Harvey's Bristol Cream.

"Oh, don't spoil it, Dad. You think I don't notice?" I asked him. "Of course, I do. I just don't want to think about it. She's such a treasure. I dread anything happening to her."

He held out his arms and gave me a hug. "Me and my big mouth. I'm sorry, love. I didn't mean to upset you."

After lunch, Peter called in, his heavy overcoat dappled with snow. He smiled and ran his hand through his damp hair. When he removed his coat, he looked so suave in his brown silk suit, cream shirt, and matching tie. *What a waste,* I thought when I hugged him. Not that I fancied him, because I didn't, but I couldn't help noticing how heads turned when we walked down the street together.

"I've just come from the hospital," he announced excitedly. "She had a little girl this morning and that means I'm an uncle." He rubbed his hands together with delight.

"Oh, that's fantastic. Are they both well?"

"Couldn't be better," he smiled. "She's gorgeous. You should see her tiny fingers and toes, oh and her face is like a little prune."

I laughed and said, "I hope you didn't tell her mother that."

I introduced him to my two brothers. "My dad's upstairs but he'll be down in a minute."

I was putting a third coat of light pink nail varnish on Maisie's hands. When I held her stick-like fingers to apply the colouring, I was almost afraid of breaking them. My dad had been right. She was getting very frail.

"Can you do mine next?" Peter asked, as he leaned over to kiss Maisie on the cheek.

"Oy, get in the queue. I'm next," Tony said, offering him a can of lager.

"Then me," Billy added.

"How are you, lad?" My dad held out his hand when he came in and saw Peter. "Our Colette's told us all about you and any friend of hers is a friend of ours, so sit down there and make yourself at home," he said, taking Maisie's bag off the chair.

"His sister's just had a baby, Dad."

"Congratulations, son," he said, giving him an extra-long handshake. "And they're both fine?"

"Oh, yeah, *father and baby* are quite comfortable," he said in amusement, explaining that, far from being a great support the baby's father, Andy, had collapsed onto the hospital floor.

"I know how he feels," Billy sympathised.

I looked at my brother in astonishment. "Oh, so how many kids have you got scattered around Liverpool then?"

"I mean, I hate the sight of blood."

"Oh yeah?" I gave him a long look.

"Did you go to the match yesterday, son?" my dad asked, indicating the coverage on the telly.

"I did. Three-one. Brilliant, hey?" Peter said.

"Can you lower your voices, please?" I whispered. "Maisie's an Evertonian."

"So's my brother," Peter informed us, "and even he was pleased that Liverpool won. Anyway, Maisie," he said, putting his thumb up and pointing to the telly, "this is the best team in the world."

From the look Maisie gave him it was obvious that she didn't agree but it was all taken in good fun.

Billy looked at his watch. "If we get our skates on, we can go and wet the baby's head. I reckon we've got an hour before closing."

"Good idea. Are ye coming down, Maisie?" Dad asked.

"Course we are," I said, reaching for our coats.

I waited for Tony to leave the room and leaned over to Peter. "Did you manage to pick the book up for me?"

"It's in the car. I hope it's the right one?"

"*The History of the Second World War*?"

"Yeah, that's it. But his birthday's not today, is it?"

I shook my head. "It's tomorrow so I'll get it off you later on and wrap it tonight. Thanks."

THAT EVENING, WHEN we took Maisie back to the home, I helped her into bed and left the curtains open so she could watch the snowflakes falling. The tree looked like a big ice-cream cone as the soft white ice settled on its branches. Outside, I helped Billy finish the life-size snowman and, finally sticking a carrot in its nose, we stood back to let Maisie admire the creation. Billy put his hand on his heart and began to serenade her through the window. "Maisie, Maisie, give me your answer do, I'm half crazy all for the love of you…"

I couldn't help sneaking up behind him, clad in my red bobble hat and scarf. I pushed him over and laughed hysterically as I put my face close to the window and blew the old lady a kiss. "See you tomorrow, Maisie." I gave her a quick wave and then ran, knowing in a few seconds my brother would be on my heels and would do God knows what when he caught up with me.

I turned and watched him scramble to his feet and brush the snow from his coat. He leaned against the bedroom window and kissed the pane of glass.

"I'm off now, Maisie. I'll see you soon."

I stood nearby in the bush and watched him stoop down and make an enormous snowball and then I turned on my heels, screaming in the night air as he came running after me.

LAST TIME I had been asked to do a night shift; this time I volunteered. I was working with Julie and the bells must have rung for four hours solid. *Fix my pillows...put my bed socks on...a bit more sugar in my tea...close that gap in the curtains...what happened in Coronation Street? I fell asleep.* Any excuse for a bit of a chat.

Julie brought in her home-made scones and they all enjoyed their 'afternoon' tea during News at Ten. We had the Golden Oldies station on the kitchen radio and made pasta for our supper. It was 3 a.m. by the time we'd finished. I settled down once again in the sitting room and continued to read the red book.

~~~

THE WEATHER EVOKED such memories. Summers reminded me of Ireland, of the cattle and sheep, and beautiful countryside–and snowy winters of the time in 1935, just four years before the Second World War broke out, when I had arrived in Liverpool with hundreds of other Irish emigrants.

I had stepped off the boat with a mixture of excitement and fear. With ten pounds in my purse and a bag containing a change of clothes, I looked around in wonder. The snow fell heavily and, with only two days to Christmas, there was a festive cheerfulness about the place.

The crossing had been choppy. The only available seat had been near the saloon doors and, despite my layers of clothes, the freezing draught from the sea had chilled me to the bone. My feet were still numb.

For a while, I stood in the freezing snow at the spot where I was to be collected by the landlady's son. Soon it began to dawn on me that I would have to make my own way to the house. Maybe, I thought, he couldn't get off from work after all. I stood under the lamp and took out the crumpled address from my pocket and tried to read it. My hands felt like ice as I stood there trying to decipher the writing.

"Are you all right, luv?" one of the dockers asked, rubbing his hands together and then blowing on them. I'd been warned about the dangers of speaking to strange men and suddenly felt afraid so I hurried on. 'Find the church,' he'd said. Now I remembered. 'If I'm not there to meet you, find the church.' I looked around me in bewilderment then I spotted the church tower. I crossed the road with a sigh of relief, walked up the steps and went in, wiping my wet boots on the mat just inside the door. My icy fingers unbuttoned my coat and I shook the snow from it onto the floor. For a moment, I stood at the back, careful not to stand in the path of the many people coming and going. An old lady knelt down in prayer near the crib in the corner and there was a constant rattle as people dropped money into the charity box beside her.

I dipped my hand in the font, blessed myself with the holy water and walked down the aisle to the front of the church, genuflecting before I stepped into the pew. The beauty and peace almost took my breath away as I gazed at Jesus on the cross, his sad eyes looking back at me. I joined my hands, closed my eyes and began to pray. I sat there on the bench for a long time afterwards.

So, Maisie O'Donnel, you finally did it, the voice in my head enthused. I did, I answered, feeling a great sense of relief, knowing the hardest part – leaving my friends and family in the West of Ireland – was now over. But I didn't do it on my own.

I opened my bag, took out my most treasured possessions and clutched the battered old books to my heart. They'd been a gift from Miss Hines, and sometimes, like that moment, I felt as if I drew my very breath from them. I looked down and smiled at the title: *The Life of Charlotte Brontë.* She was my heroine, a woman who filled me with hope and inspiration and gave me the courage to follow my dreams.

I sat and read for a while longer and, when an hour had passed, I realised I would have to make other plans.

The candles burnt in the corner. I knelt down and lit one for my mother and father. The other was a very special intention. I stared up at the crucifix for a long time and, closing my eyes, I began to pray more intently, offering up three Hail Marys and an Our Father. When I was finished, I went to the front of the altar and genuflected. Then I went out into the freezing cold.

The biting wind blew the snow into my face as I made my way back across the road to the Pier Head. I looked around in bewilderment again. Time was getting on. I would have to sort something out.

"Can we help you, Mrs?"

I turned around to see two boys of about ten years old, covered in snow. I told them the street I was looking for and they promised to take me. Just as I began to walk away from the Pier Head, I heard someone calling from behind. When the two young boys turned around and saw the man, they ran away. I nearly froze with fear as he came rushing up to me almost losing his balance on the slippery path.

"Don't be startled, luv. I'm not gonna hurt you but those two urchins were."

Anger flared inside me. "And what harm did they do to you?"

He hesitated before he spoke. "Pardon me but, looking at your travelling bag, I'm thinking you've just arrived from Ireland and those two boys are notorious for leading strangers down an alley where the real villains are waiting to rob them."

"Oh I'm sorry," I whispered.

"You're frozen to the bone. Look, why don't you come over to the café," he gestured toward the building across the road, "and let me buy you a cup of soup?"

His warning had scared me and now I was suspicious of everybody. "And how do I know I can trust you?"

"I give you my word."

I remained standing in the bitter cold, wondering whether to trust him or not. Then his hand reached out and, taking me by the arm, he accompanied me over the road.

The café was filled with a mixture of travellers and dockers coming in from the bitter cold to warm themselves. The floor was wet with melted snow and I was careful not to slip as he took my arm and led me to a table in the far corner.

"My name is Jimmy Cosgrove," he said, offering his outstretched hand across the table. "And I'm a security officer on the docks." He smiled and I found myself returning his smile.

"And I'm Maisie O'Donnel." I slipped my icy hand into his. "And I don't really know what I am at the moment."

When he returned with the cups of hot soup, I sipped the steaming liquid appreciatively. I listened to the conversations around me and felt that if I closed my eyes, I could well have been in a Dublin café, so similar was the wit and banter of the people.

He took a sip of his soup without taking his eyes from me. "Well, Maisie O'Donnel, have you a place to stay?"

"I think so, Jimmy Cosgrove."

"Well, then, Maisie O'Donnel, just so that I will be able to sleep peacefully tonight, I hope you will allow me to safely deposit you there?"

I laughed at his persistence. "Well, now, Jimmy Cosgrove, it's awful good of you to offer, but I have ten pounds in my purse and ..."

"You see?" he interrupted. "You're rich picking for the pickpockets, with 'traveller' written all over you, and you're too open and honest."

I put my cup of soup on the table and stared at him sadly. Next thing the tears were pouring down my cheeks. He reached over and clasped my hand.

"Oh God, I'm sorry. I never meant to upset you. Oh no, please don't cry." He reached into his pocket for a hankie. "I didn't mean to speak out of turn." The poor man was white with despair.

I leaned in closer, struggling to explain. "It's not your fault," I whispered. "You didn't speak out of turn. It's been an eventful day and it was sad leaving my friends and family in Ireland. They all came to the train station with me and....." I began to cry again. I had put it out of my mind all day and now it came flooding back. I looked across the table at this sad-eyed man and tried to compose myself. "They came to the station with me," I continued, "and it made me realise how much I am loved. And I thought about my best friend, Josie."

"Was she upset at you leaving?" he asked.

"No, I haven't seen her for years. She disappeared when we were eighteen but everyone knew her father had something to do with it. She was seeing a man he couldn't stand and he decided to put a stop to it. He had a brother in Cork who was about to emigrate to Australia. Everyone thought he must have paid the family to take her with them."

"That's awful."

"I always hoped she would return one day but this morning, when the train pulled out of the station, she suddenly came into my mind and it dawned on me that I was unlikely to see her again."

"You've had quite a day, haven't you?"

I looked into his eyes and nodded. "I feel better now and please forgive me, I never meant to cry."

He gave me such a warm smile. "There's nothing to forgive," he assured me. He took his cigarettes out of his pocket and offered me one. I waved my hand and watched him light his own.

"You must let me help you. After tonight, you don't ever have to see me again if you don't want to but if you don't let me walk you to your digs, I'll follow you anyway."

I raised my eyebrows and grinned at him. "You don't give up very easily, do you?" He shook his head from side to side. "All right, you've convinced me."

He covered his hand with his sleeve and rubbed the condensation from the window. "It seems to be easing off a bit now but it's still snowing."

I felt so much warmer with the soup inside me, so I pulled off my black velvet hat and shook my long hair down over my shoulders. The man seemed suddenly lost for words.

"What is it?" I asked. "Why are you staring?" When I got no response, I clicked my fingers in front of his face, bringing him out of his trance.

"Sorry," he murmured "You remind me of someone."

I leaned my elbows on the table and rested my chin in my hands. "Is that good or bad?"

He smiled. "It was an angel." The poor man looked embarrassed and quickly went on to ask me if I had any future plans.

"Well, my brother's friend lodges at this address." I showed him the piece of paper. "His landlady said I can have a bed in the parlour for a week or so until I get sorted."

"Are your parents still alive?"

I shook my head. "My mammy died when I was very young and my father passed away last year."

"I'm sorry. I shouldn't have asked."

"Not at all. You can ask me anything you like." He listened when I told him how my brother had recently married and how he had given me the fare to come over to Liverpool and train to be a nurse. "After all," I told him, "with a new wife, there'll hardly be room for me anymore."

"There are plenty of hospitals in Liverpool. You'll be spoilt for choice. We have hospitals for everything: the Eye Hospital, the Ear

Hospital, the Women's Hospital, the Children's Hospital—"

I laughed and laughed. "Musha, musha! I believe you, but d'you think you could give me some addresses?"

"I can do better than that. If you like, I can take you to a few of them and you can get some application forms."

When he looked out the window, I couldn't help admiring his good looks. Is it possible? I asked myself. I haven't been in the country for an hour, and I think I've met the man of my dreams.

The following year exactly to the day we met, Jimmy and I got married at St Nicholas' Church.

I was so proud the day I passed my nursing exams. Jimmy had waited outside the hospital for me and lifted me off the ground, hugging me so tightly I thought I was going to break.

"Smile," he'd shouted, stepping back and clicking the camera. "Once more—and again."

"Ah, Jimmy Cosgrove, will you stop?" I'd squealed, turning my back to him.

"Just once more." He ran in front of me and clicked again.

"Here, let me take one of you two," a passer-by offered.

"Thanks." Jimmy said, handing him the camera. Without any hesitation he put his arm around my waist and pulled me in close. I gasped and gently smacked his hand, then put my mouth close to his ear, and whispered, "Jimmy, will ye behave yourself! It's not that kind of photograph."

Just as the camera clicked, he managed to plant his lips on my cheek.

"Ah," I gasped. "Will ye ever stop? Ye have the poor man embarrassed."

"Oh, don't mind me, luv," he said, taking another couple of photos. "I'm enjoying it."

How glad I had been of those photos a few years later. Almost immediately after we were married, we found somewhere to live. Our top floor flat in Ullet Road was owned by a local dignitary who only let the properties to professional people. It was a pleasant area, not too far from the city centre, enabling us to get to work early in the morning. Below us lived a married couple who worked for the police force, and on the ground floor were two teachers, sisters in fact, who worked at the local college.

After I finished my nurse's training, we began to save for a house of our own so we would have more room to start a family. Come Christmas, all of our plans seemed to go out the window. It was such a special time for us – not only a time we had met, but also a time we had married. Every year on December 23, we celebrated our first meeting and wedding anniversary in that same old church, Our Lady of St Nicholas, at the Pier Head.

My poor Jimmy was killed in 1940 when a bomb dropped on our house. I was on duty at the hospital. There were so many casualties brought in that day and I knew I...

~~~

IT WAS A while before I realised the bell was ringing. Very reluctantly, I closed the book and returned to work.

I couldn't wait to tell Marion what I had read. Poor Maisie—and poor Josie. I wondered what on earth had happened to her.

~ 10 ~

THERE'S NOTHING LIKE falling into bed after a night-shift. If I made breakfast or watched TV for half an hour when I arrived home, it seemed to give me a burst of energy and I'd be tossing and turning in bed all morning. I'd be worrying if I'd forgotten to give someone a breakfast or left one of the ladies sitting on the loo. So that morning I went through the front door straight upstairs and crawled under my duvet, cuddling the hot water bottle my dad had slipped between the sheets before he'd left for work and then I went straight to sleep. I woke just after lunch then went into town to meet Marion. It was her birthday and my dad and brothers had treated her to a hair-do in Herbert's salon; a gift her mother had given her in the last few years. Afterwards we went for a meal and a couple of drinks then I dropped her home. We had to be up early for work the following day and planned a bigger celebration for the week-end. Usually if we were both off on a Saturday we went looking around all the charity shops. Between us we used to pick up loads of lovely clothes.

I was driving home and it was a while before I noticed Eddie following me. He must have been hiding on the main road outside Marion's - or maybe I was being paranoid and it was just a coincidence. When I stopped at the traffic lights, I tried not to look in the rear view mirror and kept my eyes on the road ahead.

The light turned to green and I drove on. I did a quick left turn instead of going straight down Queen's Drive but I couldn't shake him off. I hadn't seen this side of him before and I was beginning to feel afraid.

It could have been two in the morning for all the traffic that was about. My mouth felt so dry and my hands were slippery on the steering wheel. Now that I knew these "accidental" meetings on the road were more than a coincidence, I would have to do something about him.

He followed me the four miles home. When I turned into my street all prepared to beep the horn and bring out my brothers, he'd disappeared.

I went into the kitchen for a glass of water. Then I waited twenty minutes for him to get home and dialled his number.

"What d'you think you're playing at?" I asked when he answered the phone. I was standing in the hall with the sitting room door closed. I tried not to raise my voice and bring the matter to my brothers' attention.

"No, I've already told you there is nothing to talk about. It's over. Now leave me alone or there'll be trouble.... Yes, I know you're free to drive down any road you like but you're not free to harass me and if you don't stop it, you're going to be sorry."

When I hung up the phone, I was shaking with anger. There was just no getting through to him.

"Goodnight!" I called in to my brothers and went upstairs to bed.

THE NEXT NIGHT Marion and I had just pulled up outside her flat after work and I saw him slowing down by the entrance on the main road. I decided to ignore him and not to mention it to her. To make matters worse, he'd been ringing the staff payphone all afternoon. I picked up the phone and didn't say a word. I just let the hook dangle to the floor and closed the kiosk door after me.

My friend and I were now debating whether or not to go out. I yawned and wound down the window.

"I don't know if I've got the energy to be jigging around the floor tonight. God, can you believe it, I'm only twenty-eight and I'm too tired to go out. I've got to do something. I'm getting fed up covering other people's shifts because they can't be bothered to turn in for work." I moaned.

"I know how you feel. The difference it makes when one person is off sick."

"You just have to work twice as hard, don't you? And it doesn't help when you're on with this new relief nurse because she just sits on her skinny bum all day, reading Barbara Cartland novels and running up the phone bill."

"I know. She must have trained in the same hospital as Agnes." Marion looked at her watch and reached out to open the car door. "I'll tell you what, Col," she said over her shoulder, "why don't you go home and get changed and we can decide whether to order a take-away and a bottle of wine when you get back?"

"Okay," I said, turning the ignition. "I'll be back soon," I called through the car window before driving off.

They were all watching the telly when I arrived home.

"Just look at you couch potatoes," I teased. "Sorry I haven't got time for any tea. I'm going over to Marion's as soon as I get changed. We're having a girlie night in, or," I said mischievously, "maybe a girlie night out."

Billy grinned. "I wish I felt this happy when I got paid. All I want to do is bloody cry."

"You?" I responded. "You must have more money than the Queen. I'm happy because I think about what I've got. You're unhappy because you think about what you haven't got."

Tony began to laugh. Then my dad began to laugh and soon our Billy's shoulders were shaking.

"Colette, you do it every time," Tony said. "He gives you the bait and you bite away."

I realised they were winding me up so I picked up a sofa cushion and playfully hit Billy across the head with it.

"Right, I'm going back to Marion's now and then she's coming over tomorrow to do a bit of spring cleaning with me."

Tony raised his eyebrows. "It's only the first week in February."

"Yes, I know. I'm just doing it early, that's all."

Billy laughed. "No you're not, you're just doing it late."

I gasped at his cheek. "Listen, you lot, be thankful that I do it at all."

"We are, we are, aren't we?" The three men nodded in agreement.

"By the way, Eddie called. He said could you give him a ring?"

I bit my lip before I answered Tony. "The only thing I'll be ringing is his—"

"Fair enough." He surrendered his hands into the air. "Don't shoot the messenger."

I stood there twiddling with my Claddagh ring. "You don't seem to understand," I finally said. "You still think we're going to walk off into the sunset together."

"No, we don't, Col," my dad interrupted. "We respect your wishes. Next time we won't even tell you if he's called. Is that what you want?"

I nodded.

Billy and Tony exchanged glances.

"Don't worry, Col, there won't be a next time. We'll make sure he doesn't ring you again."

"Thanks, Tony."

"Yeah, leave it with us, Col, we'll sort him out."

Oh dear. I suddenly realised what they meant. "I don't want you to sort him out. Thanks anyway, but I just want you to tell him to get lost."

"Put it out of your mind. Consider it done."

I was sorry the way I'd lashed out at them. It wasn't their fault that my ex was turning into a stalker.

When I arrived back at Marion's, she looked how I felt.

"Shall we have a night in?" I suggested, and she sighed with relief.

"I've brought some wine and I don't know about you but I'm bloody starving so do you want to do the ordering? I'd like something nice and hot, like beef or chicken curry. No pizza. Not for me anyway but don't let me stop you."

Marion rang the takeaway whilst I hung up my coat and went into the kitchen to warm the dinner plates in a bowl of hot water. Then I placed one bottle of wine in the fridge to cool and poured the other into two glasses.

Marion chuckled when she saw the size of her drink.

"Just get it down your cake hole and enjoy," I instructed.

We deserved it after the day we'd had. First Mrs Stewart's ruby ring had gone missing and, after a frantic two-hour search, it was found in a secret hole she'd made under her mattress where she'd put if for safe-keeping. A burst pipe just after lunch left us with no water for two hours and, to top it all, one of the afternoon shift didn't turn up for work.

Marion put the Beatles on, and we flopped in the armchairs while we waited for our takeaway.

"By the way, Col, have you thought any more about our holiday? Because if we don't book it soon, before we know it we'll be using the money to buy our Christmas presents. Even if we only go down to Devon or Cornwall, it'll be nice to get away."

"You're right. We'll have another look through the brochures and see what we come up with. Maybe we could go over to Ireland, Cork or somewhere. Even Dublin. I've been dying to go there for years but someone said you have to go for at least two weeks because you spend the first week drunk and the second trying to sober up. Look at that stag night our Billy went on last year. They all missed the flight home."

"Ha ha. Sounds like great fun but I'm not sure my money will stretch that far. You know me mum's insurance policy only covered the funeral expenses. We used to have a bigger policy but she cashed it in when we got this flat."

"We'll go somewhere even if it's only over the River Mersey to Birkenhead." With the wages we earned that's probably all we'd be able to afford.

We had another glass of wine and brought in the spare bottle from the fridge.

When the chicken curry arrived, we dished it out on the warm plates and sat at the table near the window overlooking the park. Marion lit a tall red candle left over from Christmas and placed it in the centre of the table next to the wine. It was nice to relax and switch off from everything.

"I might have known the smell would wake you up," Marion cooed when Tiddles sidled over and sat at her feet. Stretching his long body, he circled her legs before sitting down again. "What's up, puss?" she asked, standing up to go into the kitchen and the cat trotted after her. She returned with his purple dish and scooped some of her meal into it.

"I think he was feeling a bit left out, Col. He gets like that sometimes."

What was she like? I was dying to laugh and kept a straight face for as long as I could. "Marion, it's all so tragic, you'll have me crying in a minute."

I ducked as she screwed a serviette into a ball and threw it across the table at me. And then the phone rang and she answered it.

"No, you can't," I heard her say. "Now bugger off." I couldn't help laughing. No need to ask who that was.

"Sorry he's a nuisance," I said when she returned to the table. I told her about the other phone calls.

"He what?"

"Don't worry," I said, tucking into my meal. "Come on," I indicated to her food. "He's not spoiling our night."

"Never mind ringing you, do they know he's been following you?"

"Erm, Marion, do you think he'd still be walking around on his two legs if they knew?"

"Well, you should tell them."

"They'd kill him."

"Yeah, and if you don't tell them, he might kill you."

"Oh, now you're being dramatic. I only mentioned it because he's just phoned here and besides, if he doesn't stop following me, I'm going to teach him a lesson he won't forget."

"Like what?"

"Like... I don't know. I'll think of something." I winked at her and poured some more wine. I sounded tougher than I was.

After we had eaten, I strolled over to the window to admire the view. Looking down at the park I could see the leaves beginning to appear on the trees. "Doesn't spring make a difference when the nights are a bit lighter? You get fed up going to work and coming home in the dark, don't you? The time goes so quickly." I looked at Marion and asked her what she thought we'd be doing this time next year.

"Who knows?" she answered, shrugging her shoulders. "I know, Col, while you're here, why don't you come and have a look in my mother's wardrobe and see if there's anything that might suit Maisie."

"Ooh, that'll be fun."

We picked up our glasses and the ashtray and went into the bedroom.

Boxes and bin bags were stacked beside the dressing table in the corner.

"You've been busy," I remarked, sipping my drink. My eyes scanned the pile until I came to a stack of CDs. "I didn't know your mum liked Cliff Richard."

Marion raised her eyebrows to heaven. "Well, it's not the kind of thing you tell anyone, is it?"

"Ha-ha. Our Billy loves him. He plays his music every time he gets drunk. You know, 'Got mazelf a cryin', walkin', sleepin', talkin', *livin' doll*,'" we chorused.

The room filled with laughter and Marion fell back onto the bed. Then her smile faded and she put her hand to her mouth.

"What's up?"

"My poor mother. I hope she's not offended, listening to us laughing."

"Your mother, offended? You know what she's like. She'll be looking down and saying to Gabriel, 'Look at them daft buggers, they're always laughing at someone'."

"You're right and I hope he's saying to her, 'The bloody noise out of them two, they can stop down there, 'cause they're not coming up here'."

She opened the wardrobe and we looked along the rack.

"Wow," I whispered, taking in all the colours and feeling the texture of the tweeds. "Didn't she have loads of lovely stuff, Marion? Look at that coat. It's gorgeous. That's come back into fashion now, you know?"

She reached into the wardrobe and lifted the blue coat off the rail.

"Here." She began undoing the buttons and slipped it off the hanger. "Try it on."

I swung my legs over the bed and flicked my hair back over my shoulders before slipping on the coat.

"Ooh, I wish I was tall and skinny like you. Turn around then so I can see what you look like."

I twirled one way and then the other. "It's gorgeous"

"Don't you look the bees knees? You can keep it if you like. Blue really suits you and I know my mother would love you to have it."

"Are you sure?" I asked, fastening the leather buttons and strolling over to the mirror.

"I am, and I hope it brings you luck."

I glanced at the clock and suddenly had a thought. "Shall we get a cab into town for an hour? Go on. We could have a couple of drinks and can I keep this coat on?" I asked, hugging it.

Marion hesitated only for a moment. "Why not?" She reached for the phone to dial a taxi.

THAT NIGHT WHEN I arrived home, my brothers were waiting for me. The look on their faces told me something was seriously wrong.

"What's up?" I asked. "Where's Dad?"

"Dad's in bed and he's fine," Tony assured me, "but we've a bit of sad news, Col, so I think you'd better sit down."

"What's happened?"

The two brothers looked at each other as if to ask who was going to break the news.

"Come on," I urged. "Please tell me."

"We had a call from the home tonight. It was about Maisie. I'm afraid she died in her sleep."

WORK JUST WASN'T the same without Maisie. Everybody missed her.

Her room remained locked until her affairs were sorted and they found her next of kin.

I had just returned home after working another night shift when the postman handed me a letter on his way past. It was from a solicitor by the name of Mrs. Watts, asking me to call into her office as soon as possible. I was cold and tired. I lay down on the sofa with the open letter in my hand and fell asleep. When I awoke mid-morning, I rang the solicitor and she suggested I go and see her straight away if I could spare the time, so I had a quick shower and drove into town.

I sat opposite Mrs. Watts and twiddled the leather buttons on my recently inherited blue coat. The rain beat against her office windows. I thought of Maisie, lying in the cold, in the ground.

The funeral had been so sad, with hardly anybody there except my family and some of the staff from the home. Then Mrs. Watts handed me a white envelope. I took out the letter and began to read.

Acorn House

15 January 1988
My Dear Colette,

I don't know when you will read this letter, it is entirely up to the good Lord but my eyesight is fading and I feel I must write this now before it is too late. I expect this has all come as a surprise to you.

Do you remember when I first came to live at Acorn House? You had only been working there for a few days and I think we just took to each other straight away. You were so nervous in your new job and I was so desperately sad (and afraid) at having to leave my little flat near Sefton Park and go into a home. Straight away you reached out to help me. What a difference you made to my life. You were like the daughter I never had, coming to visit me almost every day.

I shall never forget those outings to the Pier Head on a Sunday. Nothing daunted you and when the time came that I couldn't walk very far, you brought a wheel-chair in the boot and pushed me down to the landing stage and I can still recall looking across the River Mersey towards the Irish Sea. Do you remember that day on the ferry when I cried, a ghrá? I didn't mean to, you know. I was just so overcome when I thought about Ireland and that first day I arrived in Liverpool so many years before and how I'd met my lovely Jimmy. I knew I made you sad too and I'm sorry because, looking back now, they're all memories I will keep close to my heart.

You were so good to me, Colette, when you thought I had nothing. Remember the little things you used to buy me every Saturday when you went to the market, and all the chocolate and presents at Easter and Christmas, not to mention my birthday. Well, a ghrá, my mammy always used to say, what goes around comes around and now it's time for you to have your own reward.

Now, a ghrá, I must tell you about my old home in the West of Ireland, which now, hopefully, belongs to you. It is a little cottage with a fair-sized garden and a bit of land beyond, right in the heart of Bradknock village, next door to the church and graveyard. It has been rented out for years but my solicitor has been instructed that, upon my death, he is to give notice to the tenants.

Do with it what you will. You may sell it or keep it. Please, a ghrá, would you just go and see it one last time for me?
Goodbye and God bless.

All my love,

Maisie

MRS WATTS SLID the box of tissues across her desk. She seemed used to people breaking down in her office. I suppose she dealt with all kinds of tragic situations.

"Would you like a cup of tea or coffee?"

I shook my head and wiped my eyes with a tissue. "No, thanks, I'm fine," I said sadly. "It's strange. All the years I knew her, she never really talked about her past apart from the early days when she first came to Liverpool."

The solicitor shook her head. "Apparently, after her father died, her brother and his wife inherited the property and—let's see," she said, scanning the paper in front of her. "It says here that when they were both killed in a car crash in 1960, Maisie then inherited the cottage but she had been settled in England for a long time and had no desire to return so it was rented out. She was a children's nurse?" I nodded. "But she never had any children of her own?"

"No. I don't think she was married for that long. Her husband was killed when a bomb dropped on their home. She was on duty at the hospital at the time."

"Did she not even go back to Ireland for a holiday?"

I shook my head. "I don't think so. I think her brother used to visit her in Liverpool."

"She sounds like she was a very strong lady and she obviously thought a lot of you," she continued. I couldn't speak as the tears poured down my face. "If you think she was generous leaving you her little cottage in Ireland, you're in for a further shock because she has also left you two thousand pounds and this…" She opened the packet and placed the items on her desk. I looked at Maisie's wedding ring on a chain and then I gasped when I saw the gold violin brooch with a red ruby set in the bow; the very one Mrs O'Brien had given to Maisie the night of the barn dance all those years ago.

WHEN I LEFT Mrs Watts, I could hardly take it in. All those years when Maisie had lived so sparsely, hardly buying herself any clothes unless they were needed, she had been saving her money for me.

One thing's for sure, I will be as careful spending it as Maisie had been saving it. Oh yes, I told myself, wiping my eyes with the back of my hand, I'll treat it like gold.

I barely acknowledged Billy when he opened the door. I felt a wreck and my face was wet from crying. Try as I may, I could not pull myself together.

When Billy saw the state I was in, he went to the cabinet and poured me a drop of brandy. My hands were shaking when I took the glass from his hand and gulped it down.

"You'll never guess what's happened." Just as I went on to tell him, I started sobbing again.

"Come on now, Col, I know how much you cared for Maisie, but she wouldn't want you to take it like this, would she?"

"But you don't understand, Billy. You don't know what she's gone and done. Oh, she's been so good to me."

The doorbell rang and Billy went out in the hall to answer it.

I could hear muffled voices and then Marion was there hugging me.

"I've got your message and I'm telling you it couldn't have happened to a nicer person. By Jesus, I bet she's gone to heaven. Didn't I tell you that coat would bring you luck?"

When Marion let go of me, Billy put his arms around my shoulders.

"Marion just told me. Wasn't she a dark horse? The way you used to worry about her and all the time she was taking care of you."

WHEN I EMPTIED Maisie's room, I gave some of her possessions away to the other residents and, because it had such a nice view, with the owner's permission I moved Fred in there. I knew Maisie would be looking down and smiling. He sat by the window for hours watching the birds outside. He seemed to have a new lease of life.

When I'd looked in Maisie's locker for the red notebook, it wasn't there. Sure that it had been put in the office for safe-keeping, I went along to collect it but it was nowhere to be seen. I asked Agnes but she said she didn't know what I was talking about. Then I went and asked each of the staff, including ringing the off-duty staff at home. I rang the solicitor to make sure it was not in her possession waiting to be collected. It was a mystery.

A few days later, and after all else failed, I went outside to the bins and had a quick scan through the bags of rubbish before they were emptied the following day. And then I came across a blue plastic bag we used to put the shredded paper in. I lifted it out, untied the top and looked inside. I could have cried when I saw the red strips. I knew there was only one person mean enough to do that. How could she? I dragged the bag into the staff room. I was glad it was empty because I was too upset and angry to speak to anybody. I couldn't stop the tears from rolling down my face. Now I'd never know what happened. I lit a cigarette and took long drags to try and calm my nerves and, before I realised what I was doing, I was dragging the bag down to the office.

Agnes glanced up from the newspaper and turned her attention to my hands. The look on her face told me everything, so before anybody could say 'How's yer father', I lifted up the bag and tipped it over her head.

I DROVE HOME through patches of fog, wondering how she could have been so callous and then I saw Eddie's car close behind me and felt such a sick feeling in my stomach.

I wasn't scared of him and yet he was beginning to scare me more and more. It was the sudden ghostly appearance that sent a momentary shiver of terror through me. Had he stopped and waved or even flashed his lights to attract my attention, it would have been easier to deal with, but no, he just sneaked up on me like some kind of stalker. If he'd caught me on a different day, I might have felt stronger and more able to deal with him, but not today. I was tired and upset and my nerves felt jarred. I wanted to stop the car and get out and just walk – anywhere, but I continued driving and tried to ignore him. I glanced to my right and quickly crossed into the line of traffic, squeezing between two cars. My hands were shaking so I gripped the steering wheel to steady myself and drove on. I watched the car behind drop back and then do a right turn and groaned when I saw Eddie slide into the gap.

God, I thought, what has he reduced me to? I could see the traffic lights up ahead on green. My fear suddenly turned to rage and I started cursing loudly. I was not – could not - let him control me this way. As I neared the lights, I put my foot on the accelerator just enough to pick up speed and carry me through the junction. By now the lights had turned to amber and he was almost touching my bumper ready to shoot through after me. I took a deep breath, gripped the wheel and put my foot down onto the brake. Then I heard an almighty thud as he crashed into the back of my car.

I hadn't wanted my brothers to hurt him and now I wanted to kill him—well, metaphorically speaking. He always wore a seat belt so there would be more damage to his precious car than to him.

Someone hurried over and opened my door to see if I was hurt.

I was fine, actually, so I stepped out of my car, a picture of innocence and went to help the other injured driver. "Oh, my God, it's you! Are you okay?"

"D'you know him, love?" one of the good Samaritans asked. "Aw, he thinks he's broken his wrist."

"Sort of," I answered. I looked at Eddie sympathetically but he ignored me and stared straight ahead, right hand gripping left hand with pain. "I got such a shock," I said, turning to the stranger. "He just drove into the back of me."

When the ambulance arrived, they covered Eddie's shoulders with a blanket and led him into the vehicle. I hoped he was going to be all right. Maybe a broken wrist and three cracked ribs would teach him a lesson. Never drive too close to anybody – especially if you're stalking them.

THAT NIGHT, WHEN I went to bed, I lay awake for a long time. Two weeks ago my life had been going nowhere and now the possibilities were endless. I didn't need to have bosses like Agnes or boyfriends like Eddie anymore. I tried to imagine going to Maisie's cottage for a holiday. Then out of nowhere came the prospect of living there. The more I thought about it, the more the idea became fixed in my mind. I was certainly ready for change.

I didn't share my thoughts with anybody until a few days later when Marion and I were in the linen room at work, stacking the clean laundry onto the shelves. Spare quilts and pillows on the top rack; duvet covers and curtains were placed on the shelf underneath; a colourful mixture of bath and hand towels below them and then spare blankets on the bottom. It was a monotonous task but sometimes, like today when there was a lot of laundry after the week-end, it gave us a chance to have a gab whilst we worked.

"What's up, Col?" She asked me. "You look awful fed up."

"Sorry, Marion. I'm not fed up. I've just got a lot on my mind. I'm thinking of going to live in Ireland."

There, it was out.

Her mouth dropped. "Going to live in Ireland?" she slowly repeated.

"Going to live in Ireland? But you can't."

"What's the alternative?"

"What'll I do without you?"

I hated the thought of leaving her behind, imagining her in later years living in the same flat like a lonely old spinster, with her stuffed cat sitting on the sideboard. Then her eyes began to water. "I mean, you're the best mate I've ever had and good mates are so hard to find. You know all my secrets and all my faults—and I know yours—and who will put up with you like I do?"

I couldn't help laughing. I took the last bundle of pillowcases out of the laundry basket and opened the door, shoving the trolley into the corridor out of the way. "You could always come with me."

Her lips began to tremble. I could tell this was far more than she had expected when she had woken that morning, probably feeling lonely as hell, in an empty flat. She started crying and seeing those big tears rolling down her face nearly started me off, too. I handed her a clean towel and she wiped her eyes leaving a smudge of black mascara down her cheeks. "You've thought all this through, haven't you?"

I sighed. "I've thought of nothing else. Maisie has given me a great opportunity and I want to make the most of it. Will you think about it for a few days? I know it's a big step, but you know that saying, ships are safe in harbour, but that's not what they're built for. Besides, if we don't like it, we can always come back."

~ 12 ~

"WHAT'LL YOU DO with the place, pet? Will you sell it?"

I couldn't help feeling niggled. Having just arrived home from informing the solicitor of my plans, I looked at Billy for a minute before answering. "You think I would sell Maisie's house?" I asked, trying to keep the anger out of my voice.

"I can't think what else you would be doing with it."

I hadn't wanted to tell him like this. I'd planned to sit them all down together and tell them as gently as I could. Instead, I now found myself blurting it out.

"I'll tell you what I'm going to do with Maisie's house. I'm going to live in it. Yeah, that's right," I said. "With Marion." I braced myself for what was to come, but Billy didn't say anything. His face was a picture of sadness. He sat down on the chair and lit a cigarette.

In our house everybody looked forward to Friday night fish and chip supper, feet up in front of the telly and no work on Saturday. But on this particular Friday night my dad and Tony arrived home to a stony atmosphere.

"Jesus, Tony, that's all I need," I heard Dad say as he hung up his coat in the hall. "As if she hasn't had enough to cope with lately, without our Billy upsetting her even more. Maybe he didn't have much luck on the horses today."

Poor Billy.

"Well, this is a fine welcome home after a week's hard work," he said after they entered the sitting room. He sat down and rested the *Echo* on the table. Billy looked relieved to see them.

"You're not going to believe this," he warned. "She's only talking about going to live in Ireland."

Tony looked at me in amazement.

"What'll you be doing out in the bogs of Ireland?" he asked, lowering himself into an easy chair.

"Do you have to talk like that?" I asked him.

"Aw, come on now, Col," my dad said. "You'd be living in the back of beyond."

My lips began to tremble. This was not how it was supposed to be.

I looked at the three men I loved more than anything else in the world.

My dad put his arm around me. "What's happened to put you in this mood? And what's all this about Ireland? You don't really mean it do you, Col?"

I nodded.

"It's the end of the month," Tony reminded me. "Pay day. You're usually skipping around planning how you're going to spend all that dosh you've earned."

Tears began to spill down my face. I ran upstairs to my bedroom.

I FELT SO much better after a long soak in the bath and lay on my bed for a while, listening to the Bee Gees. There was so much to think about, so many plans to make. Now that I had made up my mind, I knew there was no going back. Like a train at full speed, there was no stopping me.

I took a writing pad out of the top drawer in my dresser and made a list of the things I needed to take. Just as I went to shut the drawer, the brown envelope caught my eye. I lifted it out carefully and tipped the contents into my hand. I closed my palm over Maisie's brooch, and sat back down on my bed and cried. Everybody kept telling me how lucky I was to have inherited so much. Of course, I knew they were right, but in a way, losing Maisie was a bit like losing my mother, and I grieved for the old lady.

I called to the cemetery after work every day. I could see the grave from the gates, but once it had been snowing and I hadn't been able to recognise the place where Maisie lay. People were buried every day and, because it would be at least six months before the headstones could be erected, under snow one grave looked the same as another. When I'd eventually found it, I cried as I tried to wipe the snow off the flowers and wreaths.

That day I'd bought a wooden crucifix and stuck it in the ground, making sure that no matter what, Maisie's grave would always be visible.

I put the brooch back in the envelope and returned it to the drawer.

I put on my jeans and sweater, brushed my hair into a pony-tail, sprayed on a bit of perfume and went downstairs to face the music. My dad was the first to speak. "Are you all right now, pet?"

"Course I am, Dad. I don't know what came over me. I'm sorry."

"We're sorry about earlier on, Col. We didn't mean to upset you."

"It's fine, Dad," I said, giving him a hug. "It wasn't your fault."

Billy stood up and offered me the fireside chair. Tony went into the kitchen to get my supper out of the oven. I couldn't help noticing how jumpy they all were.

"Look, if you don't all stop being so nice, you're going to start me off again."

They laughed with relief. Billy reached into the fruit bowl and picked out an apple, rubbing it on his jumper before he sank his teeth into it. I rolled my eyes at Tony and began to giggle.

"You didn't really mean it did you, Col?" my dad asked cautiously. "You know, about going to Ireland?"

I couldn't help feeling disappointed. "Yes, Dad, I did."

"But you know, lass, you wouldn't know anybody. You'd be so lonely."

"I'm with Marion. How could I be lonely?"

"Well, love," he said. "If you've made up your mind, and it's what you really want, then we'll wish you all the best, won't we, lads?"

"Aye, I suppose so," came Tony's half-hearted reply.

MARION HAD DECIDED to rent out her flat and when she offered Peter first refusal, he nearly went through the staff-room ceiling.

"Oh, have I died and gone to heaven or what? Alleluia! Just think, no more sleeping in a cardboard box down by the river. No more having to sleep with my boots on in case they get stolen while I'm sleeping." His joking aside, I am sure he was indeed relieved to finally obtain somewhere decent to live.

So the matter was settled and he was to move in at the end of March when Marion and I left for Ireland. There was only one snag. Peter was allergic to cats.

"Can't stand them near me," he grimaced. "Hay fever – nosebleeds – the lot."

"Can't we take him with us?" a blurry-eyed Marion asked me when I told her what Peter had said. I looked at her and thought for a moment.

"We could, but what if he doesn't settle and gets lost? Then you'd be blaming yourself, wouldn't you, and wishing you'd left him here."

She didn't say anything. "You never know," I tried to sound optimistic. "You might find some poor old bugger who would be glad of his company."

"I suppose so," she said miserably. "Maybe I should put an advert in the shop window or something?"

We spent almost a week clearing out her mother's possessions. She had planned to go for at least a year and we thought it was a good idea to sort through everything now in case she stayed for good.

I also had a lot of sorting to do, but it was a slow process because almost every evening someone was knocking on the door to say goodbye and wish me well. My unwanted clothes and possessions diminished as I gave people bags full to take home with them. Each night when I went to bed, I crossed another day off the calendar. I couldn't wait.

Everybody at work was talking about our forthcoming adventure and Sandy said her Irish mother was compiling a list of things we'd need to take with us because some things we would be used to could be quite scarce in the West of Ireland.

I KNELT ON the floor by the bookshelves and picked out my favourites. There were two piles—charity shop to the left, Ireland to the right. I opened the hard-backed copy of *Jane Eyre* and read the inscription:

This book is awarded to Colette Murphy for merit. Christmas 1972.

"Look, Dad. Remember this?"

He looked up from his crossword and tilted his head to one side to read the title. Taking a moment to register, he raised his eyebrows and nodded knowingly. "Oh, Jesus, don't remind me. Dear God, no! Oh, I remember all right. Every time you had your head in that book, you were crying and we were all out of our minds wondering what to do with you. And then when I tried to hide it from you, you cried even more and I had to give it back to you."

"I'm glad you did," I said, clutching the book to my heart. "I love Charlotte Brontë."

I placed it in the small wooden chest with the pair of leather-bound books I had inherited from Maisie, those very books she'd read in the church that day when she had arrived from Ireland. They just fitted together.

"I hope you're not taking any of my books," Billy warned. "I know what's there, you know, so don't be pinching any when you think I'm not looking."

"Oh, you're OK, Billy," I assured him. "I'm not really into westerns or Bruce Lee or," I said, holding up an old copy of Perry Mason with 2/6p marked on the front, "this heart-stopping page-turner."

"At least I'm only reading about old times. You're going back to them."

I snatched my dad's old slipper from beside the fire and flung it over at him. It missed him by a foot and landed on Tony, waking him with a start.

"Who threw that?"

"Don't mind," my dad consoled. "It was Teresa's lad having a bit of fun with you on his way out."

WE STILL HAD the problem of finding a home for Marion's cat. I
rang her one evening and she said she was lying on the sofa with him,
making the most of their time together. She was owed holidays from
work and had left a week earlier than me but we were constantly on the
phone to each other.

"Have you written out the cards to put in the shop window yet?"
I asked.

I could hear her voice falter. I was sorry I'd opened my mouth.
There was a long silence before she answered.

"Well, I've written out loads, Col, but they don't sound right and
I end up ripping them up. You know. Mature cat ... loving home ...
used to a lot of attention ... not used to children ... will eat only
chicken ... likes *Coronation Street* and *Eastenders* and loves *Songs of
Praise*," she sniffed. "Maybe you could help me? I just feel so cruel.
I've been getting all his things together and we've found loads of lost
toys and every time I pick anything up, his little tail perks up 'cause he
thinks I'm going to play with him and then I just drop it into a bag so
it will be ready for when he goes, and he looks at me with his little sad
eyes like he knows his days are numbered."

Now she nearly had me crying. "Marion," I said softly, "if it bothers
you that much, maybe I could ask my dad to have him for you. Our
Tony would look after him and make sure he was fed properly."

"What about your Billy's pigeons?"

"Damn, I forgot about them. Maybe we could poison them all
while he's down the pub?"

When the cards were placed in the local newsagent's window, there
was a great response. We sat in the pub and sorted through them. A cat
breeder looking for a mature ginger; a lady calling because she'd found
a mouse in her kitchen; a young mother wanting a special birthday
present for her five-year-old hyper-active son, whose last cat had fallen
out of the window and, just as she had almost given up, she had a call
from an elderly man who told her he'd spent all his life caring for cats,
assuring her he would give Tiddles a good home.

THE NEXT DAY just after we had finished eating, Teresa Regan paid
us a call. Tony and Dad were washing up in the kitchen and Billy, taking
one look at Teresa and sensing something was amiss, joined them.

Normally a woman of many words, she hardly spoke. She sat on the chair near the fire and looked down at her hands. Her marital problems were well known. That golden wedding band he'd placed on her finger all those years ago when he had promised to love, honour, and obey, was in and out of the pawnshop to help finance his drink. I sat on the chair opposite and straightened the rug with my feet.

"Ignore the mess…"

Teresa's shoulders slumped and she bit her lip.

"What's up, Teresa?"

When her eyes met mine, she began to cry.

"Who's upset you?"

"Nobody," she whispered, shaking her head and trying to compose herself. "It's just…it's just that…well, I can't believe you're really going to live in Ireland."

This was probably the fourth time Teresa had called since she had heard my news. "I know we've talked about it, Col, but I can't get used to it."

I sat on the edge of the chair and put my arm around her shoulders. She blew her nose and stuck the tissue up her sleeve. "In one way, lass, I'll be very sorry to see you go, you know that, don't you?" she said, taking hold of my hand, "And in another way, I'll envy you. When I left my Irish home in 1960, I never returned and I don't suppose I ever will." She began to cry again. "And since I heard you was going, I can't stop thinking about it…dreaming about it even."

"Why don't you come for a holiday?" I asked her.

"I've left it too long now, lass. Most of my folks are gone and it would be too painful, you know, too many memories. No," she said, "I'll leave things as they are. But I've been meaning to ask ye for a while, lass, will you write to me? I would love to get a letter with an Irish stamp in the corner." She smiled at the thought.

"Course I will, Teresa," I assured her.

"Now you won't be offended if I don't answer, will you, lass? I was never a great scholar myself…well, ye know what I mean, don't you?"

"I'll write to you every month."

THE SADDEST PART for me was leaving my job. I knew some of those residents inside out. They had been like an extended family and, in some ways, I felt like I was deserting them. They had all clubbed together and presented me with a set of crystal glasses and a good luck card signed by them all.

~ 14 ~

MY EYES MISTED over when I thought about the day ahead. I had been awake most of the night with my mind all over the place, worrying about this and looking forward to that. The fact that Billy hadn't got around to decorating my room made it so much easier to leave behind. I'd even stuck Duran Duran back on the wall, just in case I had any second thoughts.

My throat still felt dry from the excess alcohol at the party my brothers had sprung on me two nights ago. People I hadn't seen for years had been there to wish us well.

Today was the big day.

First thing that morning, I picked up Marion and we went into town to do our last-minute shopping. The air was nippy, but we wrapped up well, hurrying through town, trying to remember everything. We were due to sail at 10 o'clock that night and it seemed like we had all the time in the world, but every time I looked at my watch another hour had whizzed past.

"I've got to get those photos from Boots," I said, rummaging through my bag. "They're the last ones I took of Maisie. I thought I'd lost them and then our Tony found the roll of film down the side of the chair. Here it is." I unscrewed a scrap of paper, but it wasn't what I expected. "You'll never guess what I've found."

"What?" Marion shivered and pushed her hands deep down into her pockets.

"It's that list. I'd forgotten all about it. You know, the one Sandy's Irish mother was supposed to have written for us about certain items we'd need to take 'cause we wouldn't be able to buy them in Ireland." I scowled down the contents. "Condoms?" I said, probably a little too loud. "Coloured knickers? What the bloody hell? Well you can forget the condoms but the knickers…"

"Shush, Col," Marion whispered, taking me by the elbow and sheltering in a shop doorway.

"And look what she's put in brackets," I said, quite oblivious to the stares I must have been getting from strangers. I showed Marion the scrap of paper and waited for her reaction.

"Only sell white knickers in the West?" Marion grinned up at me.

"You can sod that for a lark," I told her. "I haven't worn white knickers since I made my Holy Communion. White knickers!" I repeated in disbelief. "If I was only going to wear white knickers, I'd have joined a convent and become a nun."

Marion looked back to the list and read the contents out loud again. "I suppose we'll get over there and Cilla Black will be number one and all the men will have quiffs and nobody will have sex until they get married."

I have to admit I began to see the funny side. "I like Cilla Black. I hope she is top of the charts." I stuck the list into my bag and we headed on up the road.

"Oh, we all know you like Cilla and so do I," Marion said, following me into Littlewoods. "It's just that you never hear any of her records and we are going back in time, aren't we?"

"Not too bloody far, I hope," I muttered.

I went straight to the underwear department and picked out lots of coloured knickers.

"Come on, Marion, let me buy you something," I said after I paid the assistant and crammed the items into my bag. "Go on," I said when she shook her head. "What d'you fancy?"

"I fancy that feller over there, but he's not for sale. A few pairs of these frilly knickers will do me fine."

With the last purchase over, we went to the cafeteria and had some lunch. I put my coat on the back of the chair and dropped my bag on the floor by my feet.

"Not long to go now," I said, seasoning my dinner with salt and vinegar. Marion handed me the sauce. "Enjoy these fish and chips because it might be a long time before we have them again."

"I bet there's loads of chippies in Ireland. Well, we know there's loads of potatoes anyway, don't we?" Marion said, dipping her chip in some brown sauce and putting it into her mouth.

"Jesus, we'll probably end up as big as houses. Maybe it's corsets we should be buying and big knickers from Evans…" I covered my mouth self-consciously at the thought that had just popped into my head. "Do you think it's true what Sandy said about nobody having sex over there until they get married?"

"We'll have to wait and see, won't we?"

THAT EVENING WE drove past the Liver Buildings and neared the check-in point at the Pier Head. Marion looked out of the window and smiled. She said she'd hardly had any sleep either but announced there would be plenty of time to catch up with that when we arrived in the West of Ireland. I felt so relieved. "I can't believe we've fitted everything in the car. I never thought we'd manage those sleeping bags. And how stupid of me to leave them till last when you think how important they are, but you know my head's been all over the place and there's been so much to think about and I just know there will be something important that we've forgotten." The sleeping bags were a must until we bought new beds. I wasn't comfy about sleeping in other people's beds at the best of times. "I even managed to squeeze in a few pairs of extra shoes." I waited for Marion's typical response of 'Oh, you and your shoes …' "Marion," I continued, "before you say anything, you must be the only female in the world who doesn't have a thing about shoes. Most women love them, not just me. Oh, and I just remembered, did you bring the iron?"

"Yes, and did you bring the hair dryer?"

I gasped. "I knew there was something I forgot"

"Oh, Col…"

"Course I did," I giggled.

We had even considered bringing the TV so Marion could watch *Corrie* and *Brookside*, but in the end she had insisted there was no point in going to live in the country if she was going to sit in front of the box all the time and she would just have to look for a new pastime. I drove over the tramlines and turned left and there was the River Mersey.

Marion did a quick intake of breath. "Is that our boat?"

"It sure is."

I checked we were in the right lane for the car ferry and pulled up by the dockside for a few minutes before we drove onto the ship. We hurried over to where the foot passengers waited and where we had arranged to meet the three wise men.

Poor Marion was fighting back the tears. It had been a long day; a long week, in fact as she'd cleared out her flat, knowing how final it all was. Goodbyes to friends and colleagues and now waiting to board the ferry, it was a sad goodbye to Liverpool.

I nudged her. "Hey, we're not going to bloody China, you know. It's only over the Irish Sea. In fact, our Billy said he'll send his pigeons over with a letter so he doesn't have to pay for a stamp and our Tony said he's just going to shout as loud as he can."

She chuckled. "They're a pair of soft gets. Knowing them two, they'll probably end up swimming over with a hundred pound bet on to see which of them gets there first."

"Here they come," I said, watching them jostle through the crowd to meet us.

"Sorry we're a bit late, luv, but we got held up," my dad said, embracing me. He looked at Marion and gave her a hug.

There was no mistaking the smell of alcohol on their breath. My heart felt heavy. It must have taken all their courage to come down and say goodbye. Tony glanced at his watch. I realised he wanted to get it over with. Say goodbye and then probably go and drown his sorrows. Billy and Dad would be hit just as hard. Tonight was going to be a sad one.

Billy tried to hurry it along. "Come on, you two! You're going to have to get a move on or you'll miss the boat." He put his hands deep into his pockets and banged his feet with the cold.

I pushed him playfully. "Glad to see the back of me now, are you? Came down just to make sure I got on the boat and didn't change my mind?"

"Aw, Col, I wish you would change your mind."

"Now don't start all that again. It was only a joke," I said, glancing at my watch, "but I suppose you're right Billy, we'd best be on our merry way."

My dad reached into his pocket and took out a thick brown envelope.

"Here, lass, put this away. It's just something off the three of us to tide you over."

"Oh, dad, I can't take this."

"Put it away safe." His voice was gentle but firm. "The more you've got, the less we'll worry."

I opened my shoulder bag and put the envelope inside.

WE WERE DIZZY with excitement when we drove up the ramp onto the ferry. We trailed behind the other cars and parked almost bumper to bumper in between two lanes of lorries. I switched off the engine and dropped the keys into my bag. My eyes wandered down the two lanes of parked lorries, and watched as the men clanged the chains around the wheels, securing them to the deck. There was something about lorries that fascinated me, and once Billy's friend had let me sit beside him down to London and back to drop off some tyres. The feeling, sitting up in that cabin as we sped along the motorway, was better than a ride on the Big Dipper at Blackpool.

Marion gently shook my arm. "Colette to earth. Calling Colette to earth."

I switched my brain back into gear and reached into the back seat of the car for our jackets. "Here, you'd better put this on. It's cold on this deck, isn't it?"

Marion wrapped her wax jacket around her shoulders and then we lit a cigarette. One of the men walked slowly towards us. "Sorry luv, no smoking on this deck. Can't you read?" he asked, shoving his cap from his brow and wiping away the sweat with his sleeve.

I dropped my fag on the floor and stomped it out with my foot. "Which charm school did you go to?" I snapped.

"Sorry I spoke," he called over his shoulder. I watched him stoop down near a lorry to check the chains were secure. "I don't make the bloody rules," he was muttering.

We looked at each other shamefaced.

"We'll forgive you," I called after him. "It's our fault. I suppose we should have known. We're a bit nervous, you see."

"And excited," Marion chirped, slipping back into her old mood.

He grinned at us. "Well, I hope you have a nice holiday anyway."

"So do we, luv," she said. "A nice long one, because you see, we're not coming back."

I turned my attention back to the car. "Right then, let's get going."

"Do you think all our stuff is safe?" she asked, surveying the other passengers.

"Course it is. They lock the car deck when the boat starts to sail and nobody is allowed down here. So I was told anyway. Here," I offered, "let me take your bag while you button up your coat."

"I can manage fine, thanks," she said, when she was clearly struggling to put on the garment.

"I know you can manage fine, but just let me help you." I eyed her curiously. "What've you got in that bag anyway?" I teased. "You'd think it was the crown jewels the way you're holding it."

She clutched the bag to her and laughed. "No such luck."

I took a closer look and asked her why it was full of holes, but she just shrugged her shoulders and told me it was old.

I looked again. "Hang on, Marion," I murmured. "I could swear I just saw something move in there."

Her face reddened and she pulled the bag protectively towards her.

"Gosh, Marion, what's wrong with you? You seem awful nervous."

And then the penny dropped.

"No. Tell me you didn't…? You wouldn't have…? Please, please, tell me you didn't. Not the cat?"

She swallowed hard. "It's going to be all right, Col. He won't be any trouble, honest. The vet gave him an injection at six o'clock so he would sleep through the night."

"But Marion, what are we going to do if he wakes up? How are we going to keep him – in a bag – on a boat?"

She squeezed my shoulder. "Don't worry, Col. I've got some more medicine to knock him out again."

"Good God, with the shock you've just given me, I could do with a dose myself."

"Aw, I couldn't have left him, Col. The poor old man was like Steptoe. Honest. And the house was so run down. You wouldn't believe the smell when he opened the door. I nearly fainted."

I took a deep breath. "Well, so did I just before." Putting my arm through Marion's, we followed the flow of car passengers up the iron steps towards the lifts.

"Anyway, he'll kill all the spiders for you. I mean, you can just imagine the size of them over there, can't you?"

"Yep!"

"And there'll probably be loads of mice and …"

"Are you trying to put me off?"

"As if."

"Come on then, we'd better get a move on before Tiddles wakes up."

We went to the check-in desk to collect the keys. I had one eye on the receptionist and another on my friend. If the cat was discovered, they'd probably put us off the ship. Or maybe they would just take him to a secure place down below until we docked in Ireland. But how could they restrain a cat? And what if Marion refused to let them lock him up? I couldn't let her go off the ship on her own.

When the receptionist offered me the keys, I quickly took them and followed the arrows up the steps and along the carpeted hallway. It was a relief when I flung open the door of cabin 42 and stepped inside. I threw my jacket on the chair, checked there were no dead bodies behind the shower curtain, flopped down on the bed and began to root through my holdall for the chicken butties. I was starving.

Marion sat down on the bunk and peeped into her bag. "He's still fast asleep, Col," she proudly announced. "You see, I told you he'd be no trouble." She took a sandwich from my outstretched hand, looked inside and then took a bite.

"Mmm, I bet your Tony made these."

"Who else?"

"I wish I had a brother."

"You can have one of mine," I offered, clicking open a can of lager. "In fact, you can have them both if you like."

Marion was thoughtful for a moment. "I wonder what my mum thinks of us going to live in the back of beyond? I mean, she's only been dead six months, hasn't she?"

"Oh, God, she'll be thrilled to bits. Do you think she wanted to see you stuck in the flat, with all your sad memories, for the rest of your life?"

She shook her head.

"No way," I continued. "Put that thought right out of your head."

She looked so sad. Then she began to cry.

"You're not sorry are you?" I asked, sitting down beside her and putting my arm around her shoulders.

"Course I'm not," she replied, reaching into her bag for a tissue and wiping her nose. "I can't wait to get there. I know we're going to have such a great time."

"Of course we are!"

"Take no notice of me. I'm like a big kid. I'm just a bit tired, that's all."

"That's okay. It might be my turn to cry tomorrow when we get there. Who knows?" I asked.

"I doubt it."

After we finished eating, Marion lay down and fell asleep.

When the Irish voice came over the loudspeaker announcing the ship's departure, I sprang to my feet and pulled back the curtain to look at the landing stage. I knew all three of them would be standing out there on the dockside in the bitter cold waiting for the ship to sail.

I put on my woolly hat and gloves and left Marion in the cabin with the cat. She must have been so worried these last few days. No wonder she was sleeping like a baby.

The sea air washed over me when I climbed the iron steps. I could barely contain my excitement when I reached the top and went out onto the open deck, clinging tightly to the rail and peering over the side. My dad and brothers were hidden behind the office buildings but I gave a tearful wave just in case they could see me.

A group of young men came and stood a few feet away. I listened to their banter in amusement. One of the lads was twenty-one and they were going to Dublin for the weekend. They were merry and loud and had obviously started celebrating before they boarded the ship.

"I hope you realise I'm missing a match tomorrow. You owe me one, Paul!"

They laughed loudly when one of the men, presumably Paul, told them they would probably lose anyway.

No doubt they were a mixture of Evertonians and Liverpudlians. Was there any family in Liverpool, I wondered, where everybody followed the same team?

The men's voices grew faint as they descended the steps and argued over whose turn it was to buy the next round.

I looked out across the river again and then I suddenly remembered that special thing I had to do. I reached into my pocket and felt around for the Eternity ring Eddie had bought me. Then I threw it over the rails into the sea.

Good riddance to bad rubbish...

I TRIED TO imagine poor Maisie when she sailed from Ireland all those years ago. Then I had a flashing image of Charlotte Brontë, and thought once again how daring and gutsy she had been when, at the age of twenty six, she had arrived in London, close to midnight, on that cold January evening in 1843. Soon she would be teaching and perfecting her foreign languages in Belgium, in preparation for the school she planned to open in Haworth with her sisters. Her temporary home had been a ferry ride and train journey away, but it must have seemed like a million miles. So many strangers. So many uncertainties.

I empathised with her as I thought how frightened she must have felt, alone on a cold night like tonight, and took comfort in the fact that my friend was tucked up fast asleep in our cabin with her cat.

A loud shout from across the deck jolted me out of my daydreams. I watched the dockers loosen the thick ropes that secured the vessel to the bay. Within minutes the ship began to inch away from the dockside and cruise into the lock.

I looked out across the river, feeling proud to come from such a great city. *In my Liverpool home*, I hummed as the waves lapped around the ship. I looked around nostalgically. Nobody could deny its beauty.

The lights shimmered on the Mersey and the ship rose as the lock slowly began to fill. The Liver Buildings looked enchanting: tall and noble, they lit up the Pier Head, giving it an almost fairy-tale atmosphere.

Across the river to Birkenhead, the cranes at Cammel Laird's pointed to the sky like machine guns and the ferry cruised across the river towards Liverpool.

I can't believe it, I whispered into the darkness. *I'm finally going to Ireland.*

The cold had driven the other passengers back downstairs, but this was an experience for which I would brave any weather, maybe tell my grandchildren about in years to come. Standing quietly, almost respectfully, I waited for the lock to fill and watched in awe as the gates opened and the ship began to cruise into the Mersey. The vessel swayed as it inched its nose with expertise, sailing through the freezing moonlit water, on and on, passing the New Brighton Lighthouse as it gathered speed and sailed into the night.

When I returned to the cabin, Marion was still fast asleep.

It wasn't long before I climbed into bed between my crisp white sheets.

With the hum of the engine and the swaying of the ship as it sailed across the Irish Sea, I soon joined Marion and Tiddles and slipped into the land of the unconscious.

Part Two

Ireland

1990

~ 16 ~

IT WAS MY birthday when I woke up in Ireland the following morning. We got dressed, had a quick breakfast and drove off the ship towards the city centre. The traffic was almost bumper to bumper as it crawled along the busy Dublin streets. We had been driving around for ages.

"How many times have we passed that floozy in the jacuzzi?"

"I can't help it, Marion. I'm following the signs, but I keep returning to the same place."

We stopped at traffic lights. When they changed colour, I went to take off the handbrake just as somebody knocked on the car window. I was sucking a Polo and nearly choked with fright when I looked at the stranger.

"Are you lost?" he asked in a lovely thick Dublin accent.

"How did you know?" I asked in surprise.

"I saw the English plate and people usually get lost driving around Dublin."

He leaned on the car as if he had all the time in the world. Then, to my astonishment, he began to wave on the cars building up behind us.

"Don't you be worrying about them. Just let's get you on the right road. Where is it you're headed?"

"County Mayo," we chorused.

"And where is it you're from?" His voice was barely audible above the hissing brakes of the lorry that had just pulled up beside us.

"Liverpool."

The man smiled. "I thought you were Scousers. I've worked over there a few times." He began to sing. "*In my Liverpool hooome...*"

I glanced at the traffic through the mirror and turned back to him.

"Anyway," I said, trying to hurry him along. I watched in disbelief when the man, cool as a cucumber, took out a cigarette and lit it.

"So you're going to the bogs of Mayo?" he remarked in amusement. "It's the West you'll be wanting then."

"Yes," we chorused.

Marion leaned over to speak to him. "You wouldn't believe how many times we've been down this road. We just keep going down roads that lead to nowhere."

He grinned and moved his long dark fringe out of his eyes.

"That's the story of my life, going down a road that leads to nowhere. Ara, but you know what you're doing wrong, don't you?" We shook our heads.

"It's left and then right over the bridge, not left and straight on. So it's left, right and another right over the bridge, straight down until you come to Heuston Station and then you stay in the left lane and follow the road out. Have you got that?"

We nodded like a pair of muppets, thanked him and drove off into the dense, slow-moving traffic, following his instructions and crossing a bridge to the other side of the Liffey. Then we stopped behind a green van at the traffic lights.

"It's like an ant nest," Marion remarked. "I've never seen so many people in all my life." She lit two cigarettes and handed me one and we continued to sit there for a minute or so, watching people passing by. "These lights are taking an awful long time. Why aren't we moving?" she asked, flicking her ash out of the car.

I agreed and strained my neck out of the window to look ahead. "Oh, I don't believe it," I moaned. "That thing in front of us is parked at the lights and here's me sitting here like Mary from the dairy."

Marion started laughing. I put on the indicator and crawled into the next lane.

"Welcome to Ireland," she said, trying to compose herself, but she couldn't stop laughing. She was soon laughing so hard that the tears were streaming down her cheeks. I kept glancing sideways at her. I suppose it was kind of funny. Before long my shoulders were shaking at the thoughts of what I'd just done and the tears began to run down my face too.

We drove for a mile and then Marion nearly jumped out of her seat. "There it is!" she shrieked. "Up ahead. Straight on. Don't dare go into another lane," she warned. "Look, it says, The West."

We soon left Dublin behind and headed towards Athlone. I had never seen such an expanse of countryside, acres and acres of bare land. I could see what was meant by the forty shades of green. Two hours into our journey, Marion needed a pee so I slowed down when we came to a farm gate and put the car into neutral.

She looked around and groaned. "It's too open here, Col. What if someone comes along and sees me?"

"Oh, they won't. Just go behind that gate. No-one will see you," I assured her.

She almost fell out of the car and hurried a little further along a path towards the gate.

"It won't open," she shouted back, "It's tied with rope."

I leaned across the passenger seat and called through the window. "So just cock up a leg and climb over."

She began to laugh and stood on the bottom rung, trying to lift her leg up, and had to let it drop again. "My jeans are too tight!" she yelled.

I giggled watching her struggle, trying this way and that, to get over the gate. I looked up and down the road. "Hey Marion, there's nobody around. Just come and do it at the side of the car."

She stopped and looked at me. "What if anybody comes?"

"They won't see you down there!"

"Well, I'm bursting to go now, so it looks like I'll have to." She struggled to the rear of the car like she was wrapped in a pencil skirt, walking slowly until she disappeared from view. I opened the map to check we were still on the right route and tried to measure the rest of the distance on the scale. Suddenly the distant drone of an engine reached my ears and I looked up to see a stream of traffic coming towards us. Human nature being what it is, the drivers slowed down as they neared our car. It wasn't long before someone caught sight of Marion and began to wolf whistle and, within seconds, all the drivers were whistling and beeping their horns.

Marion screamed as she quickly did up her jeans and jumped back into the car. "Oh, my God, I'm dying."

I looked across to the drivers. "What's the matter with you all?" I called. "Have you never seen a woman's bum before?"

On we drove, and the nearer we got to our new home, the more excited we became. We had gone from discussing buying a dog to adding sheep and cattle to our shopping list.

17

IT WAS MID-AFTERNOON when we turned off the main road and drove into the village of Bradknock, slowing down for a flock of geese that congregated in front of us. We'd only ever seen cats and dogs and budgies and goldfish, so we oohed and aahed for a few seconds as we watched them waddle across the road. We then drove on, continuing to cruise in second gear, meandering down the lane, passing houses whose only sign of life was the smoke puffing out of the chimneys.

My heart began to flutter when I spotted the church. The bushes along the far side by the graveyard obscured any further view and I drove on in great anticipation.

"Stop," Marion instructed.

I did as I was told.

We gazed at our new home in silence.

Pink roses clung to the walls of the house, creeping over the front door and surrounding the oval windows, stretching their branches around the side of the building out of sight.

A short elderly woman came hurrying towards us, waving a key in the air.

"Aw, I'm glad to see you've arrived safe and well," she said, stopping at the window. "Aren't you great for driving all this way? Them roads from Dublin are shocking. I'm Ellie," she said as we stepped out of the car, "and you're very welcome."

I introduced Marion and myself and she shook our hands with such warmth, I could tell she meant every word she said.

"Will ye come over and have a cup of tea?"

We promised to call over when we had unloaded the car.

"Well, I'll not be standing here delaying you when you've so much to do but don't forget to come over for a bite when you're finished."

I watched her walk away and then turned my attention to Maisie's cottage. For the first time since we'd left England we hardly said a word.

"It looks like a doll's house," I whispered, breaking the long silence. When I lifted the latch on the gate, bits of rotten wood came away in my hand and I didn't know whether to laugh or cry. My eyes slowly swept over the house and garden again and then I shoved open the gate and sat down on the step.

I could hardly trust myself to speak. My mind was filled with Maisie. How must she have felt leaving such a beautiful place all those years ago to go and work in England, I wondered. I didn't want to cry. Not today of all days.

I stood up and joined Marion and together we opened the front door and went inside. We stood on the stone floor and gazed silently around the room. A picture of the Sacred Heart hung above the low doorway. Home from home, I thought touching the frame. "Do you think this might have been here when Maisie was a little girl?"

"Probably," Marion whispered, wandering around the room. "It's supposed to be bad luck to throw holy relics out of your house. That's what my gran said anyway. If you want to get rid of them you have to burn them."

"And look at the turf fire and the old fire crane."

Marion went and stood by the hearth. "Someone's filled the bucket full of turf for us."

The huge black grate had been cleaned and polished so we could see the bottom half of our reflections in it. An old Welsh dresser exhibited cups and plates.

"I thought the place would have been empty, didn't you, Col?" she asked, admiring the table and chairs in the corner. "Oh, and look someone's even picked flowers for us and put them in a vase." Marion leaned close and whispered in my ear. "I feel like Goldilocks. I'm thinking the three bears are going to skip out at any minute."

Together we, and the drowsy cat in Marion's arms, looked over the rest of the cottage.

I was stunned. It was out of this world.

To the left and right of the living room were two bedrooms; the door at the back of the room led to a very small kitchen with an old enamel sink and a cold-water tap.

Looking out of the tiny window, we could see the lengthy back garden with four tall trees along the back fence. I could see through the gap in the centre of the trees onto the meadow where a wire mesh fence separated two pieces of land down the middle. There was a gate to the left of our back garden, presumably leading into the meadow

Maisie had mentioned in her letter.

I suddenly had a thought and turned to Marion. "Where's the toilet?"

We opened the back door and went outside, frightening all the birds out of the garden.

"It must be in here," Marion shouted above the noise of a passing tractor. We lifted the latch on the shed door nearest the house and poked our heads inside. It was full of turf. A chorus of little tweets drew our attention to the wooden rafters above.

"There must be a bird's nest up there," I whispered before closing the door and moving on.

"Oh, it's got to be in here," I assured Marion as I pulled open another door. An old iron bed frame and other relics from the past was all we could see.

"There's the bath anyway," Marion giggled, indicating the rusty little contraption in the corner filled with empty bottles.

I raised my eyebrows. "Oh, yeah, and look at the handles? Wow! It's portable."

We moved on to the next building, hastily scanning the dark, airless room. When we had finally searched everywhere, we looked at each other blankly. There wasn't one.

We threw open all the windows to let in the fresh air, admiring the different views as we went from room to room. I made a mental note of the furniture I needed to purchase over the next few weeks. We locked the cat in the little kitchen and started unloading the car.

MARION WAS A great one for organisation. She found a place for everything in that little cottage. The wall cupboards in each of the three rooms had been scrubbed clean, allowing the clothes and bedding to be neatly folded away.

Tractors passed along the front of the house, slowing down when they reached the cottage. Men touched their caps politely and waved as we eagerly waved back.

By the time we were finished I was dead beat.

The long drive from Dublin had taken its toll and that turf fire looked so inviting that I plonked myself in the chair beside it, stretched out my legs and yawned.

"Marion, we're like chalk and cheese. If I'd have been on my own,

I'd have emptied the car onto one of the beds and there it would have stayed."

She smiled. "Don't you be putting yourself down. I love cleaning and pottering about and besides, you did all the driving. You're the one who brought us here. You just relax in that chair while you can."

I stood up. "Gosh, I'll have plenty of time to be doing that when I'm old. In any case, didn't we promise that woman who gave us the key, Ellie, was it, that we'd call over for a quick cup of tea as soon as we had the time?"

"Good idea."

THE DOOR OPENED as soon as we reached the gate.

"God be with ye," Ellie said, shaking our hands again. "And you're very welcome. Come on in and rest yourselves. You must be worn out."

We followed her through the dark hallway, past an empty gas bottle and a bag half filled with coal, into the living room, where we warmed our hands by the fire. Two dogs and a cat ran out of the kitchen to greet us.

"Angel! Spot!" Ellie roared. She opened the back door and ordered the two dogs out. "Don't mind them," she said, closing the door again. "They're good dogs really and they keep me company in the long winter nights when there's hardly a soul to be seen."

"And what's your name?" Marion asked, stooping down to stroke the cat, but the mangy looking thing stiffened angrily before jumping up onto the kitchen cupboard.

"That's Tilly." Ellie glanced out of the window to check on the dogs and turned back to us. "Now you two don't have to stand on ceremony to me. Sit down and make yourselves comfortable while I get you a little treat." She went over to the cupboard in the corner and brought out a bottle of Paddy's whiskey.

We settled ourselves into the cosy floral armchairs and looked around the room.

I watched from the corner of my eye as our 'treat' turned out to be a drop of whiskey and the drop of whiskey turned out to be half a glass.

I was struck by her kindness and generosity. I didn't want to offend the poor woman, but I knew if I drank that much, I would have to be carried home.

Marion gave me the eye. "I can't drink that," she whispered. "I'll end up on my back. Ah, tell her not to waste it on us."

I cleared my throat and tried to sound casual. "Oh, just a drop for me, thanks, Ellie."

Ellie clucked like an old hen and gave me a sideways glance. "Never you mind. 'Just a drop for me'. It's not often we have folks coming to live here, so you just sit back and relax and enjoy your little treat," she ordered. "'Just a drop for me.' Huh!"

Soon we were sipping our drinks and, with her own good measure of whiskey in her glass, Ellie plonked herself down on the chair beside us.

"You'll have to excuse me wearing this scarf all the time, only I'm in and out to the shed all day for turf and other bits and bobs, and I find it keeps in the heat and protects my poor head from the cold. You won't find many country people with a bare head. And these old boots," she said, lifting both feet off the floor, "I've had them four years and there's never a day they've been off my feet except to go to bed, of course."

I smiled at Ellie. She obviously enjoyed the chat and filled us in on all the locals. We went up the village and down the village.

"And I wasn't born here, you know? Oh, no, good God, I wasn't. I come from Sligo, but my sister married into this village and not long after her husband died, she became ill herself. Well, I packed my things and came to look after her, never dreaming I wouldn't be going back."

"Are you settled here now?" Marion asked.

Ellie took a large swig of whisky before answering. "Ara, I suppose I'm as settled as I'll ever be. All my folks back home are gone now and my sister left me this small place, so I have to make the most of what I have. It's very peaceful here, there's only old Josie who lives in the top of the meadow behind me."

I nearly dropped my glass. Did I just hear her right? Old Josie?

"We thought we'd lost her last year after her heart attack, but when the danger was over, she refused to stay in hospital and was back home and would she take it easy? Mind you, she doesn't trouble anyone and keeps herself to herself. She has a lovely old orchard. You'll know if she likes you because she'll leave a box of apples or pears by your gate every now and again. She's no electricity and you'll see her candle burning in the window at night."

I sat there wanting to ask her a million questions. Could it possibly be *the* Josie? I would have to bide my time and wait.

Marion rolled up her sweater sleeves.

Ellie leaned over and felt the wool. "That's a beautiful jersey," she remarked.

Marion went on to tell her how it had cost her only two pounds in Oxfam in England.

"Two pounds?" Ellie repeated in disbelief.

"And I got a lovely pair of trousers with a jacket to match for a fiver," I told her. "It's dead cheap, honest. You wouldn't be bothered buying new clothes. We went to a wedding last year and I bought a gorgeous turquoise suit with a hat to match for a tenner, didn't I, Marion?"

"The gloves cost you more, didn't they?" she reminded me.

"Yeah, I paid a tenner for my outfit and fifteen pounds for a pair of gloves to go with it."

I don't think Ellie could believe her ears. "Ten pounds for the outfit and fifteen pounds for the gloves? Oh, merciful Jesus!" she roared. "Oh, aren't you two great craic altogether?"

Marion's face brightened. "If you give us your measurements, Ellie, next time we go over to Liverpool we'll get you a load of clothes."

"Not that you need them," I added hastily, just in case she took offense.

"Well, I wouldn't mind a fur coat with a hat to match," Ellie chuckled "You know, one like the Queen Mother wears for church sometimes on Christmas day, but I'd say you're hardly likely to find that in a charity shop."

"Oh, you never know," Marion replied. "We'll keep an eye out anyway."

An hour passed and I finished my second drink and placed the glass on the table. I felt a little light-headed and my movements were slow and deliberate.

"Right then, Ellie, we'd better be going."

Ellie did a loud intake of breath. "Sure, you cannot go without a cup of tea! What kind of neighbour would I be at all, sending you off without a hot drink and a little something to keep the hunger from you?"

When I went to speak, I was silenced and realised it was no use arguing, so I sat back down again.

Five minutes later we were eating apple pie and cream.

"Oh, d'you know what, Ellie, you're too kind. Nobody ever looks after us like this, do they, Col?"

"Apart from Maisie," I reminded her, "but next time, Ellie, we're going treat you."

When we were finished and ready to leave, Ellie hugged us both.

"Will I see you tonight at the Stations?" she asked, leaning her heavy frame against the hedge and waiting for an answer.

"The Stations?" Marion asked. "What's the Stations?"

Ellie clasped Marion's hand tenderly. "We have a lovely Mass in a neighbour's house and then we have a big party afterwards." She pointed across the fields. "Can you see Mrs O'Gormon's house?"

I put my hand across my brow to shade my eyes from the sun.

"Oh, it's beautiful inside," Ellie said dreamily. "You'd think you were in a palace. Ooh, you could eat your meals off the floor."

"What time do we need to be there?" I asked.

"Well now, she'd hardly expect you to be there for the Mass, knowing you've just arrived after travelling so far, but sure, don't you know everyone is dying to meet you both, so will you call over sometime?"

"We will indeed. What time does it finish?"

"Finish?" Ellie responded. "Finish? Well, I'd say if you're over before midnight the party will just be getting going."

Marion and I smiled at each other. I wondered if there would be any booze at the party, what with the Mass and all that.

As if reading my mind, Ellie said, "There'll be plenty of food and drink and the craic is always good when we get together."

I was convinced. "Say no more. We'll see you there, and thanks, Ellie, you've been so good organising everything. I'll settle things with you later on."

Ellie leaned over her gate, her face awash with excitement.

"Well, now, I can't take all the credit. All I did was a bit of cleaning and dusting and put a few bits in the press, but Sean's the one who's been going in every day, lighting the fires to keep it nice and warm for you. Anyway," she said, glancing up and down the lane, "sure, I thought he'd have been here to meet you by now."

"Don't worry, Ellie, I'm sure we'll have the pleasure of meeting him before the day is out. Toodle-oo for now and thanks for everything."

"We'll have to buy her something nice," Marion enthused as we strolled back across the road.

"Yeah," I agreed. "I'll tell them all back home to look out for a mink hat and coat from one of the stalls in Paddy's Market."

18

"HELLO THERE, AND you're very welcome."

There was no mistaking the Irish brogue that came from somewhere behind the hedge. Marion and I turned to see a dark-haired young man walking along the lane. We went down the path to meet him, exchanging sneaky, lusty glances with each other. By the time we had reached the gate, the stranger had come into full view.

"I'm Sean Tooney, and I'd have been here sooner only one of my fecking cattle got stuck in the ditch, and here's me now all covered in shite, not even having the time to get washed up and greet you properly."

I could tell Marion was dying to laugh. She put her hands in the pockets of her jeans and looked down at the floor so as not to offend the visitor.

The first thing I noticed was the donkey jacket. I hadn't seen one for years, not since my dad had worn one when I was a young girl. I shook his hand warmly and introduced us both.

"Pleased to meet you, ma'am, and I hope you'll have a very happy life here."

"Come on in," I invited, making my way up the path. "We were just about to have a drop of duty free."

Sean smiled, showing a mouthful of perfect teeth, and followed us inside.

"It makes a nice change to be welcoming people that's coming to live here instead of always saying goodbye to folks and wishing them good luck. There's more than a few people around here that'll be glad to see a light in this house at night."

"Did you know Maisie?" I asked.

Sean shook his head. "Oh, she must be gone from here before I was born, more than fifty years or so. Some of the old folk would know her. Maybe old Josie up on the hill, but don't go near her because she'll run you. Wait until you see her walking through this village, then you can ask her."

"All right," I answered but I couldn't wait. This woman had to be the friend Maisie talked about.

Sean took a chair from under the table and placed it near the fire. "I'm sorry I wasn't at Ellie's earlier on to meet you, but I'll bet she had a warm welcome for you all the same."

"Very warm. She treated us like we were her long-lost family. Really made a meal of us, didn't she, Col?"

"So she gave you a good drop of whisky, did she?" he asked pleasantly. He leaned over and took two pieces of turf out of the bucket and placed them on the back of the fire then rubbed his hands together to get rid of the turf muck before reaching into his pocket and pulling out a tin.

"She sure did," I answered, watching him roll his tobacco. His hands were big and rough from hard work.

"Ah, she's not a bad old soul." He licked the seal along his cigarette paper and folded it together. "Did you find the tea and sugar in the press?"

"Oh, so that's what they call the cupboards around here," Marion said, handing Sean a glass of brandy. "I wondered what Ellie meant."

Sean chuckled. "You'll soon get used to us. We're not that strange really." He raised his glass. "Good luck to you both, and I hope you'll have a very happy and peaceful life."

"Cheers," we chorused.

"Will you not miss your television?"

"A little bit," said Marion. "But not much," she quickly added.

"Listen, you're both welcome to come over to my place any time and watch whatever you want. Just so long as you remember I'm an ould bachelor and the place isn't up to much. My mam died last year and so I've let things go a bit. Some days I don't even bother to light the fire."

"Is your father still alive?" Marion asked.

Sean shook his head. "He died a long time ago. I've three sisters; one in Australia, two in America and I've a brother living in Wicklow. I'm the youngest of them all," he grinned.

"Do they spoil you?" I teased. There was something about him that I couldn't help but like.

"I can't complain." He grinned again, "In actual fact they're all very good to me."

"Aw, that's nice," Marion remarked. "Did you ever work in England?"

Sean raised his eyebrows. "By Jesus, I was there for years. England, Scotland, and I worked in Wales. I worked hard and made a good living and I've still plenty of good friends over there." He finished his drink and went on his way, arranging to come back and escort us to Mrs O'Gormon's house later that night.

We fell asleep as soon as he left and if it wasn't for the cat jumping on my lap and scaring me half to death, God knows when we'd have woken up. The blazing fire had dwindled to a few ashes and I switched on the light and glanced at my watch, realising we only had half an hour before Sean was due.

Marion fed Tiddles, and I put some turf on the fire and the room soon warmed up. However we were both desperate for a pee and knew we had to go outside.

"You go first then," I offered when we reached the back step.

"Aw, no, it's all right. You go first."

"No, go on, Marion. I don't mind. You go."

"Oh, all right then. But what if somebody comes?"

"I'll stand at the back door and keep watch," I whispered, "and if I see anybody I'll whistle."

She considered the suggestion and knew she didn't have any choice. She hurried out into the garden and crossed the damp grass disappearing behind the shed.

If my brothers could see me now, I thought in amusement. Quickly going indoors, I grabbed my jacket off the chair and went back outside again.

"Hurry up, Marion," I pleaded, thinking my bladder was about to burst and wishing I had gone first. A bat swooped and disappeared through a hole in the shed. I crossed my legs and leaned against the wall.

"I'm coming," Marion said, emerging from the shadows.

"Right, then. You keep watch and I'll go. And don't forget to whistle."

No sooner had I started to pee, when a loud whistle reached my ears.

By the time I hurried up the garden to the back door, Marion was leaning against it, helpless with laughter, the tears running down her face. "Sorry, Col, I couldn't resist it."

"Oh, you mean sod!" I said, chasing her through the house. "You only made me topple over into the nettles and get stung. Just wait until tomorrow when it's daylight and you're out there. I won't be looking out for you."

I was just brushing my hair when I heard the latch click on the gate and I opened the door for Sean.

"My, my, don't you scrub up well?" I teased. "I thought it was the priest calling when I looked out the window and saw you strolling down the path."

He smiled shyly.

"I've been thinking," I said, when he stepped into the room, "isn't it a bit late to be visiting someone? I mean she knows you, but we're strangers. Won't we be intruding?"

"Ara, not at all," Sean assured me. "Nobody in Bradknock is a stranger, you two included. Sure, she'd be more offended if you didn't go. She'll be delighted to see you. Honest to God, she will."

So the matter was settled. Marion kissed her cat goodbye and we left.

We walked past the church and back up to the entrance of the village, passing a pub with the sign Tansey's swaying back and to in the wind, turned left and walked along the road for about five hundred yards.

"Normally, I'd cut through the fields, but it's a bit rough for you two to be crossing this time of night."

Earlier on, Marion and I had been at a loss about what to wear. She'd wanted to go in her jeans, but I thought that maybe, because it was a kind of party, we should make a bit of an effort. The only garment that didn't need to be ironed was my knee length, three-quarter-sleeved, black velvet dress. I'd had it for years and it had never let me down. Marion put on her brown trousers suit, which always flattered her blonde hair and brown eyes. Walking beside Sean, I thought I sensed a bit of chemistry between him and Marion, and couldn't help noticing how good they looked together.

Marion suddenly slowed down and looked at Sean. "Hey, I meant to ask you, has this lady got a toilet?"

"Huh? Sure, don't you know nobody has a toilet around here?"

Oh my God! Nobody had told us that.

BY THE TIME we arrived, the Mass was well and truly over, and the party was in full swing. Mrs O'Gormon's house was indeed a sight to behold as we stepped through the front porch onto her plush shag-pile carpet. She obviously had a liking for brass: bells, horseshoes, buckles, and tankards hung from every wall in the room.

"Thank you for coming," she said, hugging us in turn. "I know how tired you must be, so we'll try and behave ourselves tonight." She laughed mischievously. "Now what'll ye have to drink? Would you like a drop of brandy or whisky maybe?" She indicated the makeshift bar in the corner. "Do you want to go and see for yourselves and then you can decide?"

We both had a glass of white wine and sat down on the chairs nearby.

A sea of faces, some of them friends and neighbours, introduced themselves. Some of Mrs O'Gormon's relations had travelled from as far as America and Australia for this very special occasion. Laughter rang through the house. The drinks flowed and people danced to the sound of the accordion.

"Can you sing?" Sean asked us.

Marion smiled. "Not much. Can you?"

"Depends how much of this I've had," he said, indicating the glass in his hand.

Mrs O'Gormon had spared no expense. Thick slices of chicken, ham, and salmon were piled high on matching oval plates; nearby were sausage rolls, meat pies and bowls of salad, not to mention the desserts of trifle and fruit salad in water crystal bowls placed on the far side of the table. Everybody in the village must have brought a cake – they sat on display like works of art almost too perfect to eat.

Mrs O'Gormon took hold of my arm. "Come here a minute, I've a surprise for you."

I could feel my face going red. All eyes were upon me as I was led through the hallway into what I thought must be another sitting room. I looked at Marion, but she seemed as nonplussed as I was. What could the surprise be? I asked myself as people looked at me and seemed to smile knowingly. The door was slightly ajar, and I very cautiously peeped inside. I couldn't believe my eyes. There on the sofa sat my two brothers.

"Oh, my God!" I yelled, throwing my arms around them. "How? Why?"

They all laughed at the shock on my face.

"But how did you manage to arrange this?"

"We had to come, Col, just to see where you'd be living and that you would be safe." Safe! I was twenty nine years old and my poor brothers were still worrying about me.

I put my hands on my hips. "I knew it wouldn't be far enough. I should have gone to China."

Marion was hiding behind Billy when I spotted her. "Ooh, you! You're getting too good at keeping secrets."

"I nearly had a nervous breakdown trying to keep this one, what with that and the cat."

Now," Mrs O'Gormon said, "come and have a drink and enjoy the party."

My brothers were in their element. Many of the villagers had spent their youth working in England and some the best part of their lives before coming back to Ireland to retire. Two of them had worked at the Liverpool Docks for a time, much to Billy's delight.

Marion had been talking to some people from Australia when I sidled over to her and whispered that I was desperate for a pee.

"I'm sorry," I moaned, "but you're going to have to come outside with me and keep watch." I couldn't believe nobody had any toilets. Still, I supposed they were used to it. "None of that funny stuff like earlier on," I reminded her. I don't know why she looked offended, as if she didn't know what I was talking about. I still hadn't really forgiven her.

"As if I would."

"Hmm, as if? OK, then," I signalled discreetly, "come on."

Outside the air was nippy and we snooped around the area looking for a safe place to squat.

"Over there." Marion pointed at what looked like a barn. Together we went behind the building so that nobody could see us.

"I'll go first this time and you keep a look out," I said, peeping around the wall and watching for anybody coming up from the house. When we were finished, we hurried out of the cold into the house.

"Good evening and God bless you all."

Ellie Ford entered the room like a Queen. "Ooh, didn't I tell you her home was like a palace?" she shouted when she spotted us.

People stood back and let her walk through to the far side of the room where we were sitting. Tony jumped up and grabbed a spare chair for her to join us, and I introduced her to my brothers.

Ellie gasped dramatically as she studied the men. "Such fine looking men," she remarked, shaking their hands. "Have either of you had the calling?"

The men were baffled and Billy looked to me for help.

"The calling?" Tony repeated.

"Sure, you'd make lovely priests," she said, to everyone's amusement.

"It was awful good of you to organise things for our Colette," he finally managed to say after he stopped laughing.

"Oh, don't you give it another thought," she told them, tightening her headscarf and sitting back in the chair. She took a swig of whisky before leaning forward. "Now I'm not one to gossip, but there are some things you should be aware of." She looked at each of us before continuing. "I'm telling you, it's not as safe in the countryside as you think."

"Is that right?" Billy asked, surprise registering on his face.

Ellie leaned forward. "I don't want to startle you, but I think you should know I was burgled here recently." She suddenly had everybody's attention.

"Aw, that's a shame," I told her.

My brothers shook their head in disgust. Burglary was rampant in England, and the elderly were frightened to open their doors, but here?

"Did they take much?" Marion enquired. Like the rest of us, she seemed very angry that such a vile thing could have happened to such a nice old lady and in such a quiet place. She looked at Ellie and waited for an explanation.

Ellie's eyes filled with tears.

"Well, I'll tell you what happened." We all leaned closer as Ellie began to tell her story. "You see, one night I went down to the village to use the phone. I wanted to ring Sam Mackey, you see, about bringing me some turf, even though," she said, raising her voice, "I could've waited and seen him the next day, and after this happened," she said, "I wished I would have waited and seen him the next day. Anyway," she said, handing Sean Tooney her empty glass without even looking at him, "when I got back I could tell robbers had been in my house."

"How?" everybody asked.

"Because the wardrobe door was open and it'd been closed when I left."

I noticed Billy and Tony exchange glances and lowered my eyes to the floor.

Something didn't sound right.

"Now," Ellie continued, "I ran back down to the phone as fast as I could and rang the Garda. That's the Irish police," she informed us.

"So they didn't take anything?" Tony asked.

Ellie's eyes widened like saucers. "Nothing," she said, to our surprise. "They didn't take nothing."

At that moment Sean Tooney returned with the drink and rolled his eyes at the others.

The old lady took the glass out of his hand and took a sip. "But I made them check all over the house to make sure they hadn't left any guns, or more importantly, planted a bomb."

Marion looked fit to burst. She'd never been good at holding it together, especially when she was with me. Once we started laughing, we couldn't stop.

I made an excuse to get a glass of water. I think we were the last to know, because everybody was grinning at me.

Her voice carried through to the kitchen and I could hear her clearly as she continued to recount the story to the others. "When the Garda left, without even thinking to put on my coat, I ran down the lane to the priest's house."

I was on my way back through the sitting room with my water and I heard Marion ask, "What for?"

I could see Ellie rest her glass on the table and fold her arms across her chest.

"Well, to bless the house, of course. They took nothing of mine, but they left something of theirs."

"Oh?" Marion sounded confused.

"Oh, yes!" she affirmed. "They left their bad spirits. Ara, look here he is," she said, almost springing out of the chair. "Here's the good man himself. Father Carol." She waved.

Glad of the distraction, all heads turned to the priest. The priest put up his hand and made his way over to us. A small, stout, grey-haired man, he winked in our direction before he greeted Ellie.

"Oh, Father, I was just telling them about that awful night I was burgled."

The priest spoke in grave tones, but there was no mistaking that twinkle in his eye as he looked around the group. "Oh, how can you even speak of it, Ellie? It was such an awful thing."

"I know, Father, but I thought it best to warn them."

"You're a very good soul, Ellie. There'll certainly be a place in heaven for you," he assured her.

"Do you think so, Father?"

He smiled. "I do."

Billy stood up and offered the priest his seat on the sofa in between me and Marion and went and sat on the arm of Tony's chair.

He smiled and squeezed in between us. "Aren't I the lucky man sitting between two lovely-looking women?"

"Ooh, Father," Ellie scolded.

"And what do you think about our great team?" he asked the men mischievously. Billy flicked his ash into the tray and looked at the priest. "Don't you mean our great team, Father? After all half of them are English."

The priest rose to the bait. "Ah, well, you're not doing that good yourselves, are you?"

"Well, Father," Tony butted in, "we thought we'd take a back seat this year and give you a chance."

"Well, now, isn't that awful good of you fellers? Let's hope they play better for us than they did for you."

Laughter rang out around the room.

Tony couldn't resist. "And hey, Father, if you like you can have one of our cathedrals."

Father Carol lit a cigar and puffed the smoke into the air before answering. "Oh, aren't you too kind to me altogether, but I think you need them more than us."

Next thing Marion gave me the eye and we excused ourselves from the happy group and went out into the garden again. My feet were freezing. This was the third time we had been outside.

"Maybe we should drink less?" I said to Marion. "At least it'll reduce the call of nature."

"We'll have to do something, because I swear I'm going to end up with pneumonia."

We hurried back into the house and warmed ourselves by the fire. Then Sean appeared with re-fills, so we accepted the drinks gracefully (what else could we do?) and began to party again.

"Where's Billy?" I asked, looking around for my brother.

Tony offered me a cigarette. "I think he's in the toilet."

"What toilet?" I snapped. "There isn't any toilet."

Marion and I rolled our eyes at each other. It was miserable enough out there without him taking the mickey.

He began to laugh so I waited to find what was so amusing. "What are you talking about? No toilet? I was there myself five minutes ago."

Do I need to tell you how flabbergasted we were?

I saw Sean trying to sneak away and reached out and caught him by the elbow.

"Sean," I said, trying to control my voice. "Did I just hear right?"

He nodded. "Aw, bejesus, I'm terrible sorry. Bejesus, I am. I meant to tell you I was only joking and then it clean went out of my head."

"What did?" Tony was confused.

"Oh, it was—"

"Never mind," I interrupted Sean, who by this time was looking at Tony and trying not to laugh. "You mean to tell me," I said, "that Marion and I have been squatting outside in the dark and the cold for the past few hours and all the time there was a toilet in the house?"

Tony began to laugh and before long Sean had joined him. Within minutes, they were near hysterical, leaning on each other like a pair of drunks holding each other up. Every time Tony went to speak, I think the thought of me squatting in the garden when there was a toilet in the house set him off again.

Sean wiped the tears from his eyes. "I'm really sorry. May God strike me down dead, I meant to tell ye."

"May God strike you down dead?" I was already starting to see the funny side and knew that in an hour, I would be laughing just as hard as them, but I didn't want to let him off too easily. "Hmm, well!" I smiled at him. "We owe you one, Sean,"

"Oh, I'll tell you what, mate," I heard Tony say as we walked away. "I wouldn't like to be you."

~ 19 ~

I HADN'T LAUGHED so much in years. Even my jaw ached from the strain of trying to keep a straight face. After a while I slipped out of the house. I felt over-whelmed and needed some time alone to process the events of the last twenty-four hours.

"Where are you going?" Marion asked, quickly following me to the door. She shivered with the cold and tucked her hands up her sleeves.

"Just for a stroll," I informed her. "It's too hot in there."

"Well, let me come with you then."

"No, I'm fine," I assured her. "Honest."

She folded her arms. "Don't believe you."

"Look, I won't be long. I just need to clear my head a little bit."

"You do it every time. One minute you're having a laugh and the next you've disappeared. You're always going off on your own and I feel awful."

"Well, you shouldn't feel awful. You know what I'm like. I can only stand crowds for so long." I felt a bit mean. It wasn't as if I hadn't been enjoying myself.

"What shall I tell Billy and Tony?" she whispered, looking back over her shoulder to make sure no-one was listening.

"Oh, I'll be back before they even know I'm gone. Look at the lovely night. And look at the moon! Have you ever seen anything like it? I want to enjoy it. All of it. I'll see you in a little while."

"Oh, go on then." She relented when I went to protest again. "But if you're not back in ten minutes, I'm going to send a posse after you."

"Twenty minutes."

She tutted.

"Never mind about me. You go on back in there and find yourself a nice bloke."

"Hey, it's you who should be looking for a bloke"

"Ha, ha! No thanks, Marion. I'm on the shelf now – old and cracked and happy."

I strolled along the lane and took in the peace and quiet. Wasn't Marion a cute one, keeping my brothers' visit a secret? And wasn't Sean

Tooney awful good for putting my brothers up in his house for the night?

I looked up at the star-filled sky. "Thank you, God," I whispered. "And thank you, Maisie. Oh, thank you."

On and on I walked and, before I knew it, I had reached the entrance to the village. I walked down past the pub, turned right, passed Ellie's pink house on the left and the church on the right and soon I was standing outside Rose Cottage once again. I found myself humming that Cilla Black song again. I just couldn't get it out of my head. *Something tells me something's gonna happen tonight ...*

I sat on the wall, kicked my shoes off and warned myself not to cry.

Talk about a run of good luck! Father Carol had even offered us a job in his sister's nursing home. I wasn't going to rush into anything. I fancied a change and needed some time to sort myself out. Marion, on the other hand, was delighted and said she'd call over to see her within the next few days.

I glanced across the field and saw the candle burning in Josie's window, just as Ellie had said. How had she lived all these years without electricity?

The view was like a Christmas card. I was longing to have a closer look, but from what I had heard the woman was a bit mad, especially when Ellie had told us she had threatened to throw a bucket of water over the priest. Still, I thought, she must get awful lonely up there on her own.

I seemed to have been sitting there for ages and slipped my shoes on to go back to the others.

I stopped and turned to have one last look.

When my eye caught the gap in the hedge, I found myself crawling through it. With the light from the moon, I sneaked across the field towards the cottage, hurrying on towards the light. The sound of music drifted towards me. I stopped and listened for a few seconds, trying to place the tune. Then I realised it was 'Marble Halls.'

I slipped off my shoes and crept up to the building, easing myself along the wall, careful not to knock over the bits of scrap iron that lay in a pile on the path. Old tin dishes with the remnants of milk told me there were plenty of cats around. Beside the front door stood a water barrel, above it an old pipe hanging down from the gutter. Sticks of wood were stacked in a heap and a bucket piled high with turf sat on the step. My heart began to race in case the old lady should come out and find me.

What would she say?

I stooped down and peeped inside the window, eyes darting here and there, heart beating faster and faster. The fire was like a kaleidoscope as it flickered, revealing different corners of the room. I could just about make out a sideboard in one corner and a brown chest of drawers, which stood facing the mantelpiece. The clutter on the table below the window obscured part of my view. My eyes struggled to focus through the half-empty milk bottle into the far side of the room. After a few seconds, the image became clear. The old lady was sitting on a stool with her back to me. She was playing the piano. I held my breath and gripped the window ledge so as not to lose my balance, moving closer until my nose almost touched the glass.

Suddenly the music stopped. I froze. Then I went into panic mode. I tried to scramble to my feet with the intention of running for my life, but I lost my balance and stumbled backwards onto the path sending the milk dishes clattering into each other.

Too late! The door handle rattled. I slowly raised my eyes and there in my line of vision stood a pair of old black leather boots laced halfway with bits of string.

I tried to gather my composure. What excuse could I give for snooping through her window so late at night? It was inexcusable. And what if she really was mad?

"I'm awful sorry," I whispered, tilting back my head so I could see the old lady's face and then panic turned into concern when I remembered Ellie had said she had a heart condition. "I'm sorry if I gave you a fright. I just heard the piano and ..."

The old lady offered me her hand.

"Get up off the cold floor, a ghrá. You'll get pneumonia down there."

I reached out and clasped her bony hand. I was soon back on my feet again, brushing the muck off my clothes. "You see, I was just going for a walk and ..."

"Is it Maisie's house you're after moving into?"

Standing face to face with this stranger, I wanted to throw my arms around her and give her a hug. Dressed in an old navy blue dress and cardigan, her snow-white collar-length hair wild and matted, she smiled a sad, joyless smile.

"My name is Colette Murphy. I used to work in the Home where Maisie lived."

Her eyes never left mine and I felt like she was looking deep into my soul.

"I was sad to hear she had died, the Lord have mercy on her." She touched my arm. "Come in, Culette, instead of standing out here in the cold. Just to warm your hands and feet. It isn't often a visitor crosses my step, and my house isn't suited for entertaining, but you're very welcome all the same."

I stepped into my shoes and followed Josie into her cottage, aware of my heels scraping on the stone floor. The smell of cabbage and bacon permeated the air and I smiled as Josie shooed the cat off the fire-side chair for me to sit down.

"And what kind of life did the poor creature have?"

How could I answer that? "A fairly contented one, I think, but maybe a bit lonely at times."

"That happens to us all, especially when you're far away from home."

I thought I was making her feel sad so I said, "She was a children's nurse until she retired."

Then she smiled. "Ara, she loved the little ones. She used to help the school-teacher out and the kiddies adored her. I think they learnt just as much from Maisie as they did from the school-teacher."

"You've a lovely fire," I remarked opening my hands and warming them appreciatively. "It's not often you see a fire in a neighbour's house in England anymore."

She took a box of matches from beside the loose tea and sugar on top of the mantelpiece and lifted the glass cover off the paraffin lamp on the table.

"A fire's the heart of a home, a ghrá," she said as she carefully lit the wick. "My fire dies once a year to have the chimney swept and on that day I have to go out of my cottage. I cannot bear to see a cold empty hearth. My mammy was the same. She kept the fire going all night, the Lord have mercy on her"

The room suddenly brightened. The clock above the fire had stopped. I could see lots of cobwebs hanging from the cracks in the walls and the faded curtains were hung with a piece of string.

She turned to me and smiled. She must have been beautiful when she was young. I could well have imagined her screaming with laughter as she ran down the path to the dance with Maisie all those years ago. There was so much I wanted to ask her. *Where did you go? When did you return?* But it wasn't the time to be raising questions about her past—a past I knew more about than I probably should have.

She remained standing near the table and, with the innocence of a child, looked from the top of my head to the tip of my toes. "That's a beautiful dress you have on."

"Oh, thank you, Josie. I made it myself."

"You must be very clever to be stitching such a garment. Take your shoes off and warm your feet, lass. I expect you're frozen to the bone after all that travelling today."

I did as I was told and slipped them off, not that it made much difference. They were thin and flimsy and not meant for crossing fields on a cold March night. Josie reached down and picked one up, turned it over for inspection and frowned. "You'll have rheumatism and bunions by the time you're thirty. Pull your chair nearer the fire while I get something to warm you good and proper."

I began telling her about my brothers' surprise visit and watched her take a bottle of whiskey from the cupboard and pour us both a drink.

"Wasn't that a grand thing to do altogether," she said, adding some boiling water from the kettle beside the fire.

When she handed me a drink I stood to offer her my seat, but she pulled the hard-backed chair over from the table and sat opposite me. We sipped our drinks quietly for a few seconds. She seemed drawn to the fire and, for a while, she looked so lost in thought I wondered if she remembered I was still there.

And then she turned to me.

"Aw, she was always good-hearted. Even when we was children she shared everything she had, and books." Josie's eyes crinkled, "She was mad on them; read everything at least twice. I said the rosary for her every night and asked our Blessed Lady to keep her safe. I knew she would end up in England; it was a place she was always itching to go. She was such a free spirit was Maisie; the best friend I ever had and do d'you know, a ghrá, that I still have something that belongs to her after all these years?"

"Wow! Have you, Josie?"

She rested her glass on the floor near the fire. "It'll mean nothing to you, lass, but it meant the world to Maisie." She went into the next room. I could hear her muttering and the sound of drawers opening and closing.

Then she emerged from the shadows and, without a word, placed a hard- backed book in my hand.

I could feel my throat contracting and swallowed hard. I knew what it was before I opened it; this story that touched so many lives.

She sat down and leaned towards me. "She'd sit in that tree at the bottom of her garden reading it over and over again. And when her father threatened to burn her books, she left it with me for safe-keeping."

"Burn them?"

"Oh, he was a grand man and it was said out of concern. She'd over-heard him talking to her brother one day, saying he was worried because she spent so much time reading. He'd never have done any such thing but Maisie was taking no chances. I was going out with my father one day and she came running over and put the book in my lap. 'Look after it,' she'd called, 'and keep it safe'."

I flicked through the old copy of *Jane Eyre*, with its discoloured paper and faded ink, then looked up from the book into Josie's watchful eyes. "You must have been an awful good friend to have kept if for all of these years."

Her eyes went watery. "We were good to each other, a ghrá."

"She kept the other copy all of her life, Josie. This was always her favourite story. Just imagine if she'd known you had kept this one too. Did you ever read it?"

"Read it? Why it's like my Bible; the only book I ever read in my life. I must have read it a hundred times. 'Tis no wonder Maisie was driven by the story, and that woman was clever to write like that, and so long ago. Aye, lass, it was the only book I ever read. Nowadays the eyesight's not as good as it was and I struggle to read the words." Another silence filled the room and then after a minute or so she turned to me and asked, "I wonder did Maisie ever meet her Mr Rochester?"

I couldn't help smiling. "She did, Josie and was very happy, if only for a short time. Did you ever meet yours?" I dared to ask.

She smiled sadly. "Oh long, long, ago, a ghrá. I didn't have to go searching for my Mr Rochester, he grew up with me in this village. He was the only man I ever loved." She turned to the fire and was lost again, as if there was so much she wanted to say and couldn't.

I glanced at my watch. I had been gone forty minutes. I'd soon have to tear myself away.

"I have to go now, Josie," I said awkwardly, "but I have some photos of Maisie you might like to see. Is it all right to pop over with them sometime?"

She looked pleasantly surprised. "Oh, that'd be grand, lass. Come over and see me tomorrow if you like. I am always here."

I reached out and gave her a hug. "Thanks, Josie, I'd love to."

I hurried back down the field. Everything seemed so unreal. Only yesterday I had been rushing through Liverpool city centre with Marion and now it seemed that my old life had stopped and I had travelled back through time.

When I reached the lane, I crawled through the gap in the hedge.

What must life have been like for Maisie all those years ago?

20

I WALKED BACK towards Mrs O'Gormon's, trying to put the sad image of the old lady out of my mind. Something caught my attention and my teary eyes began to focus on a baby rabbit, pausing on the ground in front of me. Being a city girl, the only rabbits I had ever seen were the ones in cages. I stood as still as the night air, so I could take a good look at the creature and not scare it off. Without taking my eyes from it, I slowly stooped down, thinking in my naivety that it would come to me and I could pick it up. The poor creature panicked and darted through the fence into the field. "Ah, come back here," I pleaded, climbing up on the gate. "Come on," I gently coaxed. "I won't hurt you."

"Evening, ma'am."

I nearly jumped out of my skin with fright and turned to see who was behind me.

"I'm sorry," he said, putting out his hand to steady me, "I didn't mean to startle you. I was just on my way home."

His voice was deep. I could just about see his face in the dark.

"Oh, that's okay." I giggled nervously. "You must think I'm awful mad, standing here in the dark, talking to a rabbit, in a field."

"It could have been worse. You could have been talking to yourself."

I leaned back against the fence and laughed with him. "That's true."

"Are you home on holiday?" he asked.

"Actually, I've come to live here," I whispered.

"Now I think you are mad." His laugh was warm and hearty and I couldn't help smiling as I stood there looking up at him.

"Oh, don't say that. It seems like such a nice place. Everybody's made us so welcome. Listen to them." I gestured up the road towards the music and laughter. "I've never heard people enjoying themselves so much! They certainly know how to party, don't they?"

"They most certainly do," he chuckled.

"I suppose you live around here, do you?"

"I do indeed. I'm Fred O'Gormon." I thought I heard him say.

"It's nice to meet you, Fred."

He burst out laughing. "No, it's not Fred, it's Ted–Ted short for Edward."

"Oh, sorry, Edward, I mean Ted. I'm Colette Murphy," I said, shaking his outstretched hand.

"How d'you do, Colette." He pronounced it 'Culette' just like Josie had.

"Oh," I said, "so it's your party, is it? I'm on my way back there."

"So am I," he replied. "Follow me." With a sweep of his hand, he gestured up the road. "I'm not here all the time. I have a flat above my vet's surgery in town. Now tell me, what brings you out all alone, on this dark night?"

I looked at him and smiled. "Hmm, I could ask you the same question."

"Would you believe, the moon and the stars, and half an hour's peace and quiet, brought me out alone this evening?"

"Me too. Actually, I'll let you into a little secret. It's my birthday today and I reckon it's the best one I've ever had."

"Sure, isn't that a coincidence. Just imagine." His voice rose a little with surprise. "Would you believe me if I told you it's my birthday too?"

I stopped and looked up at him. "Well, fancy that!"

When we arrived back at the house, I squeezed between Mrs O'Gormon and Marion, on the sofa.

"Are you enjoying yourselves?" Mrs O'Gormon whispered. Her cheeks were rosy from all the excitement and the drink.

"Oh, yeah, we're having a great time." And we certainly were.

ALTHOUGH WE HAD Irish blood in us, we demonstrated our lack of knowledge about the country and its politics when Marion asked Mrs O'Gormon if the man in the photo on the wall was her husband.

Mrs O'Gormon began to laugh. "Oh, the Lord have mercy on us, no! He's not my husband; he's our very own ..."

I can't even remember who it was. I just remember looking at the photo and thinking, who's he when he's out?

It was only later that we learnt what a powerful political Irish figure he had been in Ireland. How were we to know? Our history lessons in England consisted of long, boring periods about the Battle of Hastings and other irrelevant facts. We were taught nothing about

Ireland. It could have been so interesting.

One of the women began to sing and Mrs O'Gormon whispered again, only this time a little too loudly. "Now if Mary Flannagan was here, she would really steal the show. Sings like an angel, she does."

Her remarks didn't go un-noticed. People began to cough in an effort to drown out her voice, not knowing what she was going to say next.

I could see Ted sitting in the opposite corner. Every so often, I could feel his eyes on me and pretended not to notice. He was far more handsome under the light. He winked at me once and I smiled at him. I could feel my face getting hot. Oh, my God, I thought, don't tell me I'm blushing.

Ellie had been right. It was past midnight and there was no sign of anybody going home. If anything, the crowd became livelier as the night wore on.

Marion and I were standing in the kitchen enjoying some ham and chicken sandwiches with our new neighbours, Jean, the lady who sang and Imelda.

"Have you seen Mary tonight?" Imelda asked.

"I haven't," Jean replied.

"Who's Mary?" I asked.

"She lives down the lane from you," Imelda replied. "She's married to that man over there." She pointed. "The one talking to Jean's husband. She's grand and wait until you hear her sing."

"Why didn't she come tonight? Isn't she very well?"

"I was wondering that myself," Imelda remarked. "I was talking to her only yesterday and she was as right as rain. Where's Nigel?" She asked sticking her head out of the kitchen doorway. "Nigel!" I heard her call. "Where's Mary?"

"Oh, right so," she said and joined us again. "He says something cropped up. We'll probably see her tomorrow and she'll tell us all about it."

When Imelda wandered off to Stuart, Jean looked around before leaning in close to me."

"To be honest," she whispered, "Mary's not that friendly and I heard

she's a bit upset about two English people moving into the village."
I sighed. "I know how she feels."

"But - but aren't you English?"

"Nah," I stated, "We're Liverpudlian."

21

I WOKE AT the crack of dawn. My mouth felt like sawdust. God, I had never seen so much drink in all my life. Last night had been a good lesson in Irish hospitality. No wonder people came from all over the world.

I wriggled out of my sleeping bag and went into the front room.

I could hear the birds singing, so I opened the back door and went out into the cold, morning air, stooping down to inspect the cleverly spun spider webs, which were sprawled across the lawn like a fine lace.

A crow called from the top of the chimney pot and, once it had my attention, flapped its wings and flew away, soaring into the sky. I watched until it disappeared from sight.

I shivered and pulled my little nightie around me. Sandy had given me a pack of them with saucy comments written across the top. *Leave before I wake up* was the one I wore that morning.

I heard a kind of rustling noise at the top of the garden and before I knew it, a herd of cattle were standing, gawping at me. I was scared. I stood very still, momentarily hypnotised by the scene as ten cows stared back at me. Without taking my eyes off them, I walked backwards until I reached the door and, quickly turning, I went inside, my cold feet flapping on the stone floor. I turned the knob and burst into Marion's room.

"Come and see all our visitors."

Marion groaned and rolled over to face me. Her cat sat up and looked at me from the end of the bed, like a big, soft, cuddly toy.

"What time is it?" She asked, straining to see her watch in the darkened room. "Isn't it a bit early for people to be calling?" she whispered, thinking we had a houseful of people. When she tried to sit up, she collapsed back onto her pillow. "And look at the cut of me! I must look like I've been dragged through a hedge backwards. Can't they come back later?"

"Oh, don't worry about the time or the cut of you. Just come and see what's at the back fence."

I pulled back the curtains to brighten the room. She realised she would get no peace and threw back the cover and followed me.

"Oh, m-m-my God! There must be at least fifty of them."

I went up to the fence with Marion following close behind. "Do you think they're hungry, 'cause they look hungry to me?"

"Don't you go too near them," Marion warned taking a step back. "They might bite you and wouldn't that just be our luck, the pair of us eaten by wild animals on our first day in another country? Just imagine your Billy and Tony and your dad burying a set of teeth in a coffin 'cause that's all that's left of us."

I laughed and laughed. "Marion, we're in Ireland, not the outback of Australia. They're not wild bears or dingos, you know. And look at those big sad eyes. They wouldn't hurt a fly. Just look at them!"

"Look at them? Look at them? I can't take my eyes off them! Ah, but don't be so sure they won't bite you. Maybe you're reading them wrong. I mean, you're standing here in that bright red nightdress and you know that saying, don't you? Like a red rag to a bull."

"Oh, God, you're a case, you are. There are no bulls here."

"How d'you know?"

"Because bulls have horns."

"Oh well, I've heard they sometimes get them cut off."

"No, Marion, I think that's another part of their anatomy and it's called castration."

She still wasn't convinced. "Well, Col, I still don't like the way they're looking at me and I didn't come here to die."

My laughter startled the cows and they jerked back from the fence. "Hang on here a minute." I ran into the cottage and returned a minute later with one of Ellie's freshly baked soda loaves. "Here," I said to my astonished friend. "you give them that and I'll give them the rest. Come on, don't be scared," I coaxed as we approached the inquisitive herd.

"Poor Ellie," Marion lamented, trailing after me. "If only she knew."

"Ah, but she won't, will she?"

Marion shivered. After all, it was still only March. "Oh, come on, Colette, we've been out here ages and I want a cup of tea."

I stood on tiptoe and leaned over the fence. "Just let me feed this one. Ahh, its tongue's all long and wet," I squealed. "It reminds me of that feller I went out with at school."

Marion giggled and held onto her stomach. "Oh, stop making me laugh, Colette, I'm going to wet myself." She stopped and looked over my shoulder

"Who's that over there waving to us?"

I followed her eyes. "It looks like Sean," I said putting up my hand. "Oh, my God, I wonder if he saw us feeding the cows?" I asked, watching the figure head off towards the church.

We quickly threw the rest of the bread over the fence and went into the cottage.

AFTER BREAKFAST, I got dressed and went off to buy some milk. I followed the directions Sean gave me and crossed over the road by Ellie Ford's, cutting through the gap, but somehow I ended up at a farm gate. I looked around in bewilderment. Ellie's dogs began to bark.

"Is it me you're looking for?" she called from her back door. I could just about see the top of her head and smiled with relief.

"Oh, no, Ellie, I was looking for the shop to get some milk."

Ellie stepped onto the path. "Well, come on in and I'll give you a drop."

"Oh, no, don't worry, Ellie. I need some for the cat."

"Ara, sure, come with me and I'll show you where it is. I'll meet you at the front."

I walked back out onto the main street to meet her.

"Isn't it a grand morning and it's promised dry for the next few days. Begod," she said, before I could speak, "didn't we have a grand time last night? Did you enjoy yourself?"

"I had a great time. Considering we're strangers to the village, Ellie, I can't get over how kind and friendly everybody was."

"Strangers indeed! Sure now, you're no more of a stranger than I am."

On we went, Ellie, waddling along in her four-year-old boots and me in my old Doc Martens.

A maroon car came out of the churchyard and beeped its horn.

Ellie chuckled. "Ah, look! Wave to Father Carol," she instructed.

I did as I was told and the priest waved back and drove on up the road.

"There it is." She pointed when we were a little further on.

"Oh, it's closed," I said, feeling disappointed. In fact it didn't look like a shop at all. It looked like somebody's little house.

"Closed? It's never closed," Ellie informed me. She walked on past the front door and began to knock on the window.

I could see the curtains were closed and began to feel uncomfortable. Ellie waited for a minute and then stood on her toes and put her ear to the window. "Will you listen to that?" she said. "Can ye hear her snoring?" She banged her knuckles three times on the window again. "Bridie, will you ever get out of that bed? You've a customer here who's dying for a cup of tea and can't have one unless she gets her drop of milk."

After a minute or so I could hear sounds from somewhere inside the shop. I took a step back. The bolt was released and the door slowly opened.

"God bless ye, Bridie," Ellie greeted. "For a minute there I thought you were dead in the bed. With the grand day the good Lord has given us, I half expected to have seen you at nine o'clock Mass."

We strolled in behind her as she slithered across the floor in her slippers. "I need some beauty sleep, just like the rest of ye," Bridie grumbled, walking through the opening in the counter.

Ellie tittered and looked at me. "She needs it more!" she whispered.

I disagreed. Standing there in her orange candlewick dressing gown and a hairnet, which was tied at the front, she looked like she'd been asleep for a hundred years.

Ellie winked at me as Bridie put three glasses on the counter and brought a bottle of brandy down from the shelf. I watched the contents of the bottle disappear into the glasses and took a deep breath. She handed each of us a drink.

"To your good health and you're very welcome," she said, clinking my glass.

AN HOUR LATER, I hurried down the path clutching the milk and went in through the back door, breathing in the sweat smell of burning turf. I'd hardly sobered up from the previous evening and I was tipsy again. I had a strong black coffee and did a little more unpacking. I stacked some of my books on the shelves at the side of the fire, careful to leave enough space for Marion's teapots. Cutting the thick card with the scissors, I took out Maisie's photo and hung it on the nail above the fire and stood back to admire the portrait

When I looked out through the window, I noticed a woman standing just inside the gate looking into the cat basket my brothers had brought over the evening before. I knocked on the glass and beckoned to her to come up to the house. Then I hurried out through the front door.

"Hey, don't go!" I called as the woman rushed away from the garden. When she turned back, she looked embarrassed. "I was looking at your little cat, so."

"Oh, you must think we're awful cruel," I remarked after introducing myself. "But we've brought him from England, you see. We have to keep him locked up until he gets used to the place, otherwise he'll run off and he might get killed." I bent down to check that the cat was still in the container. "Actually," I said, standing up again, "he belongs to my mate, Marion. She's just gone to make a phone call. She'll be back in a minute. To tell you the truth," I whispered, "I can't stand cats. In fact," I continued, "if it was left up to me, I'd have thrown him over the ferry railings into the Irish Sea!"

She followed me along the path and into the cottage.

I turned back to her for a moment. "But don't tell her I said that, will you?"

She shook her head and her face broke into a smile. Then she introduced herself as Mary Flannagan, from up the road. I noticed a fading bruise above her eye and, as I got to know her over the months, I would notice many more.

Marion returned a few minutes later and we sat and had some coffee. She looked over to Mary and slapped her knee as if suddenly realising. "Oh, so you're Mary, the one with the lovely singing voice?"

"And who told you that?" Mary seemed surprised.

"That lady who had the Stations told us, in fact she told everyone, didn't she, Col? I can't think straight. What was her name?"

"Mrs O'Gormon. And she decided to announce how good you were when that poor woman was singing. But don't worry, she just pretended not to notice, but I saw the look she flashed her when she'd finished."

"I wonder who that was."

"I think her name was Joan or Jean. I'm not sure."

I thought I saw Mary's eyes water.

"You must have met most of your new neighbours?" she said.

"Far too many to remember," I told her. "I actually met Josie last night and then on the way back to the party, I met a man named Ted."

Mary brightened. "Oh, he's a grand feller. I'd say you'd get on very well with him. He's a great scholar."

"I think he said he's a vet?"

"That he is and a very hard-working one too. He's out in all weathers. Oh, but he's a great carpenter. Takes after his father, the Lord have mercy on him. He was a grand man; he did a lot of work in the church."

Hmm, I thought, nice looking and nice mannered and all those strings to his bow—sounded too good to be true!

Mary glanced around the room at all our bits and bobs. Black bags and boxes were scattered here and there, still waiting to be unpacked.

"How did you manage to fit it all in the car?" she asked.

"With great difficulty," Marion answered, stooping down and opening one of the boxes.

"I see you brought your hammer and nails," Mary said, admiring the pictures on the wall.

"And the drill and shears," I added.

"Oh, you'll need more than shears to keep this grass down. It grows like wildfire in the summer. There's a man around here that has goats that'll do the job for you. The only thing is they're awful messy with their droppings all over the place."

Marion tipped the contents of a small box onto the floor and Mary looked taken aback.

"Don't mind me asking, but why did you bring all that?"

I looked down at the year's supply of Tampax.

"An Irish friend in Liverpool told us you couldn't buy them over here, so we thought we'd better come prepared ..." I trailed off as Mary began to laugh. She knelt down beside the pile and counted the twenty-four boxes.

"Sandy must have been having a laugh," Marion said.

Mary was unable to speak for laughing and nodded her head.

"You mean we can buy them here?" I said, going into the bedroom and returning a few seconds later with a bundle of assorted coloured knickers. "And I don't suppose it's true that you can buy only white knickers over here either?"

Tears began to run down Mary's face when she looked at all the knickers.

"I think someone's been codding you."

"Oh, I'm going to kill Sandy Harrison!" I whispered.

Marion couldn't speak for laughing.

When the commotion was over, we cleared up the mess and made some more coffee. Mary went over to the mantelpiece and looked closely at the photo. "Isn't she lovely looking altogether? Who is she?"

"That's Maisie."

Mary's eyes widened in surprise. "You mean, the lady that used to live here?"

I nodded and told her of my surprise at finding Josie still living in the village and how I had accidentally ended up in her cottage.

Mary shook her head. "Isn't that amazing? And won't you have plenty to talk about, not that Josie talks much. She's a listener and that's if you see her at all."

"I thought she was a love," I told her and left it at that. "Where you born in Bradknock ?"

"No, I married into the place. I'm what they call a blow-in," she said in amusement. "That's a name given to an Irish person living in a different county to where they were born. It takes about twenty generations of families before you're accepted as a local and by that time I'll be dead and long forgotten."

"Hey, Mary," Marion said, "we didn't bring all this stuff, you know, although we brought most of it. Colette's brothers flew over yesterday on a surprise visit." She chuckled.

"Erm, pardon me?" I interrupted. "Surprise to whom?"

Marion laughed aloud and told Mary what had happened. "That's how I got my cat basket," she told her. "They brought it over for me."

"We're lucky really because my brother's mate works for a removal firm and he's going to Galway next week and he's promised to bring some stuff over for us. Nothing big, you know, just bits like my sewing machine and my stereo, and he's bringing stuff of yours, isn't he, Marion?"

"I hope so. He said he was anyway."

Mary sat down and took a sip of her coffee. "If I were you though,

I'd keep the cat in the house. Otherwise someone will come along and steal the little feller."

"They wouldn't?" Marion was appalled. "You mean someone would come along and steal my poor little cat?"

Mary nodded, but I think when she saw Marion's face, she wished she hadn't said anything. "I'm only warning you, that's all. In fact, it's probably safe enough."

"By the way, why didn't you go to that party last night?" I asked.

She looked a bit subdued. "Oh, it's a long story. I mean, I wanted to go. I had my hair done and bought a new suit. I spent all day getting ready. You see, there's not much else to do around here except wait for the Stations to come around. Watching the clock all day I was and then, just as I was about to go and put on my outfit, doesn't Father Carol come knocking on the door? Old Lizzie Riley had taken bad in the afternoon and even though Dr Moran had stabilised her, he wanted her to be monitored in hospital overnight. I know in England you pick up a phone and have an ambulance in about ten minutes, but not so around here. We've been known to wait an hour," she said, shaking her head. "So, just to be on the safe side, they were sending her straight away in a hackney cab and he wanted to know if I'd go along and help settle her down. Poor old Lizzie, she hates hospitals."

"Why did they ask you?" I asked.

Mary raised her eyebrows. "Well, there's a certain sneaky person from around here who told Father Carol that I was rather fond of Lizzie and that was true, because anybody would be hard pushed not to like the poor creature, but she also told him I wasn't that keen on the Stations, so that's how I ended up missing them."

"But why didn't you come over later on when you got back?"

"Sure, Nigel was back from the party by that time and he wasn't that keen on me going over on my own."

It was as if she was on this earth to please everybody else. The more she talked, the unhappier she seemed to become.

"Never mind, we'll have our own party here for you one night, won't we, Marion?"

"Dead right we will."

I STROLLED UP to Josie's later that morning. I went the proper way this time, up a lane just about wide enough for a car to drive up. Shoots were beginning to sprout on the trees and I tried to imagine what it would be like in the summer. The stone walls either side were uneven and mostly covered with wild flowers. Though I could see the cottage in the distance from my house, the bushes up the right hand side of the lane hid it from view until I reached the top and followed the bend where there were patches of daffodils beside the path to the cottage.

When I reached the door, the birds ruffled their feathers and fled towards the outbuildings.

She had the same warm welcome and was eager to hear about our first night in the cottage. We sat beside the roaring fire and she laughed and laughed when I told her about Marion's fear of the cattle and how I'd tried to feed them.

When I gave her Maisie's photo album, she hugged it close to her chest but made no attempt to open it. Maybe it was something she needed to do alone. After all, she hadn't seen Maisie since she was eighteen.

I looked at the photo on the wall. I'd noticed it the previous evening, but now, in the daylight, it was much clearer.

"That's my mother," Josie said, following my eyes. "My father's picture is in that bottom drawer and there it'll stay till I die."

I didn't ask any questions. I knew she'd tell me what I wanted to know.

"You must come down and see us sometime, Josie. You can meet Marion and we'll make you a lovely roast dinner. You can come this Sunday, if you like?"

She went to speak and then paused. "Well, I hope you won't be offended, a ghrá, but I'm not one for visiting, and I tend to keep myself to myself, and even so, I haven't been in that house since the day before I first left Ireland back in 1930. But you come up to me whenever ye want. My door will always be open to you."

22

THAT EVENING AT Rose Cottage, I sat hunched up on the window seat and looked out at the sky. Rain splashed against the glass and every so often a branch reached out and hit the pane. I rested my back against the wall and let my mind drift. I thought about Maisie and Josie again and my eyes filled with tears.

"A penny for them?" Marion was sitting by the fire, putting on her nail varnish. She shook her hands and blew on her fingers to dry it quickly. "Come on, don't be sitting there with a head full of sad thoughts. How's about we put some music on? Oh, but we can't, can we, because of these antwacky sockets, but there is an old electric fire in the shed and we could use the plug off it and stick it on the CD player."

"Mmm."

"Mmm, she says, and you're not even listening to me."

I lowered my legs and slid down from the ledge. "Sorry, Marion, but that moon is hypnotic. I keep trying to count the stars, but I get to about fifty and lose count. Do you know I've never really looked at the sky before, well, not *enjoyed* looking at it?"

"That's because there's never been anything to look at before. There's no pollution here, not like in Liverpool anyway. I bet if you looked at that sky for long enough you would see right into heaven."

We tossed a coin to see who would have the misfortune of going out to the shed.

"Sorry, Col," Marion grinned when it landed on heads.

"Don't worry, I'll get my own back." I picked up the torch, threw a coat over my head and dashed out the back door and through the pouring rain to the shed.

THOSE FIRST FEW mornings when I opened my eyes, I smiled with pleasure at my new life. The sounds of nature had replaced the hustle and bustle of noisy traffic outside my bedroom window.

We were still struggling without a toilet and had resorted to using a bucket in the shed. I had asked Sean about the possibility of having one installed and sure enough, he called a few days later to sort out the job. I was moving a pile of stones up to the top end of the garden and he stooped down to give me a hand. The sun had clouded over and it began to spit with rain.

I wiped my mucky hands on my jeans. "Will it take a long time to put the toilet in?"

"Not at all. If we put it here," he said, going back down the garden and pointing to the little pantry beside the back door, "it'd just work out nicely without you having to build an extra room for it. When do you want it doing?"

"Yesterday."

He pretended to scratch his head and then grinned at me. "It's a good job I brought my tape measure with me. Just let's finish moving these stones, and then I'll measure up."

"You're a hero," I told him appreciatively.

He smiled and then looked across the garden. "I'd say that end tree would have to come down to make way for the drains coming through."

I looked at the tall tree at the back right hand side of the garden with its tatty old piece of rope, no doubt the remnants of a child's swing from long ago—Maisie's swing perhaps. Then I remembered Josie's words and wondered was that the tree Maisie used to sit in when she read *Jane Eyre*?

"That's such a shame. Aw, it's so old."

"I know, but sure what can you do?"

He studied the tree more carefully. "We'll knock it into the field and I'll get Ted O'Gorman to saw it if you like. He'll have it done in no time and stacked in the shed."

"Oh, I thought he was a busy vet."

"He is, but he's also a very obliging neighbour and can turn his hand to anything. And he won't let you down. Oh no. He's there on the dot and won't take a penny until the work is finished and he knows you're satisfied. And offer him a drink on the job and he'll likely tip it over your head."

"Oh, thanks for the warning, Sean. I must remember that."

He turned to go and hesitated. "I've been meaning to ask you," he said, looking across to the field. "Are you going to sell your grass?"

I began to laugh. "Am I going to sell my grass? Who to and what for?"

"Well, I'll buy it off you myself if you like. I'll be taking Hanley's and Flannagan's grass, same as I do every year. You won't know this field when it's cut. It'll be as flat as a football pitch. The fellers come around and cut it down, and then it gets baled and wrapped and stored for the cattle feed in the winter."

"That's awful kind of you, Sean. Is there anything you can't do?"

He began to laugh as he walked away. "I'll be seeing you," he called over his shoulder.

I watched him until he was out of sight.

Wow, I thought. Wait until I tell our Billy; selling my grass indeed.

23

SEAN AND STUART had been working hard since eight that morning.

The first task was to remove some of the stakes and barbed wire at the top of the garden, allowing the digger entrance from Sean's land. By the time the machine arrived, Sean and Stuart had installed the toilet and waste pipe through the back of the house.

I sang as I put on the kettle and opened a carton of milk, popped the bread in the toaster and set the tray to take outside.

"Wow, he's a good mover," I remarked to Sean, watching the digger swinging into action.

"We're lucky to get him at all," he said when I handed him the tray of tea and toast. "He's a busy man and in great demand, especially this dry weather." He picked up his mug, folded his toast in half and took a bite. "It could rain tomorrow and rain for another two weeks, and then he has no job at all to go to."

He walked back up to the top of the garden and sat down with the others to eat breakfast.

When Marion and I finished, we locked the cat inside the house and sat on the back wall, watching the big yellow machine bite into the earth like a dinosaur.

"Do you know what? They've always fascinated me," I said.

"What have? Men?"

I gave her a shove. "Oh, Marion! You know what I mean. Wouldn't you love to have a go on one of them? And no, before you ask again, I don't mean the men. Ooh, it sends a chill down my spine just thinking about it."

Marion nudged me. "Well, you know what you usually say, don't just think about it. Do it."

I was aghast. "Oh, you must be joking."

"No, I'm not." The grin on Marion's face should have been a warning.

"Oh, my God, don't you dare!" I shouted, but I was too late.

I watched Marion slide off the wall and walk up the garden, waving her hand to get the men's attention. The driver turned off the engine and leaned out of the digger when Marion approached.

"Oh, Marion, I'm going to kill you," I muttered.

I felt very self-conscious, sitting on the wall, watching them cluster round the digger in conference and then, much to my horror, Marion beckoned me over.

"Come on, Col" she shouted. "He's going give you a ride on his machine."

Marion's announcement brought giggles from the men and the next minute the four of them were shouting over to me.

Oh, God, here goes, I thought, sticking my hands in the pockets of my jeans and sauntering over to them. The short journey seemed to take forever.

I carefully stepped over the tyre tracks and climbed up into the cabin. That was an experience in itself. I squeezed down beside the amused driver and tried to gain my composure and concentrate.

I was a keen learner and watched him dig into the soil.

By the third demonstration I felt I had the hang of it and took hold of the lever. The sheer thrill of being in control of such a huge machine sent ripples of excitement right through me.

If Maisie could see me now!

I sank the bucket into the ground and pulled back the lever, scooping out the earth as I helped to make way for the drains to be laid.

THE SUN WAS still shining when Mary arrived just after lunch.

I couldn't help admiring her clothes. "Oh, you look lovely. You're all dressed up and look at the cut of us?" I remarked.

"Oy, speak for yourself."

"Sorry, Marion."

"She's right though, Mary. Should we get changed?"

Mary's face started to turn pink. "Oh, take no notice of me. Can't you tell I don't get out very much?"

"Well, you could say that, Mary, or you could just say that you are well groomed and we are a pair of slobs."

"Oh, but we did enjoy playing in that muck this morning, didn't we, Col?"

I nodded and filled Mary in on what had happened.

"You really drove it?"

"I did."

"And just think," Marion said. "When they come back after dinner, they'll be finishing off the job and tonight we won't have to be squatting in a bucket in the shed."

"The only sad thing was we had to knock down one of the old trees at the top of the garden."

Mary glanced out of the kitchen window. "Well, that couldn't be helped and sure, won't it come in handy for the fire?"

I brushed my hair in the mirror and turned to Mary. "Sean said he'll ask Ted to come and saw it for us,"

We both changed into clean jeans and went off into town.

Will I ever get used to this? I wondered as we passed a field full of cattle lazing in the sunshine. We drove down the main street and parked the car beside a café. The place had an almost 1960s feel to it.

In we went and sat at the table in the far corner, taking in the awful red-and-white-checked tablecloths, full of tea stains and cigarette burns. I did a double take when I saw the statue of Our Lady watching over us.

"Is she following us?"

"I thought you were Catholics?" Mary said.

"We are, but in England, you'd never see Mary on a wall in a café. Churches, schools, and convents, and that's your lot."

When we finished, we went to look around the shops.

"How are you, Mary?" asked a passer-by, for what seemed like the hundredth time.

"Is there anybody in this town that doesn't know you?" Marion asked.

Her face glowed. "It's that kind of place."

I could see what she meant. People were so laid back and cheerful as if they didn't have a care in the world. Drivers parked their cars anywhere they wanted, even if it meant blocking somebody in.

We went into the furniture store and purchased two beds, a fridge, and some new bedding. Then we went into the post office to buy some stamps and when we came out it began to rain a little.

"There's twelve pubs in the town," Mary informed us, "so you'll never be short of a place to drink."

By the time we had familiarised ourselves with the town, the library had opened. We cut through the car park and into the glass building where Mary introduced us to Anne, the librarian.

We browsed around the bookshelves and I sat for a while, flitting through a book on gardening, trying to make up my mind whether to borrow it. I didn't have a clue about the garden, but I was eager to learn.

"I'd like to read more," Mary said when she joined me at the table, "but I never seem to have the time. I think the last book I read was the Bible."

When we made our selections and had our books stamped, we went back out into the sunshine and headed towards the car.

"What did you get, Marion?" I asked, stooping to tie my bootlace.

"This came highly recommended by the librarian. It's called *On the Pig's Back* by, let's see …" She slowed down to look at the cover. "By Bill Naughton. Anne said this is the man who wrote *Alfie*. Remember?"

"*What's it all about, Alfie?* Oh, I love the way Cilla sings that song."

"Apparently," Marion said, ignoring my bad manners, "he came from the West of Ireland and his family moved to England when he was a boy, so I'll enjoy reading this."

Mary smiled. "I got Maeve Binchy's *The Lilac Bus.*"

"And I got Jackie Collins' *Sex All Day Long.*"

Marion tutted. "What's she like?" she said to an amused Mary.

"Nah, I was only joking. I don't really go for books with sex scenes. Just reading they've gone into the bedroom together is romantic enough for me. I don't need any details. Let's see, I got—" I stopped to look at the cover, "*Goodnight Sisters* by Nell McCafferty. Anne said she's an Irish journalist and writes some really good stuff. And this other one is called, *Goodbye to Mayo.*"

We crossed the car park, deep in conversation. When I spotted Ted O'Gormon, I turned to Marion and whispered, "Hey, look who's here."

"Who?" Marion asked.

"Shush." I panicked. "We don't want the world to know. Over there," I said rolling my eyes to the left. "Putting stuff in the boot of his black car."

"Hello, Ted!" Mary called over. "Nice day."

He peered from the side of the boot and smiled at us. Then he slammed the boot shut and strolled over. Tall and lean, jeans tucked in wellies and a big sloppy navy jumper. You would think such good looks would make him vain, but he wasn't, which made him all the more attractive.

"We meet again," he said cheerfully. "I hope you're not leading these nice two ladies astray, Mary."

"Ha, ha, Ted!" She smiled. "I haven't got it in me."

We talked for a while longer and then he said, "Sean tells me he's had to knock the tree down. I've a couple of days off next week, so if the weather's fine, I'll saw it for you."

"Oh, that would be brilliant. Thanks."

He looked back to his car and called over to a tall blonde who had just arrived and was putting something in the boot. Then he said goodbye and left.

Nature's certainly been good to her, I thought as the car disappeared. She was tall and slim with golden hair down her back. Some people just look so good together.

"Is that his wife?" Marion asked.

Mary smiled. "She thinks she's going to be."

"Oh, so they're not an item?"

"Her name's Orla Riley. She's his receptionist and I'd say that's all she'll ever be. He took her out when he first moved back here but I think he's sorry he ever bothered because she won't leave him alone."

"She works for him so maybe he's giving out mixed signals," I said.

"There are two vets in the practice and she was already employed there when he bought into it."

We spent the next hour walking around and when I saw the shoe shop, I grabbed the women by the arms. I couldn't wait to see the selection in the window. "Come on, I'll treat you both."

Marion saw where we were headed and looked at Mary. "Don't go in there with her. You don't know what she's like. It takes her about three days to pick a pair of shoes. And that's only one pair. She usually buys two, at least."

Mary laughed heartily.

"I'm telling you, Mary, once you get in there with her you'll never get her out!"

"Talk about dramatic," I said, taking Mary's arm. "I promise I won't be all day. I only want to buy us all a pair of wellies. I suppose you've already got some, Mary, but I'll buy you some anyway."

We were in and out in no time and bought a pair of blue wellies each.

I nudged Mary when I saw a familiar face walking towards us. "She's the one who was singing that night," I whispered.

"She's one of our neighbours," Mary answered.

"A nice one?" Marion asked.

"That depends. She's Orla's mother, you know, the blonde, and, I suspect, the reason Orla will remain single all of her life." Mary finished just as Jean Riley caught us up.

"How did you get on after the Stations the other night?" she asked. "Didn't we have a great time?"

Poor Mary looked crestfallen and I suddenly realised this was probably that snide neighbour she had told us about. We talked for a minute or two and then Mary helped me put the shopping into the car whilst Marion and Jean stood chatting a while longer.

"I'm from Galway myself," I heard Jean say to Marion. "I come from an Irish-speaking family."

"Wow," Marion marvelled, turning to us. "Hey, Colette, here's a fluent Irish speaker."

"Well, it's so long since I've spoken it, I can't remember very much," Jean said turning to go. We said goodbye and I watched her walk away.

"That's an awful strange thing, isn't it?" I said.

"What?"

"Forgetting your native tongue? I didn't think it was possible."

"Of course it's possible," Marion said. "Didn't we forget how to speak English when we learnt Liverpudlian?"

"Ha, ha."

THE BEST AND cheapest thing I bought that day was a donkey. Honestly, I did!

We'd called into the pub and been introduced to loads of locals— Seamus and Mehaul and Paidrick and Connor, oh, too many to remember—when someone asked me if I was intending to keep cattle. I didn't mean to laugh in their faces, I really didn't, but when they saw how dizzy I was, I think they realised the absurdity of their question. The man standing next to me said quietly, "If ever you're looking for a donkey, Sam's your man." He said indicating to the end of the bar. I looked across to an elderly man, sipping a pint of Guinness. A donkey!

Now he was talking.

He must have seen my face light up, because next minute the man had joined our company and before I knew it, Sam had sold me a donkey for a tenner.

Not only did we settle the deal with a handshake, but we toasted a drink to our good health.

"You'll have to get Sean to check your fencing," Mary was advising me when we left the pub, "or the creature will be strolling into Mass on Sunday."

"Oh, yeah, as—"

"It's been known to happen," she interrupted. "We've had chickens and sheep running around the church, and one Ash Wednesday morning, this was at home many years ago, I went into church and went to bless myself with holy water, and there was a cow standing at the font, glugging away."

THAT NIGHT WE were sitting on the couch, stuffing our faces with cheese and this wonderful soda bread we'd discovered. So far we hadn't cooked that much. There was a small Calor gas cooker in the kitchen, but I'd forgotten to buy the pots and pans earlier on.

"Do you mind if I nip over to Sean's tonight to watch *Coronation Street*?" Marion asked me.

"Of course not. Why would I?"

"Just making sure, that's all."

"That's all?" I grinned.

"No need to be looking at me like that."

"Ha-ha-ha. Like what?" I asked innocently, but I knew what she meant; I was making overtures. Though I must admit there was a bit of a glow about her.

I'd seen it that first night on the way to Mrs O'Gormon's. Just a little spark between them.

"If you put on your wellies and take the torch, you can take a short cut across the back field."

"No way. I'm not getting eaten alive by a cow. I'd rather take the long way around. At least I'll be safe."

"Oh, that's true." I laughed. "By the way, what time do you start work tomorrow?"

"Not until two. I'm going in for a couple of hours in the afternoon, just to get the hang of things, and then I am working ten till six for the rest of the week."

After she left, I went into my bedroom. There was still a lot to sort out. The beds were coming after lunch tomorrow. I would have one last night on the old iron thing I had been sleeping on and dismantle it in the morning. I glanced out my window. I could see the light on in Sean's cottage.

I liked Sean. He'd been such a great help, full of energy and enthusiasm. From what Marion had said, he worked hard all day and liked to put his feet up at night and have a few beers. It made sense to me.

I enjoyed an hour on my own. I wrote to my dad and Teresa, then, I put on my wellies to go to Josie's.

24

WITH MY *GOODBYE to Mayo* library book in one hand and torch in the other, I climbed over the fence and took a short cut across the field. There hadn't been much rain for days and I enjoyed the feel of the twigs crunching under my feet. My heart warmed as I neared the cottage. I was looking forward to seeing her.

The heat hit me when I walked through the door.

"Hi, Josie, how are you?"

She was sitting at the table reading a magazine by candle-light. She put her magnifying glass down and smiled at me. "I'm very well, a ghrá." She answered. "Come and get yourself a warm near the fire."

I put my book on the table and hung my coat on the back door and went to slip off my wellies.

"Ara, will you stop worrying and come and sit yourself down?"

"I don't want to dirty your floor, Josie"

Josie laughed. "Dirty my floor? Haven't I told you before, I cannot remember it ever being clean? Now come on in. You get the biscuits from the press and we'll have a cup of tea."

I began to tell her about our afternoon in town. She laughed when I told her I'd bought a donkey. "Mary says I should wait until the grass is cut, and Sam says he'll get his friend to keep it till I'm ready."

We sat near the fire sipping our tea and munching on marshmallows. I told her how much I liked the librarian and that she'd promised to search for a book about donkeys in the main library. They'd laugh at home when they found out I was reading books about donkeys.

"I've not been to the library, lass. D'you have to pay to lend the books?"

"No, Josie, they're free," I told her. "And you can borrow two or three at a time. You can come in with me one day if you like." I picked up my book from the corner of the table and showed it to her. She suddenly seemed to sink into herself.

"Are you all right, Josie?"

"Aye, lass, I am." She sounded sad and then she said, "It's that title, a ghrá, *Goodbye to Mayo*. It just hit me hard for a second. I'm fine now. I said goodbye to Mayo once and I never thought I'd come back here but I did. I went to live in America," she said softly. "I went away feeling desolate and I came back feeling desolate."

I froze; it was the first time Josie had referred to her other life. "Oh, Josie, I'm sorry. I never meant to upset you?"

There was silence in the shadow-filled room and then she looked at me with tears in her eyes. "I'm not going to burden you with my troubles. It's not that long since you saw poor Maisie being laid to rest and I'm not laying any more misery at your door. And apart from anything else you probably wouldn't believe me. You couldn't make it up."

I reached out and touched her hand.

"You can tell me anything Josie. Honestly, I'd be really interested to hear about your life. Tell me about America. Did you go with your family?"

"No lass, I was with strangers."

"That must have been hard for you."

"I had to go somewhere, a ghrá. I had no choice. My father didn't want me around here. It broke my mammy's heart. I suppose you heard all about it, did you?"

"I heard nothing, Josie."

"Then again, that could be. Let's pretend it never happened." She laughed but a sob caught her throat. "My father tried to have me locked away in the asylum but he didn't bank on the good friends I had."

"Oh, Josie, are you serious?"

"I am, and all because I wanted to marry a man he despised."

I slowly shook my head. "I don't understand. How could your father have that kind of power?"

She sighed. "In those days they could do what they liked and they did. You see, a ghrá, my father was not a very forgiving man, or indeed a Christian man. If anybody did him any harm, that was it, they were wiped out of his life forever like the stroke of a pen. My father took me out one afternoon on my birthday and told me he was going to buy me the mare I had always wanted. Can you imagine the excitement when we set off, lass? Kissing my mammy goodbye and telling her I'd see her that evening and all the time he knew I wasn't coming back. You see, he wasn't taking me to buy a mare at all. He was taking me somewhere he thought no-one would ever find me. He wanted to lock me away forever. We'd stopped at his friend's house on the way and that's the last I remember.

"I realised afterwards they must have put something in my tea to knock me out and later I had a vague memory of stirring and someone putting a needle in my arm. Next thing I knew, I woke up shivering with the cold in the most foul-smelling place, on a dirty mattress covered in urine stains."

I opened my mouth to speak but no words came. I let Josie continue.

"I was there for a month. I cooked and cleaned all day, and you had to watch your back. I was frightened. Sometimes at night people were so deranged they tried to get into bed with me. I couldn't drop my guard for a minute.

"And then one day I tried to escape and they put a needle in my arm and I didn't wake up for two days. I felt colder than ever and realised they'd shaved my head. But you know, lass, God works in strange ways. There was an old lady working in the kitchens who took a shine to me, especially after she found out what my father had gone and done. I needed to get a message home but I knew my father would be looking out for the post. Then I remembered how Maisie used to tell the visiting Yanks her name was Jane Eyre, so that when they went home they would write to her. Some of them cottoned on, of course, and she never heard from them again, but there were others who were so infatuated with her they believed everything she said."

My head was all over the place and I didn't know whether to laugh or cry.

"Nobody knew about the letters Maisie received," Josie said. "They used to be delivered care of the post office and Maisie would collect them. Then she'd go and sit up in that tree at the top of her garden and read them over and over again. I suppose old Lilly Hanley at the post office enjoyed the excitement and encouraged her in some ways. Anyway, one day I wrote a letter and gave it to my old friend in the kitchen to post."

I gasped with surprise.

Josie nodded excitedly. "I sent it to Miss Jane Eyre, care of Bradknock Post Office."

"Oh, Josie, I don't believe it!"

"Well, I'm telling you, every word is the gospel truth."

"Sorry, Josie. Go on."

"Well, the old girl posted the letter and I never prayed so much in all my life. Maisie was my only hope. If she didn't get my letter, telling her where I was, then I was as good as dead. Who would have thought to look for me in the other end of the country? Nobody. There I was a few days later, on my hands and knees cleaning up somebody's vomit, when I heard the key in the lock and someone opened the ward door. 'You've a visitor, O'Brien,' one of the orderlies said and beckoned me to follow her.

When I arrived at the reception, there stood Miss Hines, the old school-teacher. 'Josie,' she said in a stern voice, 'I might be an old aunt but I'm a caring one, and I've come to take you out for some fresh air and there'd better be no nonsense mind, or your father will hear about it. Understood?' I was too scared to speak so I lowered my eyes. 'Now get your coat and shoes on, and we'll go out to tea somewhere.' She slid the visitors' book across the table and I watched her sign Teresa O'Brien and it was then I realised she was up to something and I had best keep me mouth shut until we were alone. When we left the main entrance, she told me to hurry towards the gate. 'Now, child,' she said, when we reached the hackney cab she had waiting around the corner, 'your father did a most cruel thing to you and if you return home, he will do it again. There is a train leaving for Dublin in ten minutes. You must get on it and never come back. Not whilst he is alive anyway.'"

I turned away from Josie. I couldn't fight the tears anymore. "I'm sorry, Josie it's you who should be crying not me."

"Well, I was crying, child. I stood on that platform like a blubbering idiot. All I wanted to do was go home to my mammy but, deep down, I knew I couldn't. She'd always feared I would go off and leave her, and now her worst nightmare was coming true. I never got the chance to say goodbye. I asked Miss Hines to pass on a message to my mammy and Maisie, but she refused, saying nobody must know. She told me Maisie knew nothing of the letter. When Lilly Hanley had received it at the post office, she was suspicious of the post mark because it had been posted from the other end of Ireland and not America like all the others. She'd opened it and when she read the contents, she took it to Miss Hines.

'I got the train to Dublin and she arranged for me to stay a few days with some people she knew. It turns out they had a daughter visiting from America and they were looking for an Irish nanny for their two children, so they arranged for me to get a passport and promised to take me with them.

'I cried when the boat sailed out of Dublin and stood on the deck long after Ireland disappeared.

'I stayed with them for twenty years, until the children grew up. They were awful good to me but I never settled anywhere. After the children left home, my employers decided to leave America. He was head of a charity and their main office was based in Delhi. They offered to take me with them but I was already too far from home. Even after all those years, I was still homesick. I knew my mammy had died but my father was still alive and I vowed to return when he was laid in the ground. I got a job as a maid but they were not a very nice family. I saved as much as I could from my wages and looked forward to the day I came home. My father died in 1965 and left me what little he had. I made sure the Parish priest always had my contact details but he was under oath not to pass them on to anybody. It was only after much persuasion I gave him permission to tell my father that I was alive and well. My father knew I would never come home while he was alive."

I stood up and put on the kettle. "I hope you found peace when you came home Josie; you certainly deserved it."

I WAS GLAD Marion was in bed when I arrived home. I was in no mood for talking. I felt drained and sat looking out of the window for a long time. How different Josie's life could have been if her cruel father had allowed her to make her own choices.

It must have been 3 a.m. when I finally took off my coat and wellies and went to bed.

25

I OPENED THE door at 10 o'clock to put out the cat and there was Ted, standing on the step. The sun shone behind him circling his head like a halo.

I'd only been up long enough to make a coffee. Marion was still in bed.

I smiled sleepily. What a lovely sight first thing in the morning.

He looked at my chest and raised an eyebrow. "Thank you very much. Don't mind if I do." He closed his eyes, puckered his lips and leaned in towards me.

I looked down at my Kiss Me nightie and grinned, quickly placing my hand on his chest and easing him back.

"No, it isn't. But come in and let me get dressed and I'll make you a coffee."

He laughed at his own cheek but declined my offer.

"I'll get started while it's fine and dry if you don't mind," he said, turning to go. "But give me a shout when it's ready."

It didn't take me long to throw on some clothes, but then when I looked in the mirror, I didn't like what I saw so I got changed again.

I could hear the rattle of the postman's diesel van through the open window, so I quickly brushed my hair back and put it into a pony tail.

He knocked and handed me a couple of letters and a jiffy envelope too big to fit through the letter box. There was a letter from my dad and one for Marion from her insurance company, which I left on the mantelpiece. I sat down and opened my dad's letter, scouring down the page, eager for news. I gasped and read over the line again just to make sure I hadn't misunderstood. They had booked a flight to come over at the end of August.

I opened the padded envelope and pulled out something wrapped in tissue paper. Ah, bless! Our Tony had sent me the bottle of my favourite perfume, which I'd left on the bathroom window ledge.

THE CHAIN-SAW REVVED like a motorbike, sending the birds scattering high into the sky. Ted was oblivious to the uproar above him.

I was looking through the window and watched him slice through the tree like a loaf of bread, tossing the logs on the heap at his side. I could have stood there watching him all day. Then I remembered I was supposed to be making coffee.

It was the beginning of April and the early mornings were still a bit chilly. I put on my wellies and duffle, went out into the garden and handed him his mug of coffee. He smiled and thanked me, wrapping his hands around the hot drink appreciatively. I felt a bit awkward, so I turned to go back into the cottage. I was not much good with the small talk. Not like these people; they had it off to a fine art.

He took hold of my elbow. "Hang on," he said brightly.

I watched him stride over to the back gate and lift his jacket off the post. I thought he was getting his cigarettes. He came back over and spread his jacket across the trunk for me to sit down.

"Thank you," I croaked, lowering myself onto the seat. I could feel my face burning and hoped he wouldn't notice as he sat astride the log to face me. I watched him take a swig of his coffee and rest the mug on the trunk.

"Tell me, are you homesick yet?"

"Don't be daft."

"I was in England a few times."

"Oh, whereabouts?"

"I shared a room at Galway University with a feller whose family had moved across to London. I went over with him a couple of times. He took me all over the famous landmarks. The Victoria and Albert Museum was my favourite." He began to laugh. "To be honest, I can't remember too much about any of the other places because we were drunk most of the time. I'll tell you what was memorable: the day we went to see Everton."

I grinned at him. I might have known football would come into the conversation.

"Who won?"

"It was a draw."

"Ha-ha, very diplomatic," I said. I told him about Maisie and my growing friendship with Josie. "Do you know Josie well?"

"Not really. I've been up a few times to look at one of her cattle. I'd say she talks to you more than to any of us neighbours because you're a stranger and you wouldn't have that much interest in her affairs."

"Maybe she would. I don't know," I said shrugging my shoulders.

"By the way," I said, wanting to change the subject, "how's your mother?"

"She's gone back to England to stay with her sister. She lives in Birmingham and I'd say my mother spends most of her time there."

"Oh, I hadn't realised."

He began to laugh. "She only came home for the stations. There's a doctor and his wife renting our house at the minute. They're waiting for their own house to be built in Galway. They both work in the city hospital, so it's pretty handy for them. I think the wife's a doctor too."

"Are you still in your bachelor pad?"

"I am indeed, along with my books and other paraphernalia."

"What do you like to read?" I asked him.

"Hmm. I have different writers for different moods. I like Stephen King and I enjoy Seamus Heaney's poems."

"Do you have a favourite novel?"

He stretched his legs and looked up to the sky as if he was looking through a library in his head. "I'd say my favourite novel of all time has to be *Ulysses*. How about you, do you read much?"

"In England I used to read a lot but since I came here I've been occupied with other things. In a way I suppose reading is a form of escape but, having said that, I do have a novel by Charlotte Brontë that I read over and over again. It's called *Jane Eyre*; she's such a wonderful character and a great inspiration for women."

So there I was, talking and listening, nodding and smiling and rolling my eyes, when I saw a car stop on the other side of the field and beep its horn.

He stood up and drank the last of his coffee. "I'm wanted over there."

"I have to be going in now anyway," I lied.

I took his outstretched hand and let him help me up.

"I'd best go and see what she wants," he said over his shoulder. "I'll be back in a minute or so, and I'll have it finished in no time."

I walked through the back gate and turned around as if to close it after me.

I could see that woman with long blonde hair walking towards him.

When I went inside, I kept having a sly look through the kitchen window as I rinsed the cups and pottered about. Then I heard the chainsaw revving and couldn't help smiling. It felt nice having him around.

When I saw the sun come out, I put on a pair of old jeans, picked up some packets of flower seeds and went into the front garden. I couldn't have felt any closer to Paradise. I wanted to cry with happiness. What I knew about flowers and gardening could fill a postage stamp, but hey, I thought, everybody has to learn. I dug a hole with the trowel and scattered a few seeds into the earth, covered them with soil and patted the little mound with my palm before sprinkling them with the watering can. I felt like a child in a sandpit and was grateful for the solitude during my first attempt at creating what I hoped would be a beautiful garden.

The soil was ground into my nails and I had forgotten to remove my Claddagh ring. I was thinking about my visit to Josie's and what she had told me. If only Maisie had known how she'd inadvertently saved her friend from a life of doom in an institution. And then I heard, "Ah, there you are. How are you doing?"

I looked up and saw two eyes peering through the gap in the bushes. I straightened up and wiped my hands on my jeans, slipped my sandals on and went out through the gate.

Ellie smiled, showing off her new dentures. "How would you like a little doggeen?" she asked, getting straight to the point.

I couldn't hide my delight. I looked at the shopping bag in Ellie's hand, half expecting her to pull out a tiny pup, just like a magician with a rabbit. It would be nice having a dog around.

"I'd love a little dog, Ellie. Why, have you got a pup we can have?"

"Well, as a matter of fact, I haven't," she said, wiping the smile from my face, "but I can always get you one. You're going to need some protection around here, and you can't have a gun, just in case you accidentally shoot yourself."

"Oh, that's true," I said, struggling to keep a straight face.

After Ellie had done her tour of inspection and had a word with Ted, she was off again, walking up the road, saying she was going to see her second cousin and promising to find me a pup as soon as she could

"Come and see this, Colette," Ted called, coming around the side of the cottage. I watched him about-turn and disappear. I finished planting the last of the packet. Well, I couldn't appear too eager, could I?

That wouldn't do at all.

When I caught up with him at the back of the garden, he was stooped down at the trunk waiting for me. He pointed to the bark with his finger and then sat back on his haunches and watched for my reaction.

I couldn't see anything and looked at him questioningly.

"Here," he said, "You're not going to believe it. Talk about coincidence."

I leaned in to get a closer look and he took my arm to steady me. "Don't worry, I won't let you fall," he assured me. "Can't you see anything?"

I tilted my head to one side and studied the carving in the wood. Though the writing was obviously very old, the message was clear.

"Oh, my God!" I whispered, as I slowly read the words. I looked again and turned to him. "I can't believe it." I read the words aloud, "I LOVE CHARLOTTE BRONTË."

My fingers traced the letters, enjoying the feel of the rough wood on my soft skin. Ah, Maisie, I thought, glancing up at the clear blue sky before turning my attention back to the tree, I feel you're sitting on my shoulder.

Ted blew the sawdust from the freshly sliced wood and rolled it to one side.

"Can I keep it?"

"Of course you can. I'll varnish it for you and you can have it as a garden seat."

My eyes were filling with tears, so I pretended to inspect the trunk again.

"Oh, there's the phone ringing," I told him and hurried into the cottage before he noticed.

The image of Maisie sitting up in that tree reading *Jane Eyre* just broke my heart. I *had* to go and tell Josie, so I hurried to the bathroom to swill my face and try to make myself look presentable and went back out into the sunshine.

There was no answer when I tapped on the cottage door, and when I peeped inside she wasn't there, so I ran around to the back of the building. The gate leading onto the field was tied with a thick rope, so I climbed over it and ran across the grass and there she was, collecting her stack of kindling wood, blown down from the trees by the March wind.

"You'll never guess what's happened, Josie!" I called excitedly and I told her what Ted had found.

"Aw, the Lord save us!" she said and blessed herself.

"Here, let me carry that for you," I offered, taking the wood from her arms.

"Did she ever leave us at all?" Josie was muttering to herself as we slowly made our way back to gate. "If I'd read this in a book, I wouldn't have believed it."

We had talked about reading *Jane Eyre* together. Josie's eyesight was not good and I enjoyed reading aloud. "Shall we start the book tonight, Josie?"

"We will," she announced cheerfully. "An' I shall look forward to it."

I left her at the cottage door. I cried all the way home. I felt like I had known her all of my life and I loved her.

WHEN MARION CRAWLED out of bed, she came and helped in the garden. Then we remembered the beds were due to be delivered and ran inside to take the old ones apart.

Ted had gone to get a spare blade and Ellie had been back to see us with news of someone who knew someone who knew someone who had a little pup and she was to collect it later on that day.

And sure enough, by late afternoon she returned with the creature crying in her bag. She lifted the ball of fluff with one hand and placed it in my outstretched arms.

"Oh, it's so cute," I said, stroking its black and white fur.

"Does it have a name?" Marion asked.

"Ah, bejesus, I forgot to ask, but it's a little bitch, so you can give her a nice name." She reached out and stroked it. "I love them when they're this size. The only trouble is, you have to keep them outside the house, otherwise they pee all over the place. Not much different to a babby, is it, except you can put a nappy on a baby? Aw, look at the little puss."

Tiddles, no doubt had heard Marion's voice and came to investigate.

"How about Jezebel?" she suggested, lifting up her cat and rubbing her cheek along its fur reassuringly. Ellie's face dropped.

"What's wrong?" Marion asked.

"Well now, that's not a saint's name, is it?" she complained, fixing the bag on her plump, freckled arm.

I chuckled. "Why does she have to be called after a saint, Ellie?"

"Ah, it would be nice, that's all."

Marion thought for a minute, and then a big smile spread across her face. "Hey, I know. Why don't we call her St. Jezebel?"

"Ah," I cooed. "That's a good idea! I think St. Jezebel would really suit her. Hello, St. Jezebel!" I tickled the pup under the chin and she moved her little head from side to side, enjoying all the fuss and attention.

"Hmm. Well, it's up to you. And I suppose I could get used to it." Ellie half smiled. "Well, I'll be seeing you," she said, walking away. "Goodbye, St. Jezebel, and good luck!" she called.

That night when I returned to Josie's, she'd placed two chairs in front of the fire and lit the lantern, in preparation for my visit. We sat together in front of the fire, and I began to read *Jane Eyre*.

26

"HEY, COL," MARION said, when she arrived home from work one evening. "Sean said he'll take us to the dance on Saturday, if that's alright with you?"

I was writing a letter to Teresa. I loved writing letters and receiving them.

When the postman pulled up, I would wait with great anticipation to read the postmark on the envelopes.

"Why not?" I answered. "It could be fun."

I picked up the pen and continued to write:

> *One of our neighbours called over this evening. He brought us some rhubarb to make some pies, so we gave it to Mary on the sly, seeing that neither Marion nor myself can bake a potato. Mary is such a dab hand in the kitchen. She just throws everything into a bowl and it comes out tasting gorgeous. She doesn't even use scales.*
>
> *Now if that was Marion and me, we would go by the book and follow the recipe word for word and by the time we'd finished, even the cat would turn its nose up at it. I suppose some people just have a knack for certain things. Don't know what mine is yet. Anyway, Mary has kindly offered to bake Sean a rhubarb tart for us, and I am going to teach her to ride a bike.*
>
> *St. Jezebel is a little devil, but Marion absolutely adores her. I have to lock my shoes away so she doesn't chew them or do something even worse in them. She is growing fast and thinks the cat is her mother, snuggling up to it at night in Marion's room.*
>
> *You would love my friend Josie. I call to see her each night and she makes me so welcome. I really enjoy taking her into town. When I collected her from the library the other day, she was sitting at the long table, sipping a cup of tea and browsing through the newspapers. Anne had her books already stamped and Josie*

picked them up on the way out.

They have a great respect here for the elderly. It's...

The phone rang. It was Imelda.

"Hang on, I'll ask her. Marion!" I called through to the kitchen. "It's Imelda and she said she's alone tonight and has two bottles of wine and if they aren't used up by tomorrow, they'll be past the sell-by date. She wants to know if we can go over and help her drink them."

Marion stood in the doorway pulling up the zip on her jeans. She always changed out of her uniform when she arrived home.

"Isn't that what friends are for, to help each other out in times of trouble?"

"We'll be there in five minutes," I told Imelda and hung up the phone.

I switched on the torch to make sure the batteries were still working and Marion grabbed some packets of cigarettes out of the cupboard.

The rain was lashing when we left the house. We slipped our coats over our heads and legged it through the dark graveyard. We arrived at nine o'clock, just in time for *The Late Late Show*.

27

WHEN SATURDAY EVENING came around, Marion was looking out the window expectantly. It had rained all day, and there was no sign of it letting up. I had spent all afternoon reading with Josie. We were up to where Jane had just arrived at Thornfield Hall, and was yet to meet her Mr Rochester. I had promised Josie I would continue with the story after the dance finished, if I wasn't too inebriated.

We'd not been able to decide what to wear, and in the end Marion had settled for her green dress and black patent leather high heels. I had chosen my blue velvet dress and matching suede shoes.

"D'you know what, Col, it's that long since I've been out, I feel like a teenager going to my first disco." She looked at her watch. "He's awful late, isn't he? What time did he say he'd be here?"

I was in the middle of pouring us both a drink. "Well, you said that he said nine o'clock, but I think he meant nine o'clock, Irish time." I giggled. "And you know as well as I do, that nine o'clock could be any time up to midnight."

I handed the glass to Marion, took a sip of my own and sat down to continued where I had left off reading the local paper.

"Do you think Mary will be there?"

I shrugged my shoulders. There was something about Mary that made me uneasy. Her husband, Nigel, seemed nice enough, but sometimes we wouldn't see her for a few days and then she'd show up with a fading bruise on her cheek or some other place and pretend she'd tripped or walked into a door. I tried asking her once, but difficult as it was, I'd learnt to keep my mouth shut, because I didn't see her for a week afterwards.

Ten more minutes passed and Marion was still standing at the window sipping her drink when suddenly the sound of an engine caught our attention.

"Oh, this'll be him." She stood on her toes, straining her neck so she could see down the lane. A moment later, she sighed and let down the curtain before turning to me. "It's not. It's just an old tractor with one light."

I looked up and rolled my eyes. "Oh, will you come and sit down and enjoy your drink and relax a bit? Come on," I urged, closing the newspaper and putting it to one side.

Marion took my advice and joined me by the fire, but still she couldn't relax and sat on the edge of the chair.

Next thing there was a loud knock on the door.

"Who's that?" I whispered, holding my glass in mid-air. "I didn't hear a car, did you?"

Marion shook her head.

We listened.

"Helloooooooooo," the voice sang.

"It's Sean!"

"But it can't be. I didn't hear his car. Unless he's left it around the corner."

I opened the door and Sean walked in. "Evening, ladies."

Marion went over to the window and looked outside. "Where's your car, Sean?"

"Ara bejesus, her battery's flat so I've had to bring old Bessie."

"Old Bessie?" I repeated. "Who's she when she's out?"

Marion giggled. She obviously knew more than I did.

I looked out the window and saw the tractor parked outside and turned to meet Marion's laughing eyes. I took my high heels off and put on my wellies.

We giggled all the way to the dance. Sean sang all the way to the dance.

"There's Imelda!" Marion said as we pulled up outside the barn. "I'll just go over and say hello."

"I reckon you should change into your shoes before you go in there," Sean suggested.

"Oh, Sean, you've gone and spoilt it now," I moaned. "I was going to let her go in there with her wellies on."

Marion took her shoes out of the carrier bag and tutted with mock disgust. She reached out and held onto the tractor so she wouldn't lose her balance and step into the mud in her stocking feet, slipping out of her wellies and into her stilettos.

She grimaced at Sean and pointed to me. "This is what you call a true friend, isn't it, Sean? Gets her thrills out of watching her mate make a fool of herself. Wants her to go into her first dance in years, where she might even meet her prince…in her wellies!"

I was so pre-occupied with the banter, I didn't notice Ted standing by the barn taking a breath of fresh air. He stepped out of the shadows and came over to greet us. I hadn't seen him for a good while, except to put up my hand when I passed him on the road.

"Hello there! And how was your ride?"

"Erm, unusual." I smiled. Then I could feel my shoulders beginning to shake when I tried to explain what had happened and I could hardly speak for laughing.

This was the second time we'd met in the dark.

I climbed back up on the tractor to get the bag with my shoes, but they were gone and so was Marion.

"Well, isn't she a sod?" I said to nobody in particular. "Talk about get your own back. She's gone into the dance and taken my shoes with her."

Ted looked down at my feet and tried not to laugh.

"Oh, what harm?" he said lightly. "Come on," he suggested offering me his arm. "We can go in together."

I looked down at my feet. "Jesus, I look like something from another century. You wouldn't dare walk in with me looking like this, would you?"

"Ara, why wouldn't I?" he replied.

"I owe you one, Ted." I bit my lip trying to hide my delight.

"Fine," he said. "Then I'll pick you up tomorrow night."

Without giving me the chance to protest, he steered me into the barn.

We received a lot of attention that night, especially me standing there in my lovely blue velvet dress and a pair of blue matching wellies.

The blonde woman approached us, or should I say confronted us, and took Ted by the arm as if to have a quiet word. He loosened her grip and glared at her.

"What happened to you tonight?" she asked. She looked more beautiful than the last time I had seen her, with her waist-long hair and beautifully made-up face.

"We made no plans for tonight," he answered gently.

"We made no plans all right. Still, I thought by tonight you'd have come to your senses, but it seems there's someone around here that's turned your head."

"Now you leave her out of this."

I was starting to see what Mary meant. I felt embarrassed for the stupid girl. She was a pest.

I thanked Ted and walked on, leaving them to it.

Forget about tomorrow night, I told myself, he's already taken, even if he doesn't know it yet.

I waved to Marion and she hurried over with my shoes. "I'm sorry, Col," she said trying not to laugh, "I just couldn't help it."

"That's OK, Marion, but you know I'll get my own back, don't you?" I warned. There was just no stopping her – she was still laughing when we sat down.

It wasn't long before we spotted Mary.

"Doesn't she look gorgeous?" I said, "Shall I go and ask her to come over for a drink?"

Marion looked disappointed. "Ah, you'd better not. She's with Nigel and some of his friends from work. Oh, and look, that feller with them has brought his accordion. Maybe he'll let me have a go later," she said, standing on tiptoe to get a better view.

Hmm. Who knew what the night held?

When Mary spotted us, she made her way through the crowd and gave us both a hug. I was so relieved to see her. "Mary, who poured you into that dress?"

"Well, it wasn't my husband, for sure. If he had his way, I'd be dressed like a fecking nun."

"Evening, ladies," Father Carol greeted us. "Are you enjoying yourselves?"

"Oh, hiya, Father. Would you like to join us?" Marion offered, moving my coat and wellies out of the way. "There's plenty of room."

He looked pleasantly around the group. "You'll have to excuse me for now, but I'll be back over to you all later on."

I watched Father Carol and thought there was probably nothing he'd like more than to have sat down amongst us and get blind drunk – to be able to let his hair down for just one night – but I guessed he'd have to keep moving, mixing and chatting and spreading his time evenly amongst all his parishioners. I knew talk was cheap and in small villages it was rampant.

Mary opened her handbag and took out twenty pounds. "Here," she said, trying to press the money into my hands. "You two get yourselves a drink on me."

"Oh, will you behave yourself? We're not taking your money. Look,"

I said pointing to the table, "Nigel's just sent a drink over."

Mary persisted. "Please! That's for all the times you've taken me to town."

"We took you? The other way around you mean?"

Mary looked towards the bar and then back to me. "Look, I've got to go. Just take it and then I'll be happy."

"I'll take it if you want, but you can have it back tomorrow."

"We'll see," she said walking away. "Be good."

"We'll try," we chorused.

A little later, when I was returning from the ladies room, I bumped into Ted again. He was sitting on a stool near the door with some friends and mouthed something to me as I was walking by.

"Can't hear you," I said, leaning in close. He rested his pint on the table and stood up, ushering me onto the dance floor. It was a smoochie and one of those embarrassing moments, like when you meet somebody new and don't know where to put your hands. He placed mine on his shoulders and put his arms around my waist and I swear to God I think if we'd been outside we'd have kissed. Then we started to move to the music. I felt good in his arms—the feel of his hands and the smell of his aftershave. When the music stopped, he kept his arms around me and we stayed for the next dance.

"Just stay for one more?" he asked after the third dance. I told him I had to get back to my friends.

"Maybe I will later, before I go home?" I suggested into his smiling eyes.

The sound of bagpipes suddenly filled the barn and everybody stood still.

I was so moved by the haunting sound, I thought I was going to cry. I smiled at Ted but his sharp eyes must have sensed my mood, because he gently took hold of my arm and pulled me closer to him. When I turned back to him our eyes locked, and something happened between us.

28

DESPITE MANY OFFERS of a ride home, we insisted on travelling back with Sean. If he was good enough to bring us, then he was good enough to take us back.

The journey home seemed to take much longer.

The full moon lit up the way, making up for having only one tractor light. The lanes were soaked and muddy, and the rain pelted down and poured through Bessie's leaky old roof. We must have looked a sight. Huddled together and clinging to the tractor for dear life, we held the carrier bags we'd brought our shoes in over our heads to stop our hair from getting soaked, as the rain dripped through the holes like a tap.

"Colette, I meant to ask you, what did Mary win?"

"What?" I could hardly hear above the noisy rain.

"What did Mary win?"

I thought for a minute. "I think it was one of those huge bottles of whisky. You know the ones? You save pennies and bits of change in them and then when you're so broke you can't even buy a cigarette, you tip it all out and go and buy a packet."

"I know what you mean."

"She's coming over tomorrow and so is Imelda. They said they're coming for the hair of the dog."

"I'll be at work," Marion moaned.

"Maybe you'll be safer."

"From you lot you mean?"

"I do!."

"You're probably right."

"Hey, Marion."

"Yeah?"

"Did you see who I was dancing with tonight?"

"You mean Ted O'Gormon?"

"Yeah."

She nudged me. "You looked good together."

That made me smile. "I think he's lovely. I saw you dancing with

Sean." I whispered into her ear.

"Hey, he's not a bad mover. I wonder where he learnt those steps?"

"We'll have to find out."

Most of the people from the dance had overtaken us, beeping a friendly goodnight when they passed.

I yawned and leaned towards Marion.

"They all think we're mad, don't they?"

Marion nodded. "That's because we are."

When Sean finished singing Danny Boy, Marion leaned forward and touched him on the shoulder. "That was lovely, Sean. Will you sing that song you're always singing about the clouds?"

"Ah, go'way," he said shyly.

"Please, Sean. Go on," she pleaded.

"Yeah, go on, Sean." I laughed, "Not putting you under any pressure or anything."

We listened carefully as he began to sing. "Rows and floes of angel hair, an' ice cream castles in the air. An' feather canyons everywhere, I've looked at clouds that way..." on and on he sang, and when he reached the chorus, we both joined in. "I've looked at life from both sides now, from win and lose and still somehow....it's life's illusions I recall. I really don't know life...at all..."

WHEN BESSIE PULLED up outside Rose Cottage, I climbed down and stepped heavily into a puddle, shrieking as the cold mud splashed the top of my legs.

"Well, thanks very much, Sean," I said good-humouredly as he put out his hand to steady me. "It's been a night to remember. I really enjoyed myself."

"You're right there, Col. Yeah, thanks, Sean," Marion echoed, struggling as she followed me. "It's one I'll never forget in a hurry. Are you coming in for a drink, Sean?"

"Yeah, you must," I said searching for my front door key and handing it to Marion. "I'm going to see Josie. I'll be back in half an hour. Oh, would you mind taking these shoes in for me?" I asked, offering her the bag.

29

MARY CAME AROUND the following afternoon. She looked like I felt.

We sipped our strong coffee appreciatively and chatted about the previous evening.

"I saw you dancing with Ted last night." She said it like she'd looked through a key hole and caught us having sex.

"Mary, it was only a few dances, besides, that Orla watches him like a hawk."

Mary sighed loudly. "Take no fecking notice of her. He's a free agent and the sooner she gets that through her head the better. Did she speak to you at all?"

I shook my head. "She ignores me."

"She'll have to behave herself because if she's not careful, she'll find herself out of a job."

An hour later, I still felt like the living dead, so we went for a walk, hoping the fresh air might do some good.

"It's always like this after a big event," Mary said. "Everybody's probably got a hangover. We'll soon be decking ourselves out for the summer festival in mid-August."

"Sounds fun."

"It is. And maybe we could do something special this year – make some fancy clothes and go as a group of nuns or we could dress up as gypsies; me, you, Marion and Imelda"

"Wow, that's something to think about. I'll look forward to it."

"Maybe you could come up with something different. You have a think about it and let us know."

On we walked up the lane. All the chimneys were smoking, but there was no sign of anybody. I automatically moved to the side when I heard a car approaching behind. It slowed down and stopped beside us. Ted was sitting behind the wheel. Mary smiled at me and leaned on the car.

"Look who it isn't," she teased, looking in the window. "Is it kerb crawling you're up to now?"

"Nope, wouldn't have the energy after last night."

She looked at me and raised her eyebrows then turned back to Ted.

"Oh, so it's not your morals that stop you then. You just wouldn't be up to it! Is that what you're saying?"

Ted laughed heartily. "I give up." He revved the engine. "I'll pick you up at eight," he said to my surprise. Then he drove off.

Mary's expression was priceless.

"Close your mouth," I giggled. "You're going to catch flies."

I strolled as far as Mary's with her and then we said our goodbyes and I went home to wash my hair. I was glad to be going for a drink with Ted. At last we'd have a chance to sit down and talk. Tonight, I felt I'd get to know him a little better.

I wasn't that bothered about what to wear until about half an hour before he was due to pick me up. I ended up doing that Julie Walters scene in Educating Rita, where she tries on every garment in her wardrobe before she makes up her mind.

He arrived half an hour late and was quick to apologise. He said it was some pregnant horse's fault. "Oh yeah," I teased and then I remembered he was a vet.

I would learn over the coming months that Irish time and English time had very different meanings.

We drove into town and decided to go for a meal. It felt good when he put his arm around me and steered me to a table near the window.

The waitress handed me a menu and took an order for our drinks while we listened to the musicians.

Ted turned to me and smiled.

"Can you play any instruments?" I asked him.

He shrugged his shoulders hopelessly. "I can bang a tambourine and that's about it. Can you play anything?"

"I wish I could," I told him. "When I was little, my dad had a friend who played the accordion. He'd take me down to the church club when he knew he'd be playing. I used to sit near the stage with my crisps and lemonade and not move from my seat all night. He let me hold it once. I couldn't believe how heavy it was. Still, I would love to have learnt how to play it."

The meal arrived and we got stuck in.

"So tell me," he said, resting his fork on the plate, "whose heart did you leave broken back in England?"

"The man I left back in England didn't have a heart."

"Is that so?"

He was watching me too closely for comfort.

"It is," I answered abruptly. "He had a problem being faithful. It seemed one woman wasn't enough."

He looked incredulous. "Are you saying he cheated on you?"

"I am," I said self-consciously.

"The fecking eejit."

"I'm not bothered anymore."

"I'd say you're not. A good looking woman like you could have anyone she wanted but I'd be thinking he's sorry now."

"Haven't you ever cheated on anybody?"

"I haven't and I never would. I can't abide a man with no back bone," he said in disgust. "You're better off without the sneaky bastard."

"I know that now. And what about you? If we're speaking of hearts, Orla is never far behind you, is she? What about her heart?"

I thought he might take offense but he didn't. I knew I'd made a fair point.

He raised his eyebrow and sighed. He seemed disappointed that I'd noticed.

"Not guilty. I know how it looks, but I swear I never led the woman on. We went out once or twice when I bought into the practice but it was platonic; she was one of my assistants, how could it have been anything else? I don't know where she gets the notion from."

We turned to the musicians and I could hear Ted singing softly. When we finished our meal, we had one more drink then went into the pub next door.

There was a darts match on and they were a couple short, so we got roped in to play on opposite teams. It was the first time I had ever played and no matter how straight I aimed, the darts went everywhere but on the board, but we had great fun and don't ask me how, but my team won.

And then I made the mistake of telling him how we used his garden for a toilet that night at the Stations. Well, did he laugh and laugh and laugh? A few minutes later, he was still laughing and wiping the tears from his eyes.

I was beginning to feel a bit stupid and could have kicked myself.

"Oh, stop it." I nudged him, "It wasn't that funny, was it?"

He coughed and straightened his face. "I do apologise. It's just…" He couldn't even finish what he was going to say. His shoulders began to shake and he was off again.

I suppose it was kind of funny. What a pair of dopes we were, believing that nobody had any toilets. Soon I was laughing with him. He put his arm around my shoulders and gave me an affectionate squeeze. "He must have been a fool," he said kissing my cheek. I presumed he was talking about Eddie.

It was ten thirty. Almost time to go home. However, much to my surprise, instead of the pub emptying, it began to fill up, and before long there was standing room only.

It seems the pub served many purposes. Farmers, builders and all other tradesmen conducted their hiring and firing and other negotiations over a pint last thing at night.

That night when he dropped me off, I reached to open the car door. He took my hand away and turned my face to his. Kissing him seemed the most natural thing in the world.

"I'm so glad you came to live here," he whispered.

"So am I," I said, returning his kiss.

"Will you come out tomorrow evening and the one after that?"

"When will I have time to wash my hair?"

"You can do it during the day," he answered as I stepped out of the car.

MARION WAS BUSY drying Tiddles' fur with the hair dryer and immediately stopped what she was doing and looked at me with an air of expectancy.

"What?" I smiled, plonking myself into the chair. The cat slid off her knee and she stood up and hurried into the kitchen.

"Don't tell me anything till I pour us a drink." She was in and out in a tick.

I took the glass of wine from her outstretched hand.

"Well? Did you have a good night?" she asked standing over me.

I couldn't stop smiling. "I had a great night," I answered honestly.

It must have been written all over my face because next thing she said was, "He's the one, isn't he?"

"I beg your pardon?" I spluttered, half choking on the drink. "Are you match-making again?"

She just stood there grinning at me. "I can tell, Col. Yeah, he's the one," she murmured to herself.

The next evening I was getting ready to go out with Ted again when I heard the drone of an engine on the field. Sure enough, when I opened the back door I could see the lights in the distance as the tractor drove up and down the meadow slicing through the long grass.

I had eight bales altogether and Sean gave me a fiver for each one. Forty quid—not bad for a bit of grass.

30

IT WAS RAINING when Sean pulled up with the horse box. I had been standing at the back door, well prepared in my anorak and wellies, hardly able to contain my excitement.

Marion and I had spent most of the afternoon clearing out the shed then Sean arrived with some straw bedding and a few bales of hay. We'd filled the water buckets and finally blocked off the draughts with bits of wood. It was perfect.

I cut through the back garden onto the field and ran across to the far side to open the gate for him to reverse in. Ted had gone to Athlone for two days and wasn't due back until tomorrow and I missed him. I leaned against the wet fence and watched Sean unlock the trailer door. Then I heard a clump, clump as the little chestnut-brown creature backed down the ramp and turned to face me.

"Oh, she's beautiful!" I said, reaching out to stroke her, but then, without so much as a how d'you do, she galloped across the meadow like she was running for her life.

I suddenly felt nervous as I realised the enormity of what I had taken on. I mean to say, a donkey? I'd never even owned a dog.

Sean rolled a cigarette. "Give her five minutes to tire herself out and she'll be back over to you, eating candy out of your hands."

He was right. When the inquisitive donkey made her way back to us, I reached out to stroke her coat and smiled as she nuzzled her nose into my shoulder.

Sean drove off and promised to return in about an hour so we could settle her into the shed for the night. I turned to my new friend and she looked at me with such intelligent eyes. I hoped she wouldn't be lonely on her own.

We jogged playfully around the field, my new friend and I, and I laughed loudly when I about-turned and she followed me.

It was almost dark when I saw car headlights slow down at the gate, so we trotted over to see who it was.

I'd have known that figure anywhere. He put up his hand and climbed over the fence.

"Hi, Ted!" I called across the field. When we caught up with each other, I walked straight into his open arms–just like that.

He kissed my wet face. I was soaked and knew I looked a mess but also knew it didn't matter. It was a good feeling.

"So this is what I have to compete with, is it?" he asked, circling the animal with an experienced eye.

He wasn't in competition with anybody. He was in a league of his own.

"I'm so glad to see you. You couldn't have picked a better time. Sean is coming back, but it seems to have gone dark awful quick, and I need to get her into the shed."

He suddenly looked like I'd shot him. "Is that the only reason you're glad to see me?"

"Oh, of course not," I protested, shoving him playfully.

We strolled over to the jeep where he collected his torch, some rope and an old towel.

The moon gave us enough light to cross the field and Sally quite willingly trotted alongside us.

When Ted led her into the shed, he rubbed her coat with the towel.

"Donkeys don't usually like the rain. Horses don't mind it because their coats absorb the water, but not donkeys. It's important to dry them off as much as possible."

I watched him proudly. I could have stood there listening to him all night. When we were finished, we locked the bottom half of the door and went over to Tansey's for a hot whiskey to warm us up.

THE NEXT MORNING I was enjoying my tea and toast when an English lorry stopped in front of the cottage.

What's this? I thought and went to investigate.

It was our Billy's mate dropping off two second-hand bikes he'd bought us in England. The man was on his way to Galway and only had time for a quick coffee.

It was such a long time since I'd been on a bike. I thought I would have to learn all over again but not so. I jumped on the saddle and rode up and down the lane and then I cycled over to Mary's for a bit of fun.

I could see her as I turned in at the gate, wiping the outside windows. I rang the bell and waved.

"Hi, Mary. Santa's come early this year. Would you like to have a go on my bike?" I asked in a little girly voice.

She touched the handlebars and rang the silver bell.

"I wish I could have a go, but I've never been on a bike in my life. My sister used to ride one all the time, but I was always too scared of falling off."

"Well, come on then," I coaxed, turning the bike around. "There's no time like the present. You'll be cycling in the Tour de France in no time. It's dead easy once you know how."

I wheeled the bike out onto the lane. "Put your rump on that," I said, patting the saddle.

"Dare I?"

"Of course you dare." I held the bike steady and Mary climbed on. "I'll hold on while you start to peddle. That's it," I encouraged as Mary moved off. "Go slow and then pick up a bit of speed. Go on," I panted, running alongside her.

She wobbled up and down the lane for the next hour and every time she fell off the bike she climbed straight back on.

"See, I told you you'd do it," I said as she once again passed the spot where she always fell off.

"How did you get on last night with you-know?" Mary asked me.

Marion had just arrived home and we had gone into the cottage for a coffee.

"You-know?" I teased. "Who's he when he's out? I don't know what you're talking about."

I was such a good liar. I hadn't stopped thinking about him all day. The way he listened when I talked, as if I was the most important person in the world. The way he held out the chair for me to sit down. The way he lit my cigarette and the way he'd kissed me at the end of the night.

"She won't tell you anything," Marion warned her. "She never does. Not about her love life anyway. She's awful bloody mean, isn't she?"

"Love life?" I gasped. "What are you two like? We've only been out a few times. And besides, what would you want to know about my so-called love life?"

"Oh, nothing at all," Marion remarked innocently.

Marion was right. I did hate talking about my love life. It was one thing to moan about a lover's tiff, but my sex life was off limits and besides, as far as sex with Ted was concerned, there was nothing to reveal—yet.

JOSIE WAS WELL pleased when I told her I'd been out with Ted. "If you were my own daughter, I couldn't have picked a nicer man for you. He comes from a lovely family and he's a true gentleman. I was at school with his grandfather and even he was a great scholar."

"Now now, Josie, we only went out for a drink," I cautioned.

Her smile told me she knew more than I did.

31

I FILLED THE bowl with hot water and stuck my head under the tap, working it into a good soapy lather, eager to get rid of all the muck and grime of the last few days. After the final rinse I felt for the towel and wrapped it around my head, then opened my eyes and groaned at the mess I'd made.

"Helloooo? Excuse me? Colette?"

Oh shit, I thought. *Who could that be?* Then I smiled with relief when I saw Mary's daughter, Elizabeth, with her graduation dress over her arm.

"Come in, come on." I beckoned, moving some clothes and magazines off the chair for her to sit down. "Excuse the mess, only I haven't tidied up yet. I'm a bit of a slob in the mornings. Well, actually," I laughed, "that's not true. I'm a bit of a slob all the time."

The young girl smiled. "Oh, now if you're busy, I'll call another time. My mam would kill me if she thought I was being a nuisance to you. I only came to drop my dress off. She says I'm to give you plenty of time so you're not rushed, because you have enough sewing to do for everyone else."

"Hold it up so I can see it. I don't want to touch it with my damp hands."

"It's gross, so it wouldn't matter anyway," she said sulkily.

"Why did you pick it?"

She shrugged her shoulders and looked like she didn't know what to say.

"It's lovely."

"To tell you the truth, my mam wasn't well on the day we went to Dublin. We went to all the big stores, you know, Clearys and Browns and there was nothing, absolutely nothing, on the racks."

"Couldn't you have left it and gone back another day?"

Elizabeth's eyes watered. "Not really."

"Have you got time for a coffee and then we can see what needs doing?"

"Thanks. That'd be grand. Can I sit over here?" She moved to the chair beside the hearth. "I do love to see an open fire. I never thought I'd miss it when we had the central heating put in. You know, no more ashes and spitting the flaming coal dust out of my mouth on a windy day when I had to go out into the rain and empty the ash bucket." The pup climbed onto her knee. "Oh, hello there, you little scamp," she greeted. "Does it have a name?"

"Tut, tut, tut. Aw, no. That's naughty St Jezebel. Get down. Come on!" I ordered. "In your bed."

"And who's this?" she asked as the cat purred at her feet.

"That's Tiddles. Do you know, Elizabeth, I don't think they know they're animals. And one word from me and they do as they like."

She laughed and put the cat back in the bed with the dog. She stooped down and stroked them both.

"Marion likes having them around. She's much better at controlling them than I am. The only thing is, she goes mad if she forgets to close her bedroom door because St. Jezebel—"

"That's the pup?" Elizabeth interrupted.

"Yeah. She goes into her room and curls up on her bed, and sometimes she's sneaked in when she's muddy and we've not noticed, and the bed's all filthy when Marion goes to get in late at night."

"Well, that's why most people cannot bear having animals in their houses, especially dogs. They're tramping through the muddy fields all day and treading their muck all over the floors."

"Oh, I know all about the muck. And I also know I'm getting them into bad habits that are going to be difficult to break."

"Don't get me wrong, I'm not complaining. In fact, I was thinking of becoming a vet, just like your boyfriend," she smiled. "Anyway," she continued, "if I don't get enough points on me leaving cert, I'll probably end up going on a secretarial course or something just as dull, but my mam says you shouldn't take your second choice in life. Work hard and get what you want; otherwise, the wrong people end up doing the wrong jobs. And she's speaking from experience. Her cousin's a psychiatrist and he wanted to be an engineer. If you heard him, you'd laugh." She chuckled and sat back to make herself more comfortable. "He comes down from Dublin sometimes on a Sunday and he can't even hold a conversation. He brings a newspaper with him and sits and reads it all day."

I couldn't help laughing at the non-stop chatter.

"I think he's really just a patient somewhere," Elizabeth continued, "and Mam doesn't want us to know. Hadn't you best comb your hair before it dries?" she said, passing the towel back.

"You're right and I'll put the kettle on whilst I'm at it."

"I'll see to the kettle if you like, while you do your hair. Anyway, I says to him once—"

"Who?"

"My uncle. The one I'm just after telling you about. Anyway, I says to him once, when you've finished reading that paper, you can read the phone book if you like, but my mam gave me such a look, I thought she was going to clonk me over the head with it, so I quickly put it back under the phone in the hall."

We went into the kitchen and I put some newspapers on the floor.

"You'll have to excuse the mess. When I wash my hair at the sink, I get the water everywhere."

The young lady surveyed the room. "Oh, I'll have that cleared up in a tick."

She picked up the dishcloth and began to wipe down the surfaces and everywhere was dry in no time.

I combed my hair back off my face. "That's the only thing I miss about England, not having a shower." I tilted back the mirror and leaned close as I parted my hair down one side.

"You can always have one put in. We had one put in last year, but the only thing was, when the eejit finished the job, and I had my first shower in our really fancy bathroom, all the tiles fell off the wall. Dad went ballistic and rang him at home in the middle of the night. Drunk as a skunk he was, of course, or pretended to be," she said mischievously, "and couldn't understand a word dad was saying, so he went over to see him the next morning."

"Did he fix them?"

"Jeez, he did indeed. If you saw my dad when he's angry, you wouldn't even be asking me that question, because you'd already know the answer. So," she asked brightly, "why don't you have one put in?"

I hesitated before I spoke. "Maybe later on," I finally said. "But to tell you the truth, I'm a bit afraid of spoiling the look of the place, you know. We've had new telephone points installed and electrical sockets put in the wall, and I don't want it looking too ultra modern."

She thought that was hysterical. "Blimey, it would take more than your shower to modernise this place, you know, like maybe a couple of hundred years."

"Oh, not you as well? It's not that bad, is it?"

"It is."

She went into the bedroom and tried on the dress, then came out looking stunning. I could see why Mary coaxed her to choose that colour.

"You see, it fits on the bottom and it's far too big up here," she moaned.

"That's easily fixed," I told her. I pinned the sides of the garment so she had a better idea how good she would look if it fitted properly. She smiled self-consciously. I don't think she was convinced.

32

AFTER SHE LEFT, I decided to go and find Sam Mackey to see about buying some turf but first things first. I put on my scruffs and went out the back to see Sally and clean out the shed.

I thought about Ted as I shovelled the horse muck into the wheelbarrow and spread fresh straw across the floor. I had slipped easily into this daily routine and often in the mornings, Sally would be standing at the back gate waiting for me. At first I'd thought she was about seven. Not that I knew anything about donkeys, but I was sure that's what the previous owner had told me. Anyhow, after Ted inspected her teeth, he reckoned she was more like seventeen.

It was handy having a boyfriend who is a vet because I was able to pick his brains about my donkey.

And the only drawback to having a vet for a boyfriend was when he covered for other vets and was away for a couple of days. I couldn't believe how much I missed him.

When I was finished, Sally followed me out into the sunshine. She kept nuzzling my pocket in search of a treat so I reached in and pulled out a pink marshmallow, her favourite and a nice change from a bale of hay.

Then I went in to get changed and walked half a mile looking for Sam Mackie's place and sure I'd missed the turning, decided to backtrack. I could see Sean driving towards me on the tractor and waved. The sky clouded over and it started to spit. When I had first arrived in Ireland, whenever it rained, I would run indoors for my coat. But now I didn't bother. I was so used to getting wet, I was even starting to enjoy it. When Sean stopped, I asked him for directions.

"You see the smoke rising from those bushes over there?"

"Yep."

"Well, that's his place, just behind them. Go down this lane and you can't miss it."

"Want a bet?"

"Ara, you'll be fine." He started the engine and rattled on down the road.

"Good luck," he called after me.

I was fine. I could hear the tap, tap, tap of his hammer before

I could see him. A black and white dog ran towards me and circled around me excitedly. I stooped to pat it, then I followed the sound and went past his cottage towards the hay shed. As soon as he spotted me, he put down the hammer and stake and came over to greet me. I had such warm feelings for this man.

I thanked him for the donkey and told him how settled she was.

He smiled and shook my hand. "It's promised heavy rain this afternoon, so I was just fixing that fence while I had the chance."

We walked across to the house and went inside.

"Oh, I don't want to hold you up, Sam."

"Hold me up?" he interrupted. "You won't be holding me up. Sit down there." He indicated a stool near the fire. "You're as welcome as the flowers in May. If you'd have called me five minutes earlier, you'd have found me gone."

"Oh, don't worry, Sam. I only came to see if you could sell me any turf? People are always telling me how your turf is the best."

"Wait a minute now," he said, scratching his head. "If ever you come here and I'm gone, unless it's a Friday when I go to town for me shopping, just go and stand the other side of that building and you'll spot me working somewhere on the land."

"I must remember that," I answered, understanding how important visitors were to him.

We talked together easily and he wanted to know all about the life I'd left behind in England. His eyes watered when I told him about my dad and brothers.

"Is it a fast country?"

"It is compared to here. It's full of people and houses and cars."

"I like to hear about England. I was the last of thirteen children and eleven lived and died across the flash." There was a moment's silence and then he asked me which country I preferred. That seemed to be what everybody wanted to know. I could only answer honestly.

"Well, Sam, at the moment I prefer Ireland, but I'm still British and proud of it."

"Well, why wouldn't you be proud of it? Nobody should be ashamed of where they come from. And d'you like it here?"

"I do, Sam. I love it."

"And what d'you think of the town?"

"Well, there's plenty to do—"

"Oh, but ma'am," he interrupted, "this town has changed. There's hardly anything to do anymore. I can remember when you'd have fair day in the summer and the square would be wedged with people. When we were children, we used to go into town and go on the hobby-horses and the swinging boat and then there was the chairoplanes. You used to sit in them and you couldn't fall out because they strapped you in, and if it was raining, you wouldn't get wet because they had a plastic cover."

"Have you been over to England?"

"No, ma'am. My mother was frightened of me going for a holiday in case it gave me a longing to leave and I wouldn't want to come back."

"Who wouldn't want to come back here?"

"Ah, you'd be surprised, ma'am, There's some that's been gone fifty years and they've not even blackened paper with a letter home."

I listened to him with great interest and an hour had passed before I knew it. As much as I enjoyed his company, I knew I had better make a move.

"Hey, Sam, do you have any turf?"

"Oh, yes, you were asking me, weren't you? I've some in the shed now, but, ara, it's no good, burns like paper. Can you wait a week till I've the good stuff ready? It'll be coming up from the bog in a few days."

"I suppose so."

"I'll tell you what I'll do. I'll get you a few bags of good turf and bring them down on my ass and cart."

"Oh, no, you don't have to do that. We'll collect it. We don't want to put you to any trouble."

"Trouble? Ara, it's no trouble at all, a ghrá. Will you be in tomorrow?"

"Well, there'll be someone there."

"Right you be. I'll call down tomorrow and I'll bring you five or six bags of good fine turf."

I thanked him and left.

When I arrived home, I saw Josie on the far side of the field stroking Sally. I went into the cottage and watched her through the kitchen window. I didn't want to spoil her moment.

When Marion arrived home from work that evening, I was busy clearing out the shed to make room for the turf.

"Don't do that on your own," she ordered. "Just give us half an hour to have my tea and I'll give you a hand."

I spat the dust from my mouth. "Aw, you don't have to. You've been working all day. Go and put your feet up. Besides, your hair will get filthy with all the dust."

"Oh, God, I'm glad you reminded me," Marion said, touching a strand of her hair. "Imelda's coming over tonight to cut a few inches off. It's really getting on my nerves lately. I've never had it so long. It grows like the grass here."

"It looks nice," I assured her.

"It looks awful, you mean. Your hair suits you long. I look daft, haven't got the right shape face for it. Oh, listen to me going on about my hair, anyway," she said over her shoulder. "Just give me ten minutes and I'll be back out to you."

"Are you going to Sean's later?" I shouted after her.

"I had planned to. He's going to give me some old clothes to make a scarecrow."

"A scarecrow?"

"So it'll keep the birds off the garden and stop Tiddles from eating them, but I'll stay and help you for a while."

"No, don't worry. Besides, Ted said he'd call round and give me a hand. You go and make your scarecrow." I turned away so she wouldn't see me laughing.

TED AND I had gone out again last night for a drink. I'd slipped into the seat beside him, expecting a drive into town to one of the local pubs, but he had other plans. We drove the forty miles to see his cousin in a village just outside Galway.

She was one of those multi-tasking mother-earth types with eleven children, all boys.

When we went to the local for last orders, somehow the men ended up playing darts in the bar and we sat in the front lounge hugging the log fire.

We chatted easily about this and that. Every so often, I'd have a sly peek at Ted across the bar and more often than not he'd had the same idea. He'd smile and mouth to me, asking if I was all right. I was more than all right. I was falling in love.

SAM WAS AS good as his word. The following morning, he arrived with his ass and cart and eight bags of turf. "I've brought you a bag of kindling wood as well. It'll help you to get your fire started first thing in the mornings."

With the rein wrapped around the iron loop in the wall, he began to lift off the bags, walked down the side of the house and tipped them into the shed. I tried to do the same.   "Oh, no, ma'am! Don't you be lifting that," he warned, taking the bag off me as I struggled down the path. "It's too heavy for you."

I didn't argue with him. "Okay. I'll go in and make some tea."

"I'll be with you in a few minutes, a ghrá."

I could hear him singing as he walked up and down the path and soon he was in the kitchen.

I poured out the tea and went back to the worktop to finish making some sandwiches.

"Ara, don't bother doing anything for me," he told me. "Just give me a piece of dry bread. I had an egg for me breakfast, so that'll just do me grand."

"Are you sure, Sam?"

"I am indeed, ma'am. I was thinking," he said when I joined him at the table. "Have you got an axe?"

I chuckled. "If you could call it that, Sam. We did have one and we split the handle, but I could always get a new one in town."

He took a sip of his tea and bit a piece of his bread. "What would you be wanting to buy a new axe for? Give it to me and I'll fix it for you. I'll call back with it tomorrow."

"Are you Jack of all trades?"

He smiled. "Well, I wasn't a great scholar. I was always scheming from school. I hated it. I hid in some building or other all day, and when I saw the kids coming home from school, I used to walk with them and me mammy never knew any different. And isn't it strange?" he went on. "Everyone reckons when you look back that school is the happiest days of your life."

When he returned the next morning, I was awestruck when he showed me the axe.

"It's nearly new," I said, admiring the handle where he had inserted a screw either side of the wood, healing the split. I ran my hands up and down the smooth surface and told him how clever I thought he was.

"Ara, not at all," he said over his shoulder. "And if you're ever stuck for anything, I hope you'll not be too ashamed to come to my door."

I stood and watched him walk on up the road with his ass and cart. He was one of the kindest people I had ever met.

THAT AFTERNOON WAS a scorcher. I put on my shorts and T-shirt and went out into the garden. It was coming along very nicely too. The flowers in the front had blossomed beautifully and I decided to do a bit of weeding in the back.

I was deep in thought as usual – thinking about Ted. I heard a noise and looked over my shoulder. I don't know how long he'd been standing there.

I stood up and smiled and he moved in close.

"No, don't come near me," I pleaded, showing him my hands. "I'm covered in muck." His blue eyes danced playfully. I turned to run but he reached out and pulled me into his arms and kissed me.

"I don't care," he said softly. "I love you. I think I've loved you since that night we met on the lane."

My heart melted. "I love you too." I whispered. "But what's brought this on?"

His answer was to turn my chin up to his and kiss me like he had never done before. "Come on," he said, leading me down to the cottage. "Let's go inside."

33

"HAVE YOU THOUGHT any more about having a float for the festival, and what we're going to wear? I've been racking my brains and our Elizabeth said we should go as Cinderella and the ugly sisters."

"Huh?" I laughed. "Did she now? You can tell her she can get someone else to fix her graduation dress, and the next time she wants to ring what's his face from here, she can get lost."

Mary grinned. "Oh, I can't wait to see her face. She won't be able to do enough for me tonight and she'll probably bake you a cake."

"Seriously, though, Marion and I were thinking, if you agreed, we could make some costumes and go as the Brontë sisters. It'd be great fun."

"The Brontë sisters?"

"Yeah. You know, there were three of them: Charlotte, Emily, and Anne. Well, five really, but two of them died when they were young. They were all famous writers. You must have heard of them? Wuthering Heights? Jane Eyre?"

Mary was thoughtful for a moment and then her eyes widened. "Oh, I saw that miserable old film all right. Isn't that the one with that mad woman in the attic?"

I couldn't help laughing. That was all anybody seemed to remember.

"But it's going to be hard dressing like them. Didn't they live in the olden days with those big frocks with sticky-out skirts?"

"They won't be that difficult to make, and look, I've nearly finished that suit I'm making for Marion."

I removed the lid from the wicker basket and brought out the green fabric. "So I could have a go at making the dresses if we're all in agreement."

Mary looked doubtful. "What about all the material? We'll need yards and yards of it to make all the dresses. And bonnets."

"Oh, listen, we can see if anybody has any old curtains they don't want and use them and if all else fails, I can ask my brothers to get some off our old neighbours. They can even go to the jumble sales, although thinking about it, they'll probably send Teresa instead."

"Is she the one I spoke to on the phone?"

"Yep, and I'm still trying to talk her into coming here for a holiday, but that's another story," I told her, folding Marion's suit back into the basket.

"You're a dab hand at this, aren't you?"

"I love sewing, but it takes up so much room. I'm going to have to get cracking if I'm making those dresses, aren't I?"

"Well, there are three of us. No, there are four of us. We can all get stuck in." Mary's face suddenly lit up. "Why don't you rent a little shop in town? Just think of all the space you would have and you could work for as little or as long as you wanted."

"Are you serious?"

"There's that many closed down and standing empty these days, you should get one for next to nothing."

Mary turned to look out the window and I caught the beginning of a smile.

I looked at her shrewdly. "What are you up to?"

"Nothing."

"I don't believe you."

"Well, I was thinking maybe I could help you out some days. We could have another line if you liked?"

"Hmm. Such as?"

"I could buy in second-hand outfits, even wedding and bridesmaid dresses, and you could alter them at the back of the shop and we could sell them nearly new."

"I like the sound of that. You're not just an ugly face, are you?"

"No, but don't tell anybody, will you?"

"No."

"Does that mean you're interested?"

"Definitely. Maybe we can have a look in town some time."

"No need to. My cousin said you can have the shop below the flat he rents out in town."

I was flabbergasted. "Tell him thank you."

"I will indeed. I'll take you over to meet him later on if you have time."

"I'll make the time," I assured her.

"Any case, going back to what you were saying about the festival, sure if there's four of us and there are only three sisters?"

"Yeah, I thought about that. Marion could be Jane Eyre. Let me see now. I could be Emily, Imelda could be Anne, and you could be Charlotte."

"Why Charlotte?"

"Because she was like a little sparrow and so are you," I told her. "Oh, you know what I mean, small and slender. You're perfect."

"That was quick thinking. You should have been a diplomat," she laughed.

"Speaking of making things, I know what I meant to show you. Come and have a look at this."

When she walked through the door and saw the scarecrow standing in the corner, she did a double take. "Jesus, Mary, and Joseph, who's he?"

"That's Cyril. Isn't he grotesque?" I said, straightening his tie. "But when you see Marion, tell her you think he's great, because it took her so long to make him and she's really proud of it."

I switched on the kettle and put some coffee into the mugs.

Mary touched the straw on its head and a bunch of it came away in her hand. "Are the men that bad around here that she has to make one of her own? Sure, if she's that desperate, you can tell her she can have mine if she wants. Hmm," she said, inspecting him, "and there was I thinking I couldn't do any worse."

"Aw, she made him to keep the birds off the garden, so her cat won't eat them."

"And, by Jesus, isn't he just the man for the job? There'll be no birds going near this feller," she said.

She followed me into the front room and wiped her eyes on her sleeve.

"Oh, look, there's Josie going past."

I put the hot drinks on the table and went to the window, lifting up the curtain and watching her stroll up the lane until she was out of sight. Lowering the net, I sighed and turned to Mary. "Oh, I do wish she would come in. I'd love to do her a nice meal and make a fuss of her, but there is no point in me asking her because she won't."

Mary sipped her coffee and looked at me sympathetically. "I think this house has too many memories for her. You never know what's gone on in her past."

St. Jezebel's bark turned our attention to the front door and the sound of the gate slamming. My hand shot to my mouth and I sprang from the chair. "Oh, I hope it's not the priest," I whispered, picking my nightdress up off the floor where I had stepped out of it earlier that morning.

Mary laughed when I ran into the kitchen with last night's wine glasses.

"In England, the priest always sends a lad on ahead to warn you that he's on his way, but here they just walk in like they're one of the family."

"Well, they are in a way."

"Oh, I know. And I think he's lovely, but I just wish he would let me know a day in advance, so I could tidy up and have the place looking nice for him."

"A day in advance?"

"Oh, all right, an hour then."

Mary began to giggle when Ellie Ford stepped into the room.

"God bless all who live here!" she announced, making the sign of the cross and at the same time, shooing the dog out with her foot. She handed me a collection envelope for the homeless in Dublin and disappeared again.

Mary stood up. "I must go. I'm on my way to Sean's to see if he'll paint the outside of the bungalow for me, but listen, I nearly forgot – all that time we were chatting this morning, it completely went out of my head. Mrs Haughey is giving her readings in a few weeks. If I can get out, will you and Marion come with me?"

"You bet we will. We've waited long enough."

Mary's smile disappeared. "But you won't tell anybody we're going, will you?"

I shook my head. "Anything you say."

"Nigel wouldn't approve … you know?"

I gave a wry smile. "What man would?"

"And I'll need an alibi."

"Consider it done."

~ **34** ~

MARY TOOK THE curtains out of the bag and unfolded them. There was no doubt about it, the Irish were a generous lot. No sooner had the idea been planted in my head than the shop was up and running. Sean did the painting, and Ted donated his carpentry skills for the new shelves and doors.

He'd loved the idea of the shop—said it gave me an air of permanence and my heart went boompty, boompty, boom.

We all met up in Tansey's the night before the opening. Everybody wanted to know what the shop was to be called, but I hadn't given it much thought. We bandied names about and as the night wore on, they became more and more silly. Then Mary made a clever suggestion.

Hmm, I thought, that has a nice ring to it. We all made a toast to The Dress Pool.

WE WERE SMACK in the middle of the High Street with a drinking hole either side. Word travelled fast and with Mary knowing half of Ireland, we soon had more than enough material for our dresses. Even Anne, the librarian, had asked some of her neighbours for their old curtains and was regularly dropping bags off at the cottage.

Sister Allen from the local convent was our first "official" customer, with some skirts for me to alter. She said her knees were full of arthritis, so I made her sit down and rest herself in the armchair Ted had rescued from his garage, and made her a cup of tea.

One of the older nuns hadn't been well and had lost so much weight the clothes were hanging off her. Poor sods. The clothes looked like they had seen better days.

I felt sorry for the nuns. At least the priest always had a few bob in his pocket and drove a fancy car. The nuns didn't seem to have anything.

When she returned a few days later, I had taken in the seams, put in a new zip and navy buttons.

"What do I owe you, Colette?"

"Oh, you don't owe me anything, Sister. I did it in no time."

She lifted her shopping bag off the floor. "Ara, no, now, I must give you a little something."

I shook my head. I wouldn't, couldn't take anything.

She mooched around in her bag.

In the end I accepted two balls of wool and a packet of Smarties.

EVERY MORNING, AFTER I fed my little donkey and mucked out the shed, I went into town to open the shop. Some days when the sun was shining, I'd leave a little earlier and cycle in. Sometimes, St. Jezebel would follow me all the way to the shop. I was afraid of her getting run over on the road, so more often than not I didn't leave the house until last minute and jumped straight in the car for work.

Mary popped down for a few hours after lunch and did her magic: cups washed, floor brushed, shelves tidied and magazines stacked neatly. We had plenty of opportunity to get to know each other and spent hours sharing stories about our lives. And then one day she came into the shop with a bruise on her face.

I wanted to throw my arms around her, but instead I put on the kettle and washed the mugs. I am ashamed to admit I did not know what to do.

"Are you all right?" I asked her cautiously. The bruising on her cheek was slightly swollen.

She looked me straight in the eye. "You know, don't you?"

I nodded. I went and locked the shop door, displayed the closed sign and finished making our drinks.

"You don't have to worry anymore," she assured me.

Her hand shook as she reached for the coffee. "Last night, when he came home from the pub, he started shoving me around the kitchen again. I can't tell you why – there's never a reason, although I'm sure he could give you a hundred. When he slammed my head into the cupboard, something inside me snapped and my fear just turned into rage. I reached into the drawer and grabbed the steak knife. I don't remember that much about it except I had him pinned to the door with the blade to his throat. I rang the Garda afterwards and they came out and warned him. You should have seen his face when he realised they could remove him from the house and lock him up." She shook her head in bewilderment. "I've been beaten black and blue for years and too ashamed to tell anyone."

"What've you got to be ashamed of?" I asked indignantly. I mean to say, a man three times her size is knocking her about and she feels ashamed.

I didn't say any more. It was her life and she was handling it.

"He never thought I had it in me, but now he knows. Having good friends like you and Marion and Imelda has given me strength," she said quietly. "And I've told him, if he ever hits me again, I'll wait until he's asleep and then I'll kill him."

I reached out and squeezed her hand.

"Don't!" she protested, jerking it away. "You'll make me cry and I'm not going to shed any more tears; no more tears ..." she trailed. "Now open the shop," she ordered. "Come on. Haven't we a business to run?"

I CRIED THAT night when I went to bed. I knew it was pure self-indulgence.

My life was wonderful and I was answerable to nobody. I made my own choices and lived with my own mistakes. I was sorry for Mary and hoped her life really had changed for the better, because now that it was out in the open, that she knew that I knew, if I ever found out that he was hurting her, I'd probably kill him myself.

I TOOK ELIZABETH'S dress over a few days later and sat in the kitchen with her mother whilst she tried it on.

Mary was standing at the sink, preparing a stew. I watched her nimble little hands working away on the chopping board. After she peeled and washed the veg, she put it all in the roasting tin to cook slowly in the oven. Elizabeth stood in the doorway and smiled at her mum, gave a twirl and finished with a curtsy. She looked gorgeous and I think she believed us this time. The dress was a perfect fit.

"Didn't I tell you you'd be the belle of the ball?"

"You're awful happy lately, Mam. You haven't got a feller, have you?"

Mary looked stunned. "Aren't I always happy?"

Mary's new empowerment had indeed put a spring in her step and I couldn't help smiling at the exchange between them both.

"No," Elizabeth replied, slouching against the door.

"Well, I'm sorry you feel like that."

Elizabeth crossed the kitchen and gave her mother a hug. "It's fine,

Mam," she assured her. "Lots of kids at school have parents who have affairs."

Mary was aghast and loosened Elizabeth's arms from around her neck. "Blessed God in Heaven, Elizabeth," she said trying not to laugh, "I'm just feeling happy. Okay?"

Her daughter shrugged indifferently. "Whatever turns you on."

"And what's that supposed to mean?" Mary asked.

"Well, if I was tied to the kitchen the way you are, I wouldn't be singing and putting steak in the oven, I'd be crying and putting my head in it."

"Will you get out of here, before I put you in the oven?"

I SAT NEXT to Marion on the bar stool in Tansey's and sipped my drink.

"How's the shop going?" Breda asked placing our drinks on the counter. "I keep meaning to call in and see you, but I have so little time to myself, sometimes I feel like I'm in a prison."

"We're doing far better than I expected, Breda, but then Mary knows almost everybody within sixty miles from here and that's a great bonus. We've got enough work to keep us going for the next three months and then in our spare time we're trying to make our costumes for the festival in two weeks' time."

Breda's face lit up. "Oh, I can't wait to see them. Did Sam say you could have the loan of his cart?"

"He did, and he said he'd lead us into town."

"Oh!" Breda smacked her hands together. "Is he going to dress up too?"

"We haven't got round to asking him yet. One thing at a time, you know?"

"Sam's got a heart of gold. He'll do anything for anybody but getting dressed up. I ain't sure about that," Breda warned.

Later that night I called over to Mary's. Elizabeth answered the door.

"Mam!" she yelled, standing aside for me to pass then sitting back down at the table to continue with her homework.

Tomorrow was our big night with the fortune teller and Mary and I were putting our plan into action.

I went into the sitting room and was greeted by Nigel.

"Come on in and make yourself at home. She'll be with you in a minute. She's just on the phone. Will you have a drop of something?"

"Oh, no thanks, I've just—"

"Course you will." He went out to the kitchen and returned with two drinks.

I stared at his hands when I took the glass from him. Those big hands he smacked his wife with. Or should I say, used to.

"To your good health," he said, raising his glass.

"And the same to you," I lied, wishing he would drop dead.

Mary entered the room in the middle of our conversation.

"I was just telling Nigel about the flower-arranging class tomorrow night. I was wondering would you like to go with me and Marion, because we won't really know anybody in the class?"

"You will of course go along with her, Mary. She'll be company for you," he said, turning to me. "Why wouldn't she?"

WE DROVE OVER a carpet of pink petals near Josie's gate and out onto the main road. I glanced at Mary through the mirror and wondered what Mrs Haughey had in store for us. I couldn't have any more good news. My life couldn't be any better.

Mary navigated the unfamiliar drive, but had forgotten to tell me the old lady lived in the middle of nowhere. '

"It's just down here," she'd said, advising me to take a left turn, just before we reached the end of the town. I drove into a lane barely wide enough for the car, expecting to stop at any minute. By now there was a soft rain falling.

"It's just around here," she kept instructing. I crawled 'just around here' for miles, silently praying we wouldn't meet any oncoming traffic. Next thing I seemed to be out in the wilds. There was a bog to the right of me and a ditch running along the left. I began to feel nervous. No wonder Ted worried when I went out to strange places.

"Oh, my God," I said to Mary, "if we fall into that ditch we're done for."

"You're doing fine," she assured me, "but try and get into the habit of keeping a rope and a knife in the boot. That way if you do slip off the road, you can get a tractor to pull you out. It happens to everybody sooner or later. You'll get used to it."

Marion whined. I thought she was going to cry. "I hope I'm not with you when you fall into a ditch," she said.

"Don't worry, Marion, we'll be fine," I told her.

We eventually pulled up at a farm gate and Mary jumped out to let us through. Then we drove for a quarter of a mile and stopped in front of a thatched cottage. I switched the engine off and heaved a great sigh of relief.

"I'll nip in with this brandy and see how she's fixed." Mary said.

She emerged ten minutes later with a big grin on her face.

"She must have had some good news," I said to Marion.

Mary came over to the car. "Mrs Haughey's not well and has taken to her bed with a cold, but her neighbour from across the way has stepped in, and says she'll be happy to do it for you. She's just read mine, only I didn't give her this," she said, taking the brandy from under her jacket. "Anyways, she said she'll do it for half the price, but you'll have to hurry because her husband's coming to pick her up soon, and he'll be spitting like an anti-Christ if he finds her telling people's fortunes."

"Oh, right then!" I said raising my eyebrows to Marion. She decided to go next and Mary quickly ushered into the house.

"What did she say to you?" I asked Mary when she came back to the car.

She sighed and slumped her shoulders. "She says I'm going on a great holiday."

"Wow, I'm impressed." I said trying to lighten her mood. "Where are you going?"

"Lourdes," she said flatly. "Fecking Lourdes. I've already been there twice."

I couldn't help laughing and looked forward to hearing Marion's news from 'Mrs Haughey's neighbour from over the way.'

Marion emerged in fits of laughter and I couldn't get a word out of her.

"You go on in now," Mary said to me with a sense of urgency. "The husband'll be along any minute and he carries his shot gun everywhere he goes."

"Quick, Marion," I said, walking towards the house and looking back over my shoulder. "What did she tell you?"

"Ooh," Marion called after me in a deep voice. "I'm going to meet a grand man, and we're going to have a grand wedding and I'm going to have five grandkids."

I laughed and laughed. "Oh, please don't start me off."

"And I'm going to go on a grand holiday to Lourdes."

By the time I reached the door I couldn't stop laughing. "I can't go in," I said to Mary.

"Oh go on," she said pushing me over the step. "It's that door facing and wait till you hear the accent. It'll crack you up even more. I could barely keep a straight face myself. I've not met this one before. She thought she had three Englishwomen coming today so she was putting it on a bit."

I walked along the hall and coughed before I opened the door in an effort to compose myself but it was no good, I knew I was too far gone and I began to laugh again. I turned to leave and there was Mary, standing at the front door, urging me to go back in. I retraced my steps down the hall and knocked on the door.

"Ah, come in, come in!" I turned the handle and stuck my head into the poorly lit room, scouring the stacks of newspapers and old tins until I saw this tiny lady sitting at a junk filled table. "Come in, come in," she said again. "Don't be shy. Come and sit across from me and I'll tell you your good fortune."

Marion's voice was still ringing in my ears and I began to laugh. I put the five pounds on the table and sat down. I had never seen anybody look so old, and yet her eyes were sharp and watchful. I was feeling very giddy and the more I tried not to laugh, the harder it became. I watched her shuffle the cards and the image of Edward Rochester sprang to mind when he'd pretended to be a fortune-teller. I half expected her to pull out a black pipe and light it.

She invited me to pick a card and I selected one from the middle and handed it to her. She turned it over and put her long tongue between her lips while she concentrated on the image before her.

"Ah!" she exclaimed. "You're going to meet a grand man and you're going to have a grand wedding and you're going' to...."

I didn't hear any more because I burst out laughing and the old lady screwed up her eyes and looked at me closely.

"Oh, I'm sorry," I spluttered, "I'm just so happy with that news." I looked at my watch and stood up. "I have to go now but thank you very much."

Marion and Mary were eagerly waiting. "What did she say?" they chorused and I told them.

"Jeez, we should've gone in together and just paid her a fiver," Mary said.

We laughed all the way into town and managed not to fall into a ditch.

Marion as usual was mooching in the glove compartment for some sweets and found the Smarties.

"They're from Sister Allen," I told her. "She gave me them when she came into the shop."

Mary leaned forward and held out her hand for some sweets. "She delivered me," she said before sticking the coloured buttons into her mouth.

I quickly glanced over my shoulder and looked ahead again. "What do you mean? She delivered you?"

"Sure isn't that simple enough for you to understand, Colette?" Mary teased. "I was seven pounds two ounces."

I was puzzled and looked through the mirror to Mary. "Were you born in a convent then, or was she a nun in a hospital or something?"

Mary almost choked on her sweets. "Sister Allen's not a nun," she said, "She's a retired nurse."

"But—I thought—"

"Don't ye see her walking around town all day carrying an old shopping bag full of rubbish?" Mary asked.

"But she lives at the convent, doesn't she?"

"The nuns felt sorry for her because she was living alone in one of the sheltered flats and she wasn't coping, so they let her board with them. She used to go to Cork or somewhere and stay with her sister for the holidays but she's in a home now. I think she stays with her at Christmas. One of the nuns drives her down there and then brings her back after the holiday."

"Aw, that's nice," Marion said.

When we arrived at the flower-arranging class, Marion suggested to Mary that we made sure everybody saw us there.

Mary raised her eyebrows, straightened the pockets on her jacket and ran her fingers through her hair. "Don't you worry. They all saw us coming down the road half a mile away."

We followed her through the dingy hall. Women gathered around the tables in groups and most people knew Mary by name, greeting her when she entered the room.

I paid five pounds and hastily tried to make a flower basket for Mary to take home as evidence. As I tried sticking the coloured paper flowers into the base, we laughed as the stems kept snapping.

"You don't do it like that," Marion said, taking the sad creation from me. "You do it like this." She bent the end of the stems and tried to get them to stand up in the bottom of the basket.

"No, you don't do it like that," Mary said, taking the basket from her. "You do it like this."

"Oh, what are you two like?" I asked, taking the basket from Mary and trying a different method.

When it was almost finished, I tied a blue ribbon around the handle and smiled with satisfaction.

"Here," I said, handing it to Mary. "Give it to him for his mother. Tell him you made it specially and he'll love you for the rest of his life."

Mary laughed and looked around to see if anybody else had heard.

"His mother's dead," she whispered, inspecting the work of art.

"Oops, sorry," I said, covering my mouth.

"There's nothing to be apologising for. Wasn't she an old witch anyway? And if she were alive and I was to buy her a present, this is all she would deserve after the way she treated me."

"Oh, thanks very much," I said.

Mary smiled. "Well, you know what I mean." She looked at her watch. "If we hurry up," she said, "I won't be expected home for another hour, so we can go to Donohue's over the road for a drink— or two."

When we went outside, we screamed laughing as the straw handle snapped off the basket and the flowers fell out onto the wet ground.

"Oh, look," Marion said, taking the basket from me and hastily sticking the flowers back in. "When you're showing him, if you just hold it underneath like that and hold the handle above it, it'll look presentable."

"Oh, hey, Marion, I don't think he'll be sitting up to see what she's made for him, do you?"

"Hrrmph," Mary muttered. "If he's waiting up for me, it won't be for flowers."

We all burst out laughing.

"Do you think someone might tell him they saw you in the pub?" I asked.

"Well, they're not supposed to say," she answered. "What ye see in town ye leave in town."

The pub was full and by the time we got served, time was getting on.

We chatted quietly amongst ourselves, occasionally being interrupted and shaking hands with friends of Mary's who came over to greet her.

"Are you going to give us a tune, Mary?" someone shouted over.

"Ara, not tonight. I'm with me friends and they've not been here before, so I'll be sticking by their sides just in case you lot try anything on with them," she teased.

"Come on! Come on, Mary!" they urged.

"Hey, you don't need to stand here with us ornaments. Don't worry, Mary, we can look after ourselves."

"Please, Mary," Marion pleaded.

"Should I?"

"You should," we said in unison. "If I had a voice like yours, I'd be up there too."

Mary was finally convinced. She handed Marion her glass and strolled over to the makeshift stage in the corner of the smoky room. The buzz of conversation suddenly died down and all eyes were upon her. When she whispered to the man on the piano, he nodded and turned the pages of his music sheets. She looked over to us and smiled shyly before she began to sing *A Mother's Love's a Blessing*

I glanced around the pub. I had never seen such respect before. Nobody moved. Nobody lifted their glasses or flicked their cigarette ash and when Mary sang the chorus, everybody joined in.

She finished to great applause and handshakes, glowing with happiness as she slowly made her way through the crowd to where we sat.

I gave her a hug and told her how amazing she was.

Marion shouted above the noise into her ear, "Oh, Mary, thanks for bringing us. We've had a great night; one of the best ever."

"I should have sung something more cheerful. We're a miserable lot, aren't we? But then I suppose we all cry after our mothers. Lord bless us and save us, will you look at the time? I'll have to be making a move."

"Ready when you are."

I DROPPED THEM home and went to meet Ted at his flat. I smiled up at him when he opened the door and he pulled me into his arms.

"Where've you been?" he asked, hugging me tightly.

"I'll tell you in the morning," I whispered lovingly.

36

THOSE LONG HOURS we spent sewing into the night had been well worth it.

We had more customers than usual over those two weeks. Everyone wanted a peek at our dresses, and came back again and again with all sorts of accessories. Someone left a bag outside the shop containing some doilies, suggesting we might like to use them as head coverings, and the Amateur Dramatic Society offered us the loan of some of their cloaks.

The sun was shining and the streets were packed when Sam led us in the parade through the town in his ass and cart. Brightly coloured streamers hung across the roads, flapping in the cool breeze, as children ran alongside us, clutching their balloons. One of them had a pig on a lead.

We made Mary a green cape and bonnet over a mauve dress and Marion wanted to be Emily (because the dress was green), so Imelda was Anne in a gorgeous chocolate satin number and I ended up being Jane Eyre in my plain grey dress and black shawl. And because it was such a special occasion, I wore the violin brooch Maisie had given to me.

When we drove up the High Street, Ted came out of the vet's surgery and took our photos, giving me a big smile and a thumb up as we drove on.

I felt so proud. We were a team: all for one and one for all.

We won a silver trophy cup for the best-dressed women and Ted had it engraved. It's still proudly displayed in my shop till this day. It sa ys: *The Brontës of Bradknock.*

We had such a laugh later on in the pubs. We Brontë sisters took our roles very seriously and insisted on being called by our "stage" names, which were pinned to our outfits, courtesy of Elizabeth and her art teacher.

"Here you are, Emily, here's your gin and tonic, and that's Jane's whisky and coke, and what did you want, Charlotte, a vodka?"

Anne supped a pint of Guinness and rolled a cigarette.

The party finished up at the cottage and spilled out into the garden. I call it a party but there were only seven of us. Nigel went home after a couple of drinks because he had to be up early the next morning for work. I still didn't like him and I knew I never would, although I made an effort for Mary's sake.

Sean, all the worse for wear, was entertaining us with his Irish rebel songs at the garden table and one by one we'd all slipped away.

Marion and Mary were cycling around the field like two mad women.

Ted and I sat on the back wall. It was such a beautiful night and it felt so right sitting together with our arms around each other.

"Let's go for a walk," he said softly into my ear.

We walked down the path and onto the lane.

"I've been wanting to tell you something for a while now," he said, wrapping his arms around me.

"And what's that?"

"You know I love you, don't you?"

I nodded.

"I mean, really love you."

Then he took something out of his pocket, got down on one knee and asked me to marry him.

The last thing I had expected when I came to Ireland was to fall in love.

I looked into Ted's eyes and couldn't imagine life without him.

"Of course I will," I answered.

He took my hand, kissed it and then slipped the ring onto my finger.

"Let's nip up to Josie and tell her," I whispered in Ted's ear.

Josie never went to bed before three and would be only too happy to see us.

Everybody else had changed out of their dresses but not me. I was only ever going to be Jane Eyre for a day, so I was determined to make the most of it.

We walked up Josie's lane wrapped in each other's arms. I began to giggle at the craziness of it all. My fantasies were becoming a reality; maybe this really was a dream and I would wake up in the morning in England.

When we reached the door, I went to take hold of the handle, but Ted pulled me back into his arms and kissed me on the lips.

Josie was incredulous when she saw the dress, and made me turn this way and that. I held out my hand and showed her the ring and she hugged me with such feeling. "Oh, Lord bless us and save us! My prayers have been answered."

Then she noticed the brooch and put her two hands up to her mouth. I was confused for a moment and then suddenly remembered it had belonged to Josie's own mother.

The memories it must have awoken in her.

When we eventually turned to leave, Josie asked me to wait for a second.

I thought she was getting some money for me to buy her bread or milk the following day. We'd had many a fight over money, but I'd soon learned if I wouldn't take her money, she wouldn't accept the shopping. But it wasn't money she placed in my hand. It was a harp-shaped brooch.

Ted rose from the chair and took it from my hand, smiling down at me as he pinned it onto my dress beside the violin.

I was fighting to keep my emotions in check. I now had those very two brooches Mrs O'Brien had presented to Maisie and Josie on that summer evening on the night of the dance many years ago.

I gave her a big hug, kissed her goodnight and left.

Ted put his arm around me when we were outside. I buried my face in his shoulder and cried.

"What's wrong, Colette?" He sounded mystified.

I wouldn't expect him to understand. He hadn't read Maisie's red notebook.

37

AS WE TUCKED into our roast beef dinner in Hanley's, I told Josie, how I couldn't wait to see my family.

I didn't bother opening on a Wednesday. It was Marion's usual day off and so it gave us a chance to spend some time together and catch up on things. This morning, however, she'd gone with Sean to his brother's wedding in Wicklow and wouldn't be back for a couple of days.

I'd given Josie a lift into town. Finally, after months of persuasion, she'd agreed to have an eye test.

"Do make sure you bring your daddy and brothers up to see me while they're here!"

"Oh, but Josie, you'll be coming down for your tea, won't you?"

Bingo, I thought. It was a good excuse to get her down to my house and spoil her.

"Oh, no, lass. Sure, you could bring them up to me? I'll get Sean to give my cottage a coat of paint. It must be ten years since it's seen a paint-brush, and I might buy a couple more seats."

"I'll make you some curtains and cushion covers if you like, Josie."

She smiled warmly. "Oh, that'd be grand. Aye, that'd be grand."

When we finished eating, Josie insisted on paying for the meal. I knew it was no use arguing. I had given her the lift and she said it was the least she could do.

We went over to the shop. I put on the electric fire and the kettle and made a cuppa. I heard the door open, and Sister Allen's voice, so I made another drink. I giggled quietly as I stirred her tea and thought of her delivering Mary.

The two women obviously knew each other very well. I could hear their voices rise and fall with merriment.

I brought an extra chair in from the kitchen and gave them both a mug of tea. I was well pleased, listening to the chat between them. Now I knew why Josie always had her Sunday best on with her blue beads and lippy; she never knew who she was going to meet.

"Isn't she a grand lass, bringing me in here to pick my own material for my cushion covers and curtains?"

"Ooh, she has some beautiful stuff behind that counter, Josie.

You'll have a hard time choosing."

I got some materials I thought Josie might like. She put down her cup, heaved herself out of the chair and came over to the counter.

I smiled and said, "You take your time and pick whatever you want. We're not in any hurry."

She liked to be home about four. We had an hour to call into the library and swap her books before we picked up her groceries.

She felt the yellow flowers on the royal-blue cloth and then turned her attention to the bottle-green material with cream sparrows.

"I like this one," she said, admiring the royal blue again. "What d'you think, Sister?"

I unfolded a bit more of the material and held it up for Sister Allen's inspection.

"Isn't it beautiful, Josie? Those flowers are so pretty. I must come out and see what it's like after all the visitors are gone."

"You'd be very welcome, Sister. Any time at all."

"Aren't you awful clever, Colette? My mother used to make the clothes for me and my brothers and sisters. She even made our Communion and Confirmation dresses, but I never had any interest in sewing myself. It takes an awful lot of patience."

I put Josie's royal-blue curtain to one side. "I could make something for you after I finish Josie's, if you like, sister."

"Oh, that'll give me something to think about. I wouldn't mind a couple of tunics or a skirt, if you wouldn't mind?"

"Consider it done," I told her.

IT WAS A week later and I had just kissed Ted goodbye before he went off to a conference in Belfast. I was tidying up the garden when I saw Josie returning from Sean's where she had left a box of apples on the wall by his gate. I hurried to greet her and together we walked past the freshly cut meadow towards her cottage.

Josie opened her gate and looked up at her house. "It's as pretty as a picture," she said appreciatively. She closed the gate behind her and clicked the new latch Sean had fixed on. I giggled when she opened and closed it again. "How will I ever be able to thank you all?"

It had taken us five days to complete the decorating and repairs, and Josie was right, her cottage was as pretty as a picture.

As we neared the front door, I watched a bunch of kittens romp playfully until the sound of our approaching footsteps sent them scattering to the safety of the hayshed.

We went into the cottage and, when Josie finished straightening the 'Welcome Home' mat she had recently purchased, she removed the tiny bits from the coloured lettering and rolled them up in the palm of her hand.

"Sister Allen's visiting tomorrow," she proudly announced. "It's a long time since I've had any visitors."

"She'll be looking forward to it, Josie. I think you're one of her favourite people."

"Did you see the beautiful cake Mary sent over?" she asked opening the tin and displaying a delicious looking fruit cake.

I leaned over and had a look. "Don't know how she does it," I marvelled. "I am useless in the kitchen, Josie. God help Ted when we're married."

Josie laughed and scolded me for putting myself down but it was true; I was useless.

I made a pot of tea and watched her straighten her mother's photograph on the wall. She stood thoughtfully for a moment and then went over to the sideboard and opened the bottom drawer.

"Do you need a hand, Josie?"

"No, a ghrá, I'm fine. There's something I've been meaning to do for a long time and there's no time like the present."

She stooped and lifted some kind of picture that had lain face down in the drawer. Her hands began to shake as she turned it over and rubbed the glass with her cuff.

"He was such a handsome man," she said of the man in the picture.

I presumed it was her father. I leaned against the table and watched her cross the room and hang the silver-framed photo on the nail next to her mother's photo.

She turned to me and sounded so sad when she said, "Perhaps it's time to start forgiving."

I went home full of high spirits, thankful that Josie was making peace with her awful past.

THAT NIGHT JOSIE and I sat by the fire reading *Jane Eyre*. We had come to yet another sad part of the story, where Jane has discovered on her wedding day that Edward is already married and has a wife living in the attic. Despite her love for him, Jane is driven by her principles and strong sense of morality and leaves Thornfield and her beloved Edward behind. Unsure where her next meal will come from, she stops at the kitchen to get some bread and water to take with her and then goes out into the world, sad, lonely and destitute.

This is the part where I usually cry but although my voice wavered, I read on through the next few pages until Jane, exhausted after sleeping under the elements for three days, sees a light that eventually leads her to her family.

I heard a sniffle and looked up to see the tears rolling down Josie's cheeks. I rested the book on my lap.

"It's an awful thing to feel so alone. She had nobody in the world and then God leads her to those good people."

I closed the book and made a cup of tea. That was enough sadness for one night.

WHEN I RETURNED to Josie's the following evening, her father's picture had been removed from the wall and returned to the drawer. I suppose some things are just unforgiveable.

38

IT SEEMED LIKE forever we'd been trying to get my dad to fly. Every year he went to Wales for a week with the local church members. Then, one year, they decided to venture further afield, but my dad remained behind when they all flew off to Lourdes. Even our Billy had tried to get him to the Munich Beer Festival – not a chance.

And now here we all were, sitting in the airport lounge.

"Cheers," my dad said. "I've been waiting 65 years for this pint of Irish Guinness."

Ted and I had brought Marion and Sean along in our car.

I'd wanted them to stay with me, but they wouldn't hear of it, telling me I had enough to do.

When we arrived at the hotel, we left my brothers at the check-in desk and went into the bar. Then Marion nipped to the shop and invited Mary to join us for a meal. We were only a few doors away, and our business wasn't likely to collapse because of an extended lunch hour.

When the meals were ordered, we had another drink and caught up on all the news.

My dad kept smiling at me and shaking his head. He said he couldn't believe how well I looked. I thought he looked older and thinner. I realised my leaving home and moving to another country must have been very traumatic for him. I hoped this visit would put his mind at rest.

Ted left straight after the meal. He had to go and check on a pregnant horse some place, I can't remember where. I was never very good with these Irish addresses. They were all the same to me.

My dad stood up to shake his hand. "He's a nice feller, Col. Is he good to you?" he asked, after his future son-in-law had left.

"He had better be," our Billy chirped in before I had the chance to answer.

I looked at him and rolled my eyes and then turned back to my dad.

"Everybody's good to us, Dad. I'm telling you, you won't want to go home."

How could I begin to tell them how kind everybody had been? In any case, I thought, they would see for themselves.

"Right, what's the plan?" Billy asked. "Are we having another drink or what?"

"The plan is to come home with me right now."

"Whatever you say," Tony said cheerfully. "Maybe we should shower and change and…"

"No, no, please, come home with me right now." I longed for us all to be together under one roof, just like it used to be.

Marion and Sean stood up to leave. She was working an afternoon shift at the home, and Sean was giving her a lift. Mary went back up to the shop and arranged to call over to the cottage later on.

I followed the three wise men up to their rooms to collect the bits and bobs they had brought over for me.

Our Billy and Tony were sharing; my dad had a room of his own. Can't say I blame him. Tony snores and Billy's feet always smell.

I couldn't believe the presents they had brought. Our Tony lifted a huge parcel, which took up almost one side of his case.

"Teresa asked me to give you this. She said it's for some old lady. Actually, Col, I think it's the one we met that night at the party. Remember? Her house had been burgled?"

"Or so she said," Billy piped up.

"Oh, my God," I exclaimed. "Is it what I think it is?" I peeled back the cellotape and opened the paper slightly so I could have a peek. It was Ellie's fur coat.

"And we brought this for your other little old friend. What's her name?"

"You mean Josie?"

"Yeah, that's her. We didn't know what to buy her, so we sent Teresa out and asked her to buy something nice."

I left that parcel untouched. It was Josie's surprise, not mine.

WHEN I TOOK them home, my dad paused on the lane and stood back to admire the cottage.

"So this is where poor old Maisie lived?"

The weather was so nice, we decided to sit in the garden. Sally was standing in the shade under the tree. My dad was chuffed when he saw her and went through the gate into the meadow to make her acquaintance. I knew Josie would be anxiously waiting for us, so I didn't leave it too long.

Her gleaming white cottage looked beautiful.

When I'd made her the curtains and cushion covers, I had also run up a bed cover and table-cloth to match. She was absolutely thrilled.

My dad gave her a bottle of Brandy. When she opened their present, she found a navy cashmere cardigan with a matching silk scarf.

Well done, Teresa!

We crossed Mary's cattle grid and strolled down her tree-lined path. The garden was the same as the house – immaculate. When we knocked on the door, they all came into the kitchen to greet us. I was so proud of having such a lovely friend. .

My dad was very impressed with the house and was given a guided tour. Our Billy and Tony were talking to Nigel about football, fishing, darts and snooker and every other man sport. They were merry and loud when we left four hours later. My dad was close to tears when he thanked them for their hospitality. I knew exactly how he felt.

They really enjoyed working on the garden. Tony bought me a plastic greenhouse and spent hours erecting it. My dad started a vegetable patch and planted some tomato seeds in the pots. He crammed so much activity into that week. Ted took him on some of his calls, and at every farm they visited my dad was invited in for a drink.

14 *

~ 39 ~

IT WAS A cold December morning and it had taken me ages to warm up the shop. I'd been over to Galway again the previous night with Ted and hadn't got back until late, so I was running a bit slow. Just to make matters worse, my car would not start, so Ted had to knock Sean up to give us a lift into town. However, it only needed a jump-start, and Sean had us on the road in no time.

Ted had wanted me to stay at the flat last night, but my house was warmer and much cosier than his. We had been discussing where we were going to live when we married. There were lots of options; Ted said we could live in his family home, or build an extension onto my cottage. We were even considering building another house on the back field.

I was going to be a June bride, and these days, it was all I could think about.

What had started off as a fairly reasonable number of guests had now risen to over two hundred. Of course my family were coming over from Liverpool. We had even booked Teresa on the flight. She had to be at my wedding. I told my Dad if she refused, I would fly over there myself and drag her over. Then there was Ted's side, including half the vets in Ireland.

I sat in front of the electric fire, flicking through the bridal magazines. I was making the bridesmaids' dresses, but was undecided whether to make my wedding dress, or buy it. Mary and Marion were horrified. They said they'd never heard of anybody making their own wedding dress. I was instructed to let them know when I came to my senses, and we would all travel up to the Wedding Shop in Dublin to pick out a gown.

What I hadn't told them was that I still had my mother's wedding dress, but my family didn't know. Several years after she'd died, my dad, with the encouragement of my brothers, decided it was time to donate my mother's clothes to charity. The job was hastily done, just in case he changed his mind, and when the bags were left in the hall ready to be collected, I had a quick look through when nobody was about. I saw the wedding dress and veil, and sneaked them up to my room, hiding the bag in the back of my closet. It wasn't until I was twenty one, when

I was having a sort out, that I tried it on. The smell of her perfume had brought tears to my eyes. I wished she hadn't died so young. I'd stepped into the ivory lace dress and stood before the mirror. It was such a perfect fit. We were more alike than I'd imagined. I looked like her wedding photograph; we were both tall and slim, with auburn hair. I felt like her double.

And now, flicking through yet another magazine, I'd seen hundreds of dresses, but none as nice as my mother's. I so wanted to wear it but I had my dad to think about. How would he feel seeing me walk down the aisle in my mother's wedding dress? I decided to run it by my brothers; to wear it would be a dream come true.

The door opened. I put the magazine to one side.

"Hi, Kelvin," I greeted the local blacksmith when he came to collect his jacket. He was so shy. I was surprised he had the courage to come in the first place.

I'd given up making conversation with him. Some people just didn't want to speak unless they had to, and that was fine by me. He slipped his arm into the sleeves, and now that loosely fitting jacket fitted him perfectly.

"Give us a twirl," I teased, picking a bit of loose cotton from the shoulder. He smiled and turned a dark shade of red, paid me and hurried out of the shop.

Sister Allen arrived to collect two flannelette nighties just before lunch. She was having them altered for her sister, compliments of the nuns. We went through the same rigmarole: her trying to pay me and me refusing, and I ended up with a bar of chocolate and a couple of balls of wool.

"Thanks, Sister," I said popping the chocolate into my bag for Marion.

The odd balls of wool had been accumulating over the weeks. She didn't know I was crocheting a shawl with all this wool she was giving me. I thought it would make a nice gift for her sister. It was coming along nicely and would easily be finished for her to take on her Christmas visit.

I smiled when she said she remembered me in her prayers every night. That was payment enough for me. Even if she was a self appointed nun, she was one of the best.

There was a funeral on, so I dimmed the lights. We stood in the doorway until the hearse had passed the shop. Funerals always seemed sadder when it rained.

Jean Riley came through the door just as Sister was leaving. Although I hadn't had many dealings with her, I'd never really taken to her or that daughter of hers, Goldilocks.

"I'm glad I caught you," she smiled. "Can you put new zips in these for me?"

I was surprised she was being so nice to me. Only that morning Ted had confided that Orla had taken a van from work and crashed it; she was about to be sacked.

I took the garments from her and promised they'd be done by the end of the week. I didn't offer her a cup of coffee because I didn't really want to encourage her to stay any longer than necessary. Still, she didn't seem to be in a hurry and strolled along the clothes rack, admiring some of the dresses due to be collected.

We chatted about the weather and other boring things. Then she came and sat down near the counter and I continued glancing through my magazine.

Don't make yourself too comfortable, I thought, 'cause you're not stopping here for long.

"I don't think I've had a chance to congratulate you yet."

"Oh, thanks," I said off-handedly. I did not like her and she knew it.

"You're going to have to keep an eye on him," she said slyly. "With his history, he'll have another woman before the ink's dry on the marriage certificate."

I looked up and gave her my full attention. "What is that supposed to mean?"

"Well, he's engaged to you, and last weekend he's in a hotel with our Orla."

"And lots of other women" I told her.

He'd gone to Belfast for the weekend to cover for an old university friend who was getting married. I was supposed to go too but I had an awful cold and just wanted to stay home. I should have made an effort because I felt so guilty all over the weekend. He'd even returned on the Sunday evening instead of Monday morning, and I'd been so pleased to see him.

I looked at this sour little woman with her cold eyes and her mean mouth. Some people just couldn't stand the thoughts of anybody else being happy and by God, was I happy.

"I'm just trying to stop you making a big mistake, that's all."

"Aw, that's awful thoughtful of you."

I opened the shop door. "You can take your garments with you because I'm not doing them," I told her.

She stood up and swept the clothes off the counter before walking out of the shop.

~ 40 ~

"WOW! OUR FIRST Christmas in Ireland and it's snowing."

It was Christmas Eve. No, it was two o'clock in the morning so it was Christmas Day. Like a pair of ducks, we waddled along the lane in single file so as not to spoil the snow with our footprints.

"Jingle bells, hm hm hm, la la la la laaaa! Oh, what fun it is to ride on a one horse open sleigh, Oh ..."

I stopped singing. "See, you're glad of your wellies now, aren't you?" I said, lifting my big foot in the air and stomping it down in front of me, careful not to slip on the ice underneath the fresh snow.

"Dead right I am. Anyway, where are we going?" Marion asked, blowing the snow off her face and rubbing her wet nose with her glove. She said her head was feeling better now that we were out in the open, even if it was freezing.

"You'd better not let Ellie see you with that tea cosy on your head."

Marion glanced over to Ellie's and quickened her step. "Oh, I know, and it took her so long to make it, but I couldn't find my hat and it was lovely and warm on the tea-pot. I just couldn't resist it."

I turned around and we walked on.

I missed Ted. He'd been called out late afternoon and, as the snow fell thicker and thicker, he'd rung to say he didn't know if he could make it back before morning.

"Hey, Marion, who ever heard of going out at ten o'clock in the morning on Christmas Eve to do the shopping and coming home at eight that night, blind drunk and not a Christmas cracker in the house?"

"It's a good job we'd bought most of it already. I mean, we can easily make our Christmas crackers if we have to, can't we?"

I laughed again, louder this time and put my hand to my mouth to quieten the sound. My hangover was wearing off and I was beginning to see the funny side. When we had called into Tansey's that morning for a celebratory drink, all the plans we had made had gone out of the window. Swept along with the day, when we announced we were off, someone bought us 'one for the road'. And so did every other neighbour.

"We can just go around the block if you like."

We passed the church, which, two hours before, had been packed to the brim for midnight Mass. "It's the only time I ever go," I said, stopping in front of the building. The highlight for me had been watching Ellie going to the altar for Communion in her fur coat with matching hat.

"Look," I said, pointing to the ground all around me. "It just goes to show how heavy the snow is when all our footprints are gone."

Tiddles came from nowhere and circled Marion's feet, his long tail standing up with pleasure.

"Look, he must be freezing." She reached down and scooped him up, tucking him inside her coat. "Ah, listen to him purr. He's telling us he's enjoying his first Christmas here too."

On we walked.

"He knows how lucky he is," I whispered. "He could have been spending this Christmas in the bottom of the Irish Sea. After all, he was a stowaway and he was caught."

"By whom?"

"By me."

"You cruel thing," Marion whispered, hugging her cat closer to her.

I laughed and put my arm around my friend's shoulders to give her a hug.

"I didn't mean it. You know I love your cat. I'll tell you what, though, he loves his Guinness, doesn't he?"

Marion stopped still. "What d'ye mean, 'He loves his Guinness'?' Is that why he slept all night? You gave him Guinness?"

I surrendered my hands in the air. "It wasn't me, honest."

"Don't tell me. It was Sean."

"I'm saying nothing."

"You don't have to. I've told him about it before. He's going to turn my poor cat into an alcoholic. He used to put it in the cat's dish and now he's got the poor thing sitting on his knee, taking sips from his pint."

I listened to Marion getting all fired up about what she was going to say to Sean tomorrow. If only she knew what I knew.

When she'd gone to the loo in Tansey's this morning, Sean had given me a sly look at her Christmas present.

"Oh, you dark horse," I whispered when I saw the engagement ring.

"Don't crack on," he warned, returning it to his pocket.

"Certainly not."

Who'd have thought when we came to Ireland that we'd both be engaged by the end of the year?

WE WERE FROZEN to the bone when we reached the cottage and hurried out of our wet things and into our jamas.

The Christmas tree dominated the room with its sparkling lights and glittering tinsel. Unfortunately, the chocolate figures, which nobody could wait to eat, had dwindled with each passing day until only half the original number remained. The Christmas cards, so many from England, hung across the chimney breast like streamers.

Marion poked the fire and placed a few pieces of coal around the turf. That extra heat made all the difference as the embers took longer to burn. She swept the hearth and emptied the dustpan onto the fire, making the flames rise for a second before they settled down again. We needed to keep the fire going all night so the place would be nice and cosy on Christmas Day. Mary had invited us all over for a drink in the evening.

I made us both a cup of tea and put hot water bottles into our beds. Then I began to wrap the presents. I did Josie's blue tea-set first and slid the box under the tree. I planned to take it to her later with her Christmas dinner. Ted's watch was easy to wrap, as was Mary and Imelda's perfume. I'd hidden Marion's TV at Ted's, and I imagine she'd hidden my present at Sean's.

We'd had lots of parcels from Liverpool. My dad sent me Claddagh earrings and a gold bracelet. My brothers sent me a box of chocolates, with two airline tickets for England. I had bought the three of them sweaters from the wool shop in town, and wrapped them around a bottle of Paddy's whisky. I knew my dad would enjoy that when he sat down to watch the Queen on TV after his turkey dinner.

I yawned and glanced at my watch. "It's half past two."

Marion tutted. "What about the turkey? We'll have to be up in a few hours to stick it in the oven."

"We might as well do it now." I uncurled my legs and stood up, stretching my arms into the air and yawning.

"If all had gone to plan, we should have done it yesterday."

"I know, but let's put it down to experience."

"And one I'll never forget." Marion laughed, glancing out at the snow.

"We've had lots of fun here, though, haven't we?"

Marion giggled. "We have, but next year, we'll do the shopping before we go to the pub, not after. Just think, Col, this time next year, you'll be Mrs O'Gormon."

I couldn't help smiling and I nearly said to Marion, and just think, this time next year, you'll be Mrs Tooney. That is if she accepted, of course.

Marion began to cry.

"Aw, what's the matter?"

"I'm thinking how gorgeous you looked when you tried on your mam's wedding dress. Even Mary was crying, wasn't she?"

"I know. Everybody has cried over this dress, especially my dad."

"He cried with relief didn't he, Col?"

"He did."

"Aw, fancy feeling guilty for throwing it out and all the time you'd been looking after it."

I smiled and choked back the tears. "Every time he phones me he says he can't wait to see me walking down the aisle in it."

Marion squeezed her hands together with excitement. "Oh, I can't wait either."

"Me too," I said and gave her a big hug.

When the turkey was stuffed, we wrapped it in foil and placed it in the oven.

"Don't forget to turn it on," Marion said, fiddling with the dial and closing the oven door.

"Oops! Marion, what would I do without you?"

The snow began to pile up on the kitchen window. Marion, true to form, gathered the spare breadcrumbs into her hands and went outside to put them in the little bird house.

I stood at the back door and looked out across the snow-covered fields. This is the stuff dreams are made of, I thought.

When I went to bed, I left the curtains open and lay for a long time, watching the snow fall.

I'd have liked nothing better than to wake up in Ted's arms Christmas morning, but I just told myself there would be many more of them.

I was drifting off to sleep when I thought I heard a tap on the front room window. I thought I must have imagined it and turned over and snuggled down again. Then I heard it again. I got out of bed and put my jeans and sweater on over my pyjamas. When I opened the door, he was standing there like the abominable snowman, and I fell into his freezing arms.

"You made it," I cried. "Oh, I'm so happy to see you."

"Put on your coat. I want to show you something."

"Wh—?"

"Just do it, please?"

I stepped into my wellies, put on my duffle and hat and let him take my hand like a child and lead the way. I didn't ask where we were going at three o'clock in the morning on Christmas Day. It didn't matter. He could have walked me to the end of the earth. Within seconds, we were covered in snowflakes as we made fresh tracks through the back-field.

I stooped down and gathered a handful of snow, giggling as I shaped it into a ball.

"Don't you dare," he warned, but he was too late. I threw it with all my strength and hit him in the chest.

His snowballs turned out to be far bigger than mine, and soon we were having a snowball fight. We laughed and laughed, battering each other until, laughing so much, we both slipped over in the snow.

When we reached the building, he felt inside that familiar place where we kept the torch. Then he took off his gloves and covered my eyes. I heard him pull back the bolt on the bottom gate. He slowly guided me into the building. When he removed his hand, it took me a few seconds to focus. I gasped when I saw the tiny donkey lying next to Sally on a bed of straw. I wanted to stroke it, but we were so cold and wet, we'd have given the poor creature a heart attack.

"So this was your emergency, was it?" I whispered, leaning over to kiss him. He was so kind and thoughtful and I felt the happiest woman alive.

"Does he or she have a name?"

"No, *she* doesn't."

"Well then," I chuckled, "I think I'll call her Charlotte."

We walked back across the field with our arms around each other, me and my Edward. We had so much to look forward to.

WHEN WE GOT up a few hours later, the snow had stopped falling and everywhere looked beautiful and white.

Marion had gone over to Sean's to see what time he was coming for his dinner, and Ted and I were in the kitchen slicing the turkey. The sudden rush of cold air on my legs told me someone had come in from outside. I thought it would be Marion returning from Sean's so I poured her a drop of sherry and took it in.

I stopped dead in the doorway. There in the middle of the floor, after an absence of over sixty years, stood Josie.

For a moment I could only stare. When she turned to me and smiled, I quickly put down the glass and gave her a hug.

"God bless you all!"

"Oh, Josie—"

"Don't go to all that trouble of bringing my dinner up, a ghrá. I'll join you down here, if that's all right?"

"If it's all right?" I repeated. "Josie, you've made my Christmas."

I helped her slip the coat from her shoulders and hung it on the hook behind the kitchen door to dry.

"Merry Christmas, Josie," I said, throwing my arms around her again and hugging her tight. "Oh, merry Christmas!"

"And the same to you, a ghrá!"

Made in the USA
Charleston, SC
11 July 2012